D0863411

FARRAR, STRAUS & GIROUX, INC. *Book Publishers*

HILL & WANG

JONATHAN GALASSI
Executive Vice President
Editor in Chief

Dear Friends,

I feel lucky to have been asked to say a few words to you about Niall Williams's FOUR LETTERS OF LOVE because this means I get to be the first person to tell you about this enormously fresh and touching novel. It is not very often that I'm moved to tears by a novel. I was, though, by FOUR LETTERS OF LOVE. The book is so genuine, so ardent in its portrayal of overwhelming emotions, that I felt truly joyful reading it, and I think you will have a similar experience.

FOUR LETTERS OF LOVE is being published worldwide this fall with enormous enthusiasm. Once you've read this lyrical and visionary love story, I feel certain you'll feel the same.

Sincerely,

Niall Williams

FOUR LETTERS OF LOVE
AN UNFORGETTABLE FIRST NOVEL
ABOUT THE ILLUMINATING
POWER OF LOVE

William Coughlan abandons his wife and his son to paint the pictures he believes God has commanded. He disappears into the west of Ireland on a mission, following a prompting that may or may not have been real to daub the canvas and stare at the Atlantic light.

On an island off the west coast, a boy gifted in music falls mute and lame while playing with his sister. It is a moment that scars the heart of Isabel Gore, as she helps her brother Sean home across the island to meet the disbelief and sorrow of her parents.

Two moments, two stories, each apparently as random and uncertain as the other. *Four Letters of Love* brings them together in a lyrical effusion of bracing freshness and power. This is a novel about destiny, acceptance, the tragedies and miracles of everyday life, and about how all our stories meet in the end.

NIALL WILLIAMS was born in Dublin in 1958. He is the author of four books written with his wife, the artist Christine Breen, about their life in County Clare, including *O Come Ye Back to Ireland* and *The Luck of the Irish*.

6 x 9 / 352 pages
HARDCOVER 0-374-15817-7
$23.00/NCR

BY NIALL WILLIAMS AND CHRISTINE BREEN

The Luck of the Irish
O Come Ye Back to Ireland: Our First Year in County Clare
The Pipes Are Calling; Our Jaunts Through Ireland
When Summer's in the Meadow

FOUR LETTERS OF
LOVE

FOUR LETTERS OF
LOVE

A NOVEL BY

NIALL WILLIAMS

FARRAR, STRAUS AND GIROUX
NEW YORK

Farrar, Straus and Giroux
19 Union Square West, New York 10003

Copyright © 1997 by Niall Williams
Published in England in 1997 by Macmillan
Distributed in Canada by Douglas & McIntyre Ltd.
Printed in the United States of America
Designed by Jonathan D. Lippincott
First American edition, 1997

For my mother
hidden among the stars

Lovers pave the way with letters.

—OVID, *The Art of Love*

FOUR LETTERS OF
LOVE

1

When I was twelve years old God spoke to my father for the first time. God didn't say much. He told my father to be a painter, and left it at that, returning to a seat amongst the angels and watching through the clouds over the grey city to see what would happen next.

At the time my father was a civil servant. He was a thin man, tall and wiry, with bones poking out into his skin. His hair had turned silver when he was twenty-four and given him a look of age and severity which were later to deepen and increase to such an extent that he could not walk down a street without being noticed. He looked touched by something, an impression furthered by the dazzling blueness of his eyes and the fewness of his words. Although I had no brothers or sisters, from the first twelve years of my life I can remember little of what he ever said to me. The words have vanished and I am left mostly with pictures of my early childhood: My father in a grey suit coming in the front door from the office in the fog of November evenings, the briefcase flopping by the telephone table, the creak in the stairs and across the ceiling above the kitchen as he changes into a cardigan and comes down for his tea. The great shelf of his forehead floating up above the line of a newspaper in response to some question. The New Year's Day swims in the frozen sea at Greystones. I hold his towel and he walks his high frailty into the water, his rib cage and shoulders like a twisted jumble of coat hangers in an empty suit bag. His toes curve up off the stones, off the ends of his arms he seems to carry invisible bags. Seagulls don't move from him and the pale gleam of his naked body as he stands before the blue-grey sea might be the colour of the wind. My father is thin as air, when a high wave crashes across his wading thighs it might snap him like a wafer. I think the sea will wash him away, but it never does. He emerges and takes the towel. For a moment he stands without drying. I am hooded and zippered into my coat and feel the wind that is freezing him. Still, he stands and looks out into the grey bay, waiting that moment before dressing himself into the New Year, not yet knowing that God is about to speak.

He had always painted. On summer evenings after the grass was cut, he might sit at the end of the garden with a sketchpad and pencils, drawing and cleaning lines as the light died and boys kicked a ball down the street. As an eight-year-old boy with freckles and poor eyes, I would look down from my bedroom window before crawling under the blankets and feel in that still, angular figure at the end of the garden something as pure, peaceful, and good as a nighttime prayer. My mother would bring him tea. She admired his talent then, and although none of his pictures ever decorated the walls of our little house, they were frequently gifts to relations and neighbours. I had heard him praised, and noted with a boy's pride the small WC that was his mark in the corner of the pictures, pushing my train along the carpet, driven with the secret knowledge that there was no one with a dad like mine.

At twelve, then, the world changed. My father came home in his grey suit one evening, sat to tea, and listened to my mother tell how all day she had waited for the man to come to repair the leak in the back kitchen roof, how I'd come home from school with a tear in the knee of my pants, how Mrs. Fitzgerald had called to say she couldn't play bridge this Thursday. He sat in that rumpled, angular quietness of his and listened. Was there a special glimmering of light in his eyes? I have long since told myself I remember there was. It cannot have been as simple and understated as I see it now, my father swallowing a second cup of milky tea, a slice of fruit loaf, and saying, "Bette, I'm going to paint."

At first, of course, she didn't understand. She thought he meant that evening and said "Grand, William," and that she would tidy up after the tea and let him go along now and get changed.

"No," he said quietly, firmly, speaking the way he always spoke, making the words seem larger, fuller then himself, as if the amplitude of their meaning was directly related to the thinness of himself, as if he were all mind. "I'm finished working in the office," he said.

My mother had stood up and was already putting on her apron for the dishes. She was a petite woman with quick brown eyes. She stopped and looked at him and felt it register, and with electric speed then crossed the kitchen, squeezed my upper arm unintentionally hard, and led me from the table to go upstairs and do my lessons. I carried the unexploded fury of her response from the kitchen into the cool darkness of the hall and felt that gathering of blood and pain that was the bruise of God coming. I climbed six steps and sat down. I fingered the tear in the knee of my trousers, pushed the two sides of frayed corduroy back together as if they could mend. Then, my head resting on fists, I sat and listened to the end of my childhood.

2

"I'm going to paint full-time," I heard my father say.

There was a stunned pause, a silence after a blow. From beyond the door on my perch on the stairs I could see my mother's face, the flickering speed of her eyes in panic, the tight bustle of her energy suddenly arrested, stunned, until:

"You're not serious. William, you're not serious, say you're not . . ."

"I'll sell pictures. I've sold the car," he said.

Another pause, the silence loading like a gun.

"When? Why—how can you just—you're not serious."

"I am, Bette."

"I don't believe you. How . . . ?"

She paused. Perhaps she sat down. When she spoke again her voice was edged, swallowing the broken glass of tears. "Jesus, William. People don't just come home one evening and say they're not going back to work. You can't, you can't say that and mean it."

My father said nothing. He was holding his words in that narrow, thin chest of his, while lowering the great dome of his head into the palm of one hand. My mother's voice rose.

"Well, don't you think I should have some say in it? What about Nicholas? You just can't . . ."

"I have to." His head had come up. The phrase thumped out on our life like a dead child, and a sick silence swam around it. Then, in a voice I hardly heard, and told myself later I hadn't, had imagined it in the half-dark of my bedtime when my prayers were said and the streetlamps edged the curtains with golden light:

"I have to do it. It's what God wants me to do."

3

The following days I came home from school to find the house in a state of transition. God had moved in overnight. The garage was full of the living-room furniture, the Venetian blinds had been taken down to let in more light, carpets were taken up, and a great board table was set up on concrete blocks in the corner where the television had been. Our telephone was disconnected and sat forlornly on the floor for a month inside the front hallway. My mother had taken to bed. I was given no explanation for this by my father and took the burned rashers and fried egg he cooked for my mother up the stairs to the bedside like some coded message crossing the drawbridge into the place of siege. A furniture lorry came and emptied the garage. Neighbours' children stood around the gateway and watched the old life of the house being taken away. "You've no telly," a boy jeered at me. "Coughlans have no telly!" "We don't want one," I shouted back, and went to stand between the makeshift goalposts of two jumpers thrown on the grass, holding up my hands and squinting at goals that went flashing past.

Then it was early summer. My mother got out of bed, my father went away on the first of all those trips in springtime and summer, disappearing into the yet blank canvas of the season and leaving my mother and me in the colourful but faintly rotting mess that was our house four weeks after God arrived.

"Your father, the painter, has left us," my mother would say to me, and then, with heavy irony, "Only God knows when he'll be back." Or: "Your father, the painter, doesn't believe in bills," when I came from the dentist mumbling and holding out a small brown envelope.

In a week we tidied the house. There was a small room off the hall that had kept its carpet and chairs, and it was to there my mother would retire in the evenings, sitting alone after I had gone to bed, watching the lights in the neighbours' houses and wondering what would become of the bills when the furniture money ran out. Across the hall was now my father's room. I had not, in that first month, stepped inside it. From moments when he opened the door, I had glimpsed rolls of canvas, timber stretchers, a little mountain of half-squeezed tubes of dark oil paint, others curved like dying slugs on the bare floor below the table. Now, as I lay in bed with the summer night never darkening, it was to that room my imagination took me, and in the first two months of my father the painter's absence I could imagine him in there, working away all the time, having never left us for a moment.

When the summer holidays came, my school report signalled the collapse of my education. I had failed everything but English, and in English was told I suffered from too much imagination. "An Elephant in Our House" had been the title of my essay.

As I was sitting across the kitchen table with my mother one Saturday morning, she told me in an urgent whisper that I was the little man of the house now. I had to work hard in school and get a good job and make money. I was twelve years and seven months old, and watched her pretty round face contort with the huge grief and anxiety God had put there. All her loveliness, the jolly nut-eyed smile and quick laugh that had ringed my childhood were vanished that summer. She was suddenly a tired engine of a woman. Her hands held each other tightly; if one of them got free it flew up to her face, rubbed the side of her cheek, ran down, and held at the thin line of her lips. Our neighbours did not call or come in. And for a time our house seemed an island in the street, the place from which William Coughlan had gone off to paint. When I was sent down the road to the shop, always deliberately getting there in those last empty moments before it closed, wheezing bosomy Mrs. Heffernan turned and looked at me over her half-moon glasses and added a free bag of jellied sweets to the single tin of beans or soup my mother had asked for. "There you are, love," she'd say across the swirls of her perfume, "eat them all up yourself."

Within a month or so, at the turn in the road before the shop I had learned to toss my hair, pull out my shirttail, rub a little dirt on the sides of my neck and around my mouth. This never failed to bring Mrs. Heffernan from behind her counter, tut-tutting and breathing loudly, lifting the corner of her apron to her mouth and cleaning me up before giving me a bag of assorted apples and oranges to improve my health.

That first summer we were not sure if my father would return at all. My mother, of course, told me he would, and how happy we'd all be again, and how he'd be delighted to know I was reading schoolbooks all summer and becoming so clever. The more she told me that, the more I read, leaving aside the goalkeeper's gloves on the dresser beside the window and devouring books in a vain search for any boy who had a painter for a father.

10

The days were golden. It was a famous summer in Ireland. Our lawn mower had been sold and a daisied wildflower meadow sprung up in our front garden. The grass grew three feet tall, and sometimes in the evenings I went out and lay hidden inside it, feeling the soft waving motion of its sea around me and above me and watching the blue of the sky deepen to let out the stars. I kept my eyes open and thought of my father, out there, painting the hood of night over me.

4

By the middle of August we had had two postcards. One from Leenane, County Mayo, one from Glencolumbkille in Donegal. Both of them told us he was doing well, working hard at painting. Both of them said he would be home soon. They were put, message outwards, on the windowsill next to the table in the kitchen, and in the mornings before I went back to school I read and reread them, sitting with a mug of milk-rationed tea and, a little anxiously, fingering the grey patch on the knee of my trousers.

Then, on the first wet school morning of September, I came downstairs and heard banging and knocking sounds in my father's room across the hall. He had come back during the night, a thin figure with a hat and a small bag, sloping up the path to knock on his own front door. My mother must have thought him a beggar or a thief. She heard him knocking and didn't move from her bed, half-imagining she dreamt the long-awaited sounds that had woken her sleep. When he let himself in around the back and she heard him move through the kitchen and across the bare floor of the hall, she knew it was him. He left his bag at the bottom of the stairs and came up to the bedroom. He looked in on me, I imagine, imagining too his long-fingered cool hand reaching across the bedroom dark to smooth my hair. Then, backing out, from the dark of the room to the dark of the landing to open the bedroom door. A figure in a drenched raincoat and dripping hat, he stood in the boots that had brought him from the west and looked at my mother. He was expecting insults, curses, any kind of coldness. She propped herself on one elbow to look at him and was a moony whiteness in her nightdress on the sheets. There was a moment she waited to be certain she wasn't dreaming, then, "Thank God," she said, and held out her arms to him coming.

I didn't know all this yet, of course. That damp morning I heard the noises in his room and thought in a flash of panic we were selling his things. I opened the door to look in and found him banging away, making a large frame with stretchers. He didn't see or hear me. I opened my mouth to call out his name but found the sound gone. Instead, gaping in the doorway, I watched him, how he seemed to be bent over, lost in the concentration of making, banging away at the wood like some still, frozen figure in a painting, heedless of all the world clamoring past. I stepped away and closed the door. I went into the kitchen and made my breakfast in silence with swirls of terror and joy inside me. When I opened my mouth to eat, I felt them rush upwards and gag me; my face bulged. A stream of unvoiced words gushed around. Had he come back, then? Was life to resume order and peace once more, or was he frantically banging the stretchers apart and not together. Was his painting all over? Had God spoken again?

My eyes read the postcards on the windowsill as they had done for weeks now, and then I felt his hand alight upon my shoulder.

"Dad," I said and, turning, felt burst in tears the watery balloon of emotion. Onto the damp turpentine smell of his thin chest I clung and cried, until at last he patted my back and held me out from him. He looked me up and down, and dabbing the tears with the fraying sleeve of my grey jumper, I hoped he could see the summer of study glowing off me. I hoped he could see how I had become the little man of the house, how I had fooled Mrs. Heffernan into pounds of fruit and sweets, and how I knew all along that he would come back to us.

Holding me back from him, he let those blue flecks of his eyes examine me for an age. His hair had grown long and in the morning light seemed white not grey. Even his eyebrows seemed lightened. A pale translucence was in him now, so that the more I looked at him, the more he seemed to disappear, to be a quality of light not a person, to be what I had begun to imagine was something like God.

"No need to go to school this week," he said. "What do you say? All right?"

Of course it was all right. It was marvellous. Mother came down from her bed in a green dress I had never seen. She sent me to the shops for potatoes and carrots, and I came back with a turnip, too.

My father had sent his summer's paintings by train to Dublin, and so later that morning he took me with him to meet them at the station. It is the first real journey into the city that I remember, sitting upstairs on the double-decker bus in the front seat with thin branches of sycamore and chestnut trees brushing against the window, how they loosed their leaves behind us onto the little housed roads along the way. I put my hands on my knees and forgot about the patch, turning a glance at the still silent figure of my father. I could not say he looked happy to be back among us. He was a man of such thin bare stillness that his emotions themselves seemed to fall lightly into the day, as soft and soundless as little swirls of unseen leaves spiralling down in the half dark of autumn afternoons. You didn't see his feelings, but somehow noticed a great littering of them all around you in the aftertraces when he was gone. Just so then, I can say he hated the city. Something in him despised the fact that he had been born there, that there he had gone daily to work in an office and wasted so many days of light.

From him on that late-morning bus journey I took my own anger at the city. What a leafless grey fright it was, a huge changing puzzle of concrete muddled with little hurrying lines of people in brown coats and wet faces. I wanted to hold his hand when we stepped from the bus, but didn't tucking cold fists deep into the pockets of my duffle coat and trying to match the long, purposeful slap of his strides. He had not shaven in over a week and his face was finely silvered with beard, the wisps of his white hair blew sideways in a little wind to show pink patches of his skull. He wore no hat down the streets and caught the eyes of passerby along the quays, as if the oddity of his looks, long hair nearly to his shoulders and those blue flints of eyes, was a guarantee of some celebrity. I think he took note of nothing along the way to the station, not the wail of the sticky-mouth baby in its mother's arm or the oily splash that an incoming bus painted across both our trouser legs. He was, I imagined, like me, and my mother back at the house, picturing the pictures. Perhaps he was already there, in the open landscape of browns, greens, and purples, standing in the places where day after day he had tried to hold and lay the coloured light on the canvas.

We entered the great windy arch of the railway station and my heart leapt at the sight of the trains. At a railing before an engine he told me I could stand and look while he went to see about his packages.

The slow heavy arrival of the trains, uniforms, loud distorted announcements, place-names from out there beyond the end of the long platforms.

"Right, then."

The back seat and boot of a taxi were already loaded with a series of brown papered canvases. We crowded into the front seat next to the driver. I sat upon my father's sharp knees and he leaned forward and rubbed the haw of our excitement off the windscreen, leaving us a small smudged circular view of the streets as we sped along. I was full of pride then; these paintings we were ferrying home were to be the trophies of the summer's grief. My mother would look at them and clap and raise her hands to her mouth. The paintings would all be sold in a week, we'd have carpet in the hall and a red car in the garage. I bubbled with the soapy happiness of it all as the car weaved its way into the quiet serpentine estates of semi-detached houses, where all the men had gone to work and all the children were locked in school.

5

Ours was not, in the ordinary way of speaking, a religious family. Until I was ten, my father and mother had accompanied me to Mass on Sunday mornings. We sat in the polished cedar pews amongst our neighbours and stood and knelt and sat at all the right places. Sometimes, when the priest's sermon grew too dull or his invective too hot, my father would practice a kind of loud deep breathing that shut the sounds from his ears and caused those nearby to think he was sleeping with his eyes open. He was not; he was controlling rage, I heard him tell my mother. Besides, wasn't breathing, he said, the purest form of prayer.

"God, Nicholas," he told me later, "does not live in red-brick churches in the suburbs." It was a summer afternoon. We were out walking, my mother was taking a nap. We took my father's favorite route, a steep hill towards the countryside. Once we were beyond the estates, the rings and loops and labyrinths of new houses, the air changed. My father straightened and seemed to grow, to expand, a giant of deep feeling moving silently past the tumbling red blooms of wild fuschia and yellow woodbine. The broader skies seemed to suit him, his strides lengthened in the sunlight. He pulled the sticky leaf of a laurel hedge and kept it, rolling it between his fingers like a memory. I knew he was happy then. And when he said the sentence about God and churches, leading me round a corner of sunshine that was slanting over a hedgerow thick with birdsong, I didn't think twice. I knew he was right.

We stopped going to Mass sometimes after that. And a little afterwards, it seemed to me, God came to live in our house. He was not often spoken of, and was never addressed. And yet we knew he was there. Not exactly holy, not exactly prayerful, but a kind of presence. Like central heating, my mother said. When my father was gone, He stayed.

In the wrapped canvases in the back of the taxi I knew we carried home the proof of God.

When we arrived, my mother was upstairs; she was in a fluster, and of the two main crisis reactions of her personality, retiring to bed or gearing herself up into a kind of mindless superactive machination of cleaning, sweeping, brushing, and dusting, she had chosen the latter. She was cleaning the bedroom window without looking through it, without seeing the parade of brown squares and rectangles making its way from the taxi to the room off the hall. She believed that upon them, those fragile coloured pieces of his art, lay all our family's future, that behind the brown paper wrapping were the pictures that had tossed and turned the sea of her sleepless mind since the night before. Unseen, they were a kind of torment to her, and yet now, at the moment when she might have run downstairs and opened the door to us, torn off the wrapping and stood back to let peace swim in over her mind, she dared not. She rubbed the window she had already cleaned.

When the taxi man had been paid and the still covered paintings stood like tilting tombstones around the bare room, my father stood for a moment looking at them. His long arms hung down by his sides. It was ten minutes to three o'clock. Standing, waiting for instructions, I watched him across the pale light of the room and smelled the smell of trains and oil. The window was behind him. Wild wisps of his hair stood into the light and haloed his head. I wondered if he was waiting for my mother.

"Will I call Mammy?"

He moved and I realized how still he had been. "No," he said, "you can help me. Fold the paper when I give it to you, all right?"

On one knee, then, with those thin boney long-fingered hands slowly undoing the wrapping, he went around the room revealing the pictures. I heard my mother come downstairs and begin to sweep energetically in the hall. Following a step behind my father, I folded the sheets of brown paper in silence. I didn't dare speak; I barely looked. When we had uncovered the last one, my father took the single wooden chair and placed it in the midst of them. He sat down and folded his arms and was gone from me, breathing deeply, lost inside a fog of silence. I went outside and closed the door after me.

In the hall my mother was still sweeping. There was no little pile of gathered dirt, instead, she swept the floor in long lines back and forth, back and forth, pushing ever ahead of her the moment when she would have to go inside and view the pictures. She didn't let herself look at me when I came out but glided past, brushing the bare floor and fixing her brown eyes downwards as if expecting a blow on the head.

I went upstairs to my room. I sat on the edge of my bed and let what I had seen crash in on me. For my father's paintings had not been the field and mountain, sea and shore images we had expected. There were no green fields dotted with cattle, no grey peaks rising into Connemara clouds. Instead the thirty canvases that ringed my father in his silent chair were to my twelve-year-old eyes a confusion of colours, a wild and eccentric fury of featureless daubings so forcefully done, so full of suddenness and energy that they were not pictures at all. Had he really painted these? I had looked at them and looked away, not wanting to see displayed for all the world the incipient madness that I feared would now sweep us away. After the first shock I had deliberately avoided looking, telling myself I didn't understand, that really they were wonderful, and concentrating on folding the brown paper in exact lines, finding comfort in being neat. Flashes of grey and brown, colliding slashes of angry mauve and black kept catching my eye and I stared. What brutal compositions they were, all black above, splashed, dribbled with brown, stippled blue then purple, washed across with a wave of white. Another, in green and red, broad arcs of colour flowing off the edge of the canvas, yellow run amok everywhere, and again black. So much black and brown. They were the paintings of a demented child: I could make out nothing in the furious nexus of coloured curves and lines and after a few moments looked no more. By the time I had left the room and gone upstairs I had convinced myself it was some trick of the light that had kept me from seeing. I sat on the bed clinging to the last traces of the faith I had had coming from the railway station. My father was a genius. He was a great painter. We were all going to be happy and rich and famous.

When my mother at last stilled her nerve and entered the room where my father had not yet moved from his chair, she pushed the sweeping brush ahead of her and was halfway toward the far wall when she stopped. She was wearing a yellow apron. The afternoon light was quickly fading and the paintings around the room had taken on the grim air of the dying day. She stopped, as if to let the dust settle a moment before the brush, and chanced the look that all summer she had been waiting for. Her small brown eyes travelled the paintings like a bird, staying nowhere, moving quickly from one to the next and on again. She circled the whole room without moving from her place. The silence was charged and immense, and within it she felt herself fall and land in the little dusty pile of her broken spirit. She gripped the handle of the sweeping brush, she found breath and moved her legs. Without a word, without a sign, she turned and swept herself out of the room.

My father, watching her from the throne of his immense stillness and quiet, made no gesture or effort at explanation. He sat still, angled slightly forward, with the palms of his hands pressed between his knees, his shoulders aslant, the bones of his elbows poking out like wings. Only his eyes were moving, only his eyes were telling her it would be all right.

6

Isabel was born on an island in the west.

When I thought of it later, adding the fragments she told to the ones I imagined, I would see her childhood like some fine cloth spun of sealight and sand, frayed and ribboned with beauty and grief. Hers was the place my boyhood eyes had pictured my father painting, hers the great expansive skies, the little stonewalled fields trapping the runaround summer breeze, the endlessly felt presence of the hushed or crashing sea. Looking up from running or skipping or chasing on the little white hoop of sand that was the eastern shore, Isabel would see the grey hulk of the edge of the country and wonder at the world that awaited her.

The island was small and quiet; it had no cars. From a little rough pier in the early mornings fishing boats sailed on the slapping waters, dancing round the island and off into the sea of loneliness and rain, disappearing to the west toward the unseeable horizon of America, where in the rising falling waves the fish were netted and brought home.

With her brother she would cross the island sometimes after school. Their father was the Master, and while he tidied the schoolroom or stopped in at Coman's for two short glasses of Irish whiskey, they would leave their schoolbags over a low place in a wall and walk across the hill at the back of the houses. She was eleven, he was ten. Down the labyrinth of rough gravelled pathways where even bicycles would hardly travel, they made their way, across the cragged stretch of grey limestone to the western shore of rock and foaming sea. They walked to the island's edge, a sharp jut of high stone with a sudden drop to shiny black rocks the tide made vanish under the tumbling waters. The shoreline itself appeared and disappeared like magic below them as the waves crashed. There, they had a favorite place to play, a little sea gallery of stone steps, levels, platforms. They were the King and Queen there. In the majestic hush and beauty of the land's end they could imagine themselves ruling a fabled kingdom of fiddlers and poets. Men like their father, women like their mother. They spoke in Irish, and in the spoken phrases of their game a little Gaelic world took life. Playing numerous parts for each other, they were now chieftains, now bards, now blacksmiths and bakers. Isabel danced on the high slab of rock to Sean's imaginary fiddle. They issued commands, and turned around to obey them. Sometimes, in the afternoons of early spring when sudden bounds of new life seemed to come at them across the surface of the sea, they would pretend they were invader and defender of their island, one grappling the other in mock fight, crying out to unseen armies of men and plundering the riches of the kingdom. Seabirds screamed in choruses overhead, and the fabulous light of the spring skies made a tapestry above them. Clouds white and fast were the sails of ships come to visit.

When Isabel danced on the rock's edge she felt the wind dance with her; she felt it touch her legs and run the danger through her. Her cheeks burned, her eyes fixed on the far sea and her hands down by her sides. In his squat position behind her Sean sawed the pretend fiddle in perfect jigtime. He knew the tune well, had played it and dozens of others for gathered crowds in Coman's pub on Saturday nights. For he was one of those children, an ordinary-looking, freckled, round-nosed boy with ears like cup handles stuck to the sides of his head by whose hands God seemed to play music. He played whatever he picked up, fiddle, whistle, flute, bodhran, banjo, spoons, and played each effortlessly well as he released the notes in the dead instrument and looked around him in mild bemusement at the dancing or gaping adults ringed around. For his sister, Isabel, he was happy to pretend, and made himself giddy by changing the instruments he played as she was dancing. Now he was fiddling, next whistling, and so on through all the instruments without his losing the tune or Isabel the steps.

"Sean!" she shouted in mock annoyance, crossing the rock in her jig steps without looking at him. How she loved to dance, she thought, leaping on the grey edge of the Atlantic.

They played the game for an hour or so on those rocks above the sea. For a time Sean teased her. She was dancing farther back from the edge, he said.

"Is meatachan tusa," he said, calling her a coward. The next tune he jigged he hurried the music out of time, going faster and faster, letting a little laugh break into the notes, shaking his head.

"Sean!" Isabel called as the music sped on and she tried to dance with it, crossing the edge of the bare rock back and forth like a tormented puppet, dancing as fast as he could play, on and on, back and forth, faster and faster, until suddenly he stopped. She sighed, exhausted. What wonderful dancing! God, how she loved it. The silence swept up the cliffs over them, and when she turned around she saw that he had taken a fit. His face was a sticky white, his eyes were gone back into his head, and his whole body shook stiffly on the stone. At first she thought he was pretending, that it was some further facility he had developed, this wild horror, the stuff that was drooling from him. But when she reached her hand to touch his forehead her fingers knew; the illness came off on them, the filmy sweat of his disorder that she brought to her lips, then cried out.

It seemed forever, but was over in minutes. In minutes Sean's body had slumped back on the rock, limp and slimy as fish. His eyes had come back, returned from another world with a glassy expression. He gasped. He tried to talk but couldn't when at last he managed her name, it was a thick mumble, as if stuffed in his mouth was the useless lump of someone else's tongue.

Isabel lifted him. He was light and weak, the wind might have carried him into the sea. Gulls had landed on the platform above them, watching, waiting for the rain that was about to fall. Now, as she ringed her arm around her brother and helped him make stumbling progress over the broken gravel track that led back across the island, the heavens opened. The rain came as it always came, travelling across the horizon in swift soft veils of water, joining the sea and sky in a seamless grey and curtaining the island from the world. It poured down on them. Sean walked shakily at his sister's side, making slow steps as if each was a separate new creation. They made their way home across the quiet of the island. They left their schoolbags in the puddled place by the wall and carried on to the house where their mother and father had begun to worry for them.

Off Isabel's arm, Sean flopped onto the flagstones of the kitchen floor. Margaret Gore cried out. She bent to help, but her husband was there before her, picking up the boy and carrying him quickly from the kitchen to the bed. For a moment Isabel sat there, slumped and wet on the floor, the long mass of her dark hair tangling down across her face as her mother rushed over. What had happened? What in God's name had happened?

She was out of her clothes, wrapped in towels, shivering before the fire. Her father had gone out into the rain to the post office to telephone the next island for the doctor. Her mother was sitting across from her at the fire, getting up and sitting down, going in and out of the boy's room, where he lay lifeless in a stupor beneath the blankets. The rain lashed down. *What had happened? What had happened?* At eleven years of age, Isabel Gore had no idea. She stared into the fire as the boat bearing the doctor thrashed across the angry sea. She kept her face close to the flames until the heat began to burn her and she felt the pain, saying nothing at all, staring into the orange glow of the turf and thinking, I caused this. I've hurt my brother.

7

That winter, while my father stayed at home, my mother stayed in bed. There was no money for central heating and our now three beds were piled high with blankets, coats, spare towels, and anything else that could be found. In the mornings the cold on my face woke me, I shivered into chill damp clothes and walked downstairs thinking I felt a breeze blowing around my ears. My father sat across the breakfast table in his coat and sometimes his hat. Usually he said nothing more than my name, or Here, or This is for your mother, or Take this up. It was not that he was morose or unloving. He had entered the winter phase of his inspiration, the cold season after returning, which we would all three come to know so well. Novembering, Decembering, that period of cold weather in him, the days and nights he would sit in his studio and look at the summer's paintings and begin to doubt: had God been with him at all?

A clear white frost came inside him, his thinness made him seem brittle, and he walked from room to room with infinite delicacy, slow and careful and quiet, as if he might crack, flake with the pressure on his soul.

In the absence of conversation the radio had become my mother's only luxury. She preferred radio, she told me confidentially, to two cups of coffee, and propped herself up in the bed in the mornings as I left for school, craning her ear to the fading sounds of the world coming through the sticky crackle of the transistor's weakening batteries. There was a chat show on in the mornings. The host was a genial man with a soft voice, and among his mannerisms was a whole series of rhetorical questions, a plethora of well-you-know-yourself-don't-you's and well-I-never-heard-the-the-likes-of-it-did-you's? and so on. To these now my mother had taken the habit of giving answers, leaning sideways on the hump of pillows and speaking carefully into the radio as if it were the dark semi-deaf earpiece of her closest friend.

With my mother speaking to the radio, and my father silent and frozen in the aftermath of his inspiration, I left the house each morning and joined the ragged line of other schoolboys cycling into the day. I did not mention my parents to anybody, or raise even an eyebrow when during Religion Brother Maguire stood at the head of the class and asked every boy to close his eyes and think, think, of Holy God coming into our daily lives.

8

On the island of quietness, Isabel began to feel a prisoner of what she had done. Somehow, she felt, her dancing had been the cause of her brother's illness, and after each day's school she came home to his bedside. In the small damp bedroom Sean lay motionless beneath a great layering of woollen blankets, looking up into the clear white aftermath of his fit as if the world had suddenly been laid bare for him. The music was gone and he was as stilled and useless as an instrument laid aside, God gone to play on someone else. He took food with difficulty, dribbled watery mashed-up meals onto a baby's linen nappy about his chest, then lay back again into his deep drift of quiet, not noticing the little clusters of sorrow-faced men and women in wet coats and head-scarves who leaned in the bedroom door to look. Rumblings of rosaries and other prayers hovered over him.

Alone next to his bed, Isabel whispered in his ear. At first it was only: Get well, Sean, feel better, or the words of her sorrow, "Sean, *ta aifeala orm.*" But as the first weeks stretched into months and it began to seem as if he would never recover himself again, she tried to offer him as recompense the whispered words of her secrets.

On a still blue September day, Muiris Gore took her by boat to the mainland to enroll in a boarding secondary school in Galway. Isabel had always known she would be leaving, and yet as the little ferry bounced across the water and the small walled fields of the island became a featureless grey hump in the distance, she felt banished. She sat on the bench at the side of the boat beside her father with the soft spray washing over them and a flock of gulls screaming in a trail behind. She clutched the handle of her bag and wondered if she fell overboard would it float. After three sips from the flask in his coat pocket, her father warned her about the nuns. He spoke in English and told her to do the same.

"Issy," he said, "you'll be good, won't you? You'll show them up, you'll show them we know a thing or two. There'll be girls from the city there, and all over, but you'll be smarter and better than all of them." He looked to the sea behind them. "We're not ignorant or backward or stupid, Issy, remember. You'll be better than all of them."

She couldn't look at him. She knew the patterns and rhythms of this speech already, had with all her classmates heard a hundred versions of it in the small green schoolroom where the map of Ireland hung on the wall. It was her father's main theme, the pride of their place and the unsurrenderable conviction of who they were when they ventured forth from the small intimacy of their world. She knew, and knew too that the whiskey and the journey were adding new emphasis. In a moment he might have stood up and stammered it out for the handful of other passengers, speaking with a kind of self-conscious careful deliberation until the swaying of the boat would toppled him against the railing and over, stammering on into the sea.

When he looked at her she nodded. He did not say anything about Sean. From the day of the accident he had never quite known what to think. What had happened on that shelf of rock by the sea to rob his only son of speech and movement was still one of God's mysteries to him. In the first days afterwards he had sat in the kitchen and heard Isabel tell it over and over, how she had danced as she always danced, how Sean had sped the music in fun and she had kept with it, crossing the rock in front of him, leaping into the wind until the music suddenly stopped. For Muiris some clue was absent, and in his weaker moments in Coman's he had wept openly at his grief and frustration in being unable to understand it. For a time he thought it was a judgement on his vanity, his pride in his son, the gifted musician, the prodigy now lying gaggling and drooling in the songless bedroom where the window let in the low sounds of the sea. Was there not something more, something Isabel was not saying, he wondered sometimes. He looked down the classroom at her, he watched her walking home. How different she seemed from other girls. She had something wildly beautiful about her, a quality he took for pride and independence. She would be stubborn, he thought, like her mother, a woman who combined hasty fire and brutal commonsense in such proportions that he had long abandoned debate with her. He was the Master. He was a man of substance on the island. To him, he imagined, fell the awesome responsibility of kneading, rolling, and moulding the raw rough stuff of the island mind. He had read more books than anyone, including the priest. He could recite poems in Irish of a hundred lines and more, and often at weddings or wakes was called upon to deliver those late-night age-old verses that would still the house and make women cry. He loved himself for it. He had tried to give his children his love of poetry and song; their game at the island's edge he had all but showed them himself. Now, sitting on the boat crossing to Galway under the September sky, he looked at his daughter and flushed with terror and pride at what he might have created. She would be beautiful, he knew. Her eyes were already extraordinary, her hair was thick and dark, and she walked even as a young girl with her head upright and a certain aloneness in her stride. She was polite with him. She answered him in few words. But something in her face filled him with the feeling that she was full of secrets he would never penetrate.

To his wife this was nonsense. The girl was quiet, that's all. She had had a bad fright, she would be back to herself in a short while. Besides, Galway would change her, she had told her husband. The mainland changed all the island girls. They left as children and never came back quite the same. Their childhood was left on the island, and coming back they could only visit it anymore, she said, thumping the iron to her words while he sat saying nothing by the fire. Perhaps she should stay back another year in his school, he thought, but didn't say it. He knew what his wife's response would be. Besides, Isabel was quick and clever, and even quiet and apart in her seat, she had been among the best in the class.

The brown suitcase had been taken down and packed while she slept. In the morning before the two passengers left for the ferry, Mrs. Gore gave each of them fresh scones in paper bags in their pockets. She held her daughter to her tightly, holding her there against her so that Isabel could not see her face, nor how the tears kept coming and how the mother tilted up her head so that they might drop back silently and unseen into the great grieven wells of her eyes. For a moment, the girl's father stood beside them like a useless extra. His cap on his head, the suitcase in his hand, the lump of the scone bag in one coat pocket and the whiskey flask in the other, he seemed for a moment a figure entirely adrift, cut off from the massive closed circle of emotion that locked itself between mother's and daughter's arms. He swallowed thickly and stared. Neither Isabel nor her mother had spoken a hundred words together about her leaving; it was he who had sat her opposite him in the parlor to talk, he who had walked alongside her across the white arc of sand in the summertime, telling her to think of Galway. Yet now, in this locked embrace without word or sound,

Muiris Gore saw with amazement the hopeless inadequacy of the human mind to fathom the miracle of love. When Isabel let go of her mother, she turned to him and seemed at once to have lived ten years in as many instants. Her face was not wet with tears, those dark and extravagant eyes were not swollen or red, but somewhere there she wore the grief of her going and it became her like a black stole. One last time she asked to see Sean, and ran in through the house to his room. She was no more than a minute. He lay on his bed and took her kiss and the squeeze of her hand with a broken little wail of sound and a sweeping roll of his eyes. Into the cup of his ear, as always, she hummed the few notes of a tune, and then hurried back to where her father was waiting.

Out the door then, down the little stone path, and pulling open the small white iron gate that her father always said he must oil, out down the slope of the island to the pier. Three of their neighbours had seen them off. Two other girls were going to the nuns also. The Master would take them too. There was a flutter of Irish, the last sounds of the island and then the roar of the engine.

As the ferry bumped in against the wall of the mainland Muiris Gore stirred himself out of his memories. His daughter was standing beside him watching as the man threw the knotted rope and tied it to its mooring. Gathering himself up and quickly summoning an air of authority and importance, Isabel's father placed his hand on her shoulder, faltered back a step with the rushing realisation that the whiskey and nostalgia had unsteadied him, and stepped onto the mainland holding on to her as his buoy.

They sat down on the pier. The two other girls were giddy and light-headed with freedom. They stood and bumped against each other and giggled. Isabel, as always with her father, said nothing. She waited for the air to bring him back; she had seen him like this before and knew it was nothing. And yet, even as at last he stood right and smiled and led them off into the city where Isabel was to spend the next six years of her life, she had fortified even stronger in herself an idea of men, pale rhapsodical creatures, figures touched by God, with weak sickening bodies and musical, immortal souls.

9

My schooldays were not the happiest days of my life. Mr. Curtin, the vice principal, a man of sixty with thinning grey hair and full dark eyebrows that were combed outwards into outlandish wings, thrummed above the days. He was a man who couldn't sit down, who liked to pace with hands together butterflying gently behind him until he turned his eyebrows upon you and you felt them coming for you, hands and eyebrows, blackbirds of anger or accusation. He walked around us, keeping the eyebrows to himself for a while, listening to answers, hands flickering behind. He stopped and stood so close you felt the sourness of his breath and saw speckled bits of yellow between his teeth. "Come with me, you," he said, leading one away.

In those large white rooms with cracked ceilings and naileddown windows began my growing up. Mr. Curtin's eyebrows flew about us. He walked his restless suspicion in creaking shiny shoes, endlessly circling. He made us demonstrate the comic hopelessness of our understanding of the Irish language. We were the ridiculous boys of 4B, astounding him with our stupidity and sending the eyebrows ever higher with the outlandish absurdity of our answers. *How could you think that, but how, tell me, please!*

In that room in 4B, under the glowering of Mr. Curtin, I first realised that God must have something special in store for me too.

That winter my father stayed at home. He rose in the mornings before me and moved about the freezing kitchen in his vest and trousers, making tea and toast that I brought upstairs to my mother and her radio. He said almost nothing to me that I remember from that time. I had not altogether lost my confidence in him, but ever since his return at the end of summer I had realised that happiness for us was not meant to come simply, that in some way our little family had been singled out. We were a sort of test unit for God, I imagined, a kind of three-person Moses or Job or somebody, a little household upon which He had decided to lay the burdens of His presence because in some way my father was chosen. When we froze or caught cold, when I grew hungry or tired of thinly buttered stacks of toast, I sat upstairs in my room telling myself to learn the lesson that there was no such thing as fairness in life. Beauty or genius, cleverness or stupidity were visited upon the deserving and undeserving alike, I told myself; a family could go to sleep, switch out the lights in a fairy-tale cosyness of loving, and wake in the morning amidst the ruins of all that they had cherished. It was a mystery, that was the thing. But more and more I began to wonder what in all the mysterious ways ahead was specially intended for me?

When I went to school my father went into his room. Sometimes when I came home in the darkened gloom of the winter afternoons, cycling home through the coal smoke on the air and the little avenues of skeletal trees clawing the sky, I was afraid he would be gone again. I came inside the house and listened for him, standing with my ear to the door for the tiniest sounds of his brush moving on the canvas. I heard the rattle and small swish in the glass jar of his turpentine and stood back. He was in there. He was painting. Light came out under the door. In the darkened house where there was barely enough money to pay the electricity to heat our food, he kept himself in a room of five lightbulbs or more, working eight hours in a brilliant whiteness of false light and urging on the faith that an inner voice was guiding his hand.

I never entered his room anymore. I had no idea then that he was still working on the canvases he had brought back from the west. I didn't know that what my mother and I had seen were only the rough underpaintings, the crudest renderings of what all winter long he would try to bring forth as his remembered vision of the glory of God. I didn't know. I realised, I suppose, that he was in there struggling, and that was all. In a way, it was enough. His struggle, like everything else about him, seemed to my boyhood eye cast on a monumental scale.

On weekends he would sometimes take me with him on walks. I cannot remember exactly how it started; I remember no invitation, but somehow it happened and became a habit, the two of us leaving the house for three-or four-hour rambles while my mother slipped out of her bed and in a pink dressing gown came down on a once-weekly reconnaissance of the squalor and wreckage that was once her home.

My father and I set off at a brisk pace, heading always for the hills beyond the housing estates, striding away so quickly we were always breathlessly ahead of the possibility of our dialogue. When we returned we would see the signs of my mother's visit, the traces of her energy in the perfect still lifes of cups on saucers, stacked plates, cutlery back in a drawer.

She did not know that she was losing her mind, that the firmness of her grip on the little interior world of the household had become maniacally tight. She returned things to their places with such a concentrated and urgent energy that it seemed each week the setting of cups back on their saucers was the last-chance risky business that kept her sane. It was in fact a sign of the very opposite. This woman, on the weekend afternoon, swept down the stairs with a fierce light in her eye, a ruthlessness for order. It was as if all week the jumble of our collected life had amassed in the drawing room of her mind, blocking out the white space in which ideas might have lived and charging her down the stairs at the end of the week to clear her head. She washed the clothes, she ironed with a kind of genius, pushing creases to the farthest edges of the world and folding my father's paint-stained and tattered shirts, as if preparing him for Monday at the office. She scrubbed around the sink until the plumpish fingers of her left hand were swollen and bright pink, rising above the golden hoop of her wedding ring so that it appeared embedded into her hand. She ironed socks and underpants, folded everything, swept imaginary mounds of dirt back and forth across every floor in the house except the studio, and reached a state of exhausted exhilaration, a dust-free heaven of pure order, as the evening darkness was drawing in. When she went back upstairs to her bedroom her mind had been swept clean of the clutter of the present. She sat on the bed's edge gazing out the window with the beatified expression of a serene angel, staring out beyond the rooftops to the distant hills and falling back into the sweet dream of the past.

10

When my mother met my father she was sixteen. He was four years older than she and had already begun his ill-fated career in the civil service. He was a proper boy, her mother had told her. He was honest and hardworking; he came from hard-working people. He was quiet, but yes, they liked him. They liked the way he came to call for her on time, the dark blue suits he wore, the clean-shaven boyish look of him with his thinning hair combed back already showing the massive dome of his forehead. Mrs. Conaty liked the way he brought flowers for her daughter, how he stood, the great gangling length of him in the porchlight, cradling the tulips across his arm like an infant, saying the few obligatory words to her with such weighty deliberation that she knew he was bursting with love. Her daughter was too young yet for this quiet prince, but in a few years they would make a match; she decided it as if choosing a wallpaper. She encouraged my mother and told Granda to do the same. He was a nice fellow, this William Coughlan. Granda asked him about his job and didn't listen to the answers, smiling blithely through the first stages of his imminent deafness, nodding and grinning while the awful realisation that his youngest daughter was grown tore out his heart.

Amidst the bright rays of her parents' approval my mother suddenly lost the excitement she had felt the first evening she had seen this man walk into the dance hall. She was afraid of something. His quietness drew and repelled her. She fell in love with drawing him out of himself, and like many of her school friends mistook the new delight of seeing her effect on a man's heart for the ecstasy of being in love. When she sat in school waiting for Friday night, it was the thought of how she would tease him from that stiff high silence of his that excited her. She became addicted to the warm flush in her cheeks when his face collapsed with pleading or she said she didn't love him.

There was a little season of nights then, those Friday and Saturday nights of her girlhood when she walked out with this quiet man beneath the almond-scented trees of the springtime avenues. She mocked him unmercifully, flirting in a yellow dress with red shoes, tossing back the wavy curls of her hair to look sideways at him, drawing out a long strand of hair between her fingers and turning it in front of her face intentionally as she asked him how much he loved her.

She had a laugh he loved. She skipped a few steps ahead of him and he came lankily hoofing along after her, calling out for her to stop. He was no fun, she told him, when he preferred not to go dancing, insisting instead they should use the bright summer nights to walk as far as the sea. He always wanted to walk. And if after two years of courtship in which she had dictated the pace of loving, allowed or not allowed the kisses, directed his hand and his lips, the truth was that she did not really know him as he knew her.

It was he who was in love. In this girl of eighteen William Coughlan had found the first evidence of the life-changing power of beauty. She flashed upon his life with an electric energy, shattering every day's effort at work and leaving a kind of glimmering burning feeling all day and night around the edges of his heart. He sat in his office distracted to the point where for two years of courtship he performed his office duties in a kind of disinterested stupor, all the more remarkable for not being noticed by his superiors. It took him a week to write a letter; he disappeared into the library and file room for hours every day, turning over sheets of paper upon which he imagined he saw glimpses of her face. For whole weeks he was sick with waiting to see her, a kind of inflated longing took over his insides, ballooning up in the thinness of his body until he had to sit and close his eyes and wait for it to pass. Across the desk from him a man called Flannery thought my father was dying, and after work introduced him to a short whiskey. He was the first person to whom my father explained that he was in love, saying the words out loud in The Fleet bar and feeling the rush of relief pouring out of him until he was able to go home laughing, kicking his long, lanky legs out in a little skip-dance beneath the million-starred canopy of the December night. He was in love with her. By the time he reached home that night and had turned the key in his parents' small house on the edge of the city she was already a part of him. That Friday night he asked her to marry him.

She said no. She teased around true reason: he didn't like dancing, he was too tall, he didn't like parties and never introduced her to friends. (This last was a thing she hated him for until the day of their wedding, when walking up the aisle she looked around and suddenly realised with the swiftness of a blow that he had none.) No, she could not marry him. She stood back beneath the streetlamp that was shaded with a sycamore and bit her lip. The huge leap into his life was beyond her. Her eyes filled with tears as she saw the heart of this tall man collapse like a skyscraper before her. He could say nothing; he could not even plead, and stood there a little apart from her, tilting alarmingly as the flecks of cold sweat gleamed on his forehead.

"I'm sorry, William," she said. "I just can't say yes, like that."

He stood there, mute and hopeless as the trees, the life draining out of him, the big shiny shoes alone keeping him upright on the world.

"You shouldn't have surprised me like that," she said, turning the blame back on him even as she was blaming herself. Why, why could she not simply have said yes and end the pain? She took a breath, the leaves whispered. But no, no, she couldn't; she wasn't prepared, not right at that moment anyway. My father could not breathe. It seemed to him that his world had come crashing headlong to this moment on the suburban night street. He could not imagine a string of tomorrows without this girl, for although he did not know it yet, he had invested in her all of his imagination. He had created her, this girl in the yellow dress, to become the woman into which flowed all his dreams. He could not move from the footpath. Cars passed.

It was she who moved first, taking his arm and steering them in a stiff and floundering silence down the street beneath the lamps and the trees. At the door to her house she leaned up and broke a kiss on his cold cheek and said her good night, leaving him to move like a man on stilts down the path and out the garden gate into the ruins of his fallen-down world.

He did not rise for work the next day, nor the one after that. When he did finally arrive at the office, Flannery sitting across the table from him saw at once the embedded dagger of one-way love still hanging from between my father's ribs. When he opened his hopeless downturned mouth, the butterflies of love might have escaped. Flannery offered advice, a liquid lunch, and the music of Bach, for no woman, he pronounced sagely, was worth it, and he himself had no intention, no intention at all of ever being hooked, hitched, or otherwise yoked.

Still, my father could not rally. He had a gift for intense feeling, for looming over the pain, and as he loped through the office corridors his forehead glistened, his pale eyes staring away like a pilgrim's. He could not work, the pen in his hand jaggered like a pulse graph; he broke in sweats and fits of dryness and sounded silently his own name in the way she said it.

When at last he could bring himself to write, sitting in the silver suit with his sharp knees pressing into the creases of his pants and his left hand holding from falling the immensity of his head, he began without address or name with the three words that had been flying around and around the rooftops of his mind like a madness:

I love you.

Just that. *I love you.* Perhaps he thought to write nothing more, for there is a marked pause, a change of ink and a handwriting that slants to the right, as if ever so gently toppling out the emotions, when the words resume.

I love you. You must know that. I love you so that I cannot imagine my life now without you. I cannot sleep, I lie awake all night turning and turning about and saying your name. I have never felt like this before and understand now how a man could cut off his hand or slit his throat in the torment of such feeling. I love you. I say it over and over in my mind and see you standing there under the tree and the streetlight and suddenly it seems as if I can hardly breathe. Everything of the world that is beautiful to me is bound up in you. You are those trees, that light, the loveliness of everything I am cut off from if you say no. I tell myself that in those moments on Friday night when my ears were ringing and my mouth dry I heard you say "Not yet, William." It may not be true. But I hope with all my heart it is and know that I can wait, however long, for you.

I will not call to your house nor write again unless I hear from you.

I love you,

William

He signed the letter in a shaky hand and sealed it inside a department envelope, stepping outside in his grey suit and striding down the bright raucous street to post it, staring straight ahead of him, not yet knowing that he carried in his hand the first true turning point of his life.

11

All of this I learned from my mother. I saw the letter and heard her repeat fragments of it to herself in the solitary bedroom when she thought only the ghosts of the past were listening. The letter had won her heart. She had taken it from her mother's hand upstairs to her bedroom and laid her face into it with a smile. How wonderful it was to have him write like that to her! She rolled over on the bed and suddenly exploded into tears, crying uncontrollably until her mother's soft knocking came on the door. It's all right, she called, standing up with the letter still in her hand and going over to the door in the terrible dawning realisation that she had already chosen to marry this man.

The wedding was in the little church of St. Joseph on an April Saturday pouring with rain. Flannery was my father's best man. In her small white bag, clutched before her, my mother carried the letter like the absolute certification of love.

Now, in the upstairs bedroom in the swept-clean house, my mother remembered. It was the only time she left the radio switched off, and in the following few years my ears grew tuned to that silence of her memories. I came in the door from school and listened at the foot of the stairs, hearing, if the radio was off, the dead voices of the past whispering in my mother's head and the scenes of her girlhood loving flashing past her gazing eyes.

It was gradually of course that I understood all this. At first I interrupted her, coming into her room with red cheeks from walking and the smell of fresh air and the countryside in my hair. In the half darkness she would be looking out the window; if she turned to see me, there would always be the same smile, a smile from before I was born and perhaps a phrase issued across the expanse of innocence and hope when all her life was still an excitement of flowers and chocolates and the marvellousness of a man sickening for her kiss: *Is he downstairs waiting for me?*

If my father noticed this, he did not say so. He waited for me to realise it on my own, and then acted as if we had had a lengthy conversation about it and everything was understood between us. On those days when we walked together there was, for the most part, no talking. Up in the hills, away from the houses, the afternoon light was a thin clear serenity along the roads. Children's voices died away in the distance, the football games on the streets where I might have kept goal vanished behind us as we strode on, putting a hurried breathless mile between us and the cataclysm of our home life. We almost never met anyone. It seemed prearranged. The trees I remember are the trees of winter, their bare limbs aloft in a kind of mute beseeching, as if the spring would never come and no leaf or bird ever move again in the dream of April. There was a pale, suspended emptiness we walked through, emptying me in turn, pulling free the tight-gathered knot of worries and imaginings the week had spun inside me. It felt clean. And although my father seldom spoke and never in any way referred to or urged on me the benefits of these marches, I felt the cleaning wind blow through the thinness of him too.

There were many things I wanted to say to him. Already I had felt for his great quietness the same irresistible attraction that had so drawn my mother to him in the end. It was as if his wordlessness held within it a boundless wisdom or grief; it was his silence that so made you want to tell him things, the silence that made you want to break it and return him to the ordinary world. But I said nothing. I didn't tell him how school was going, how Mr. Curtin's eyebrows and butterflying hands still pursued me through the corridors, how he showed up in the yard, pacing with a fury, fluttering his hands behind him, while we took turns to dare mimic at his back, how it seemed certain I would fail the summer exams.

No, I told my father nothing. I walked with him on weekends, I took the breakfast he made for my mother up the stairs in winter. And that was it. Still, as we turned the last corner to home and his hand sometimes reached out to touch the back of my coat, ever so slightly guiding me onto the road, or down a kerb, or in the gate home, I shuddered from head to toe, flushed and giddy with a boy's warmest feeling of all his father's love.

12

It was three months before Isabel returned to the island. Then it was Christmas and the crossing barely manageable. The sea churned. The passengers, all old women and young children, sat huddled in the three-sided cabin with the life jackets fallen out on the floor. The mainland vanished in a wash of grey behind them as they rose and fell sideways into the Atlantic, coming home. At the pier it took half an hour to moor the ferry, and even then the climb from the deck onto the rough worn steps of stone was treacherous. The boat rocked away from the wall and a deep drop opened into the water. The children jumped the distance lightly, hurrying up into the squall of rain where their parents were standing in soaking raincoats to welcome them. Irish fluttered on the wind. Second coats were spread over wet shoulders and the groups dispersed up the rough path into the island in black-coated clumps like half-curraghs, heading off to the small white houses where the fires of Christmas were already burning.

Isabel's father was waiting for her. He had whiskey inside him and paid no attention to the bitter and hard rain that had needled through his coat and numbed the redness of his face. He had watched the ferry coming from the window of the pub and, with his third glass of warmth beginning to fill inside him, felt like a wounded general watching in pride the return of his victorious army. He had taught every one of the children now sailing back to the island. There were his emissaries in the greater island, and he left the pub, coming out in the fierce weather and down to the pier to meet them with a perfect smile of welcome. He shook their hands and called their names, smiling at how they had grown and were no longer the scrawny white-faced children in short pants and knee stockings to whom he had given their first lessons in the world.

When at last she came along the pier, Muiris threw his arms around his daughter and pressed her to him. She hugged in to his chest, and in the familiar smells of him, smoke and chalk, whiskey and onions, she suddenly realised how unhappy she had been and felt the spring of tears. She held on to her father a long time, as he in turn held on to her.

As the ferry pulled out they made their way home. It was Isabel's first return, and as she felt the rough gravel of the path under her feet, the cool cleanness of the sea air thrashing across the treeless island, she told herself through her tears that she never wanted to be away from it again. She would marry an island man, she told her mother that night. Galway was not the great place people thought it was, she said, knowingly delighting her father in his listening place across the hearth from her and making herself a little giddy with the homeliness and comfort in speaking Irish words again. The nuns were hard, they scolded them for everything. They hated island girls the most, she told them, they didn't like the way she talked, they wanted her to cut her hair. They said she looked untidy if over her uniform she wore the long wine-coloured cardigan her mother had knit for her. The Irish teacher was hopeless, the food was a sloppy bubbling brown stuff in great black pots with stringy meat and mushy potatoes. Isabel poured it all out to them, translating her delight in being home into a tirade against her life on the mainland.

Later that evening she sat in the chair by Sean's bed and told a different story. It wasn't what she had imagined it to be. The city was not friendly, it was dirty and noisy to her. People were always bustling through it. But still, Sean, she told him, whispering in his ear and watching the little lights of his eyes, there was something about it that was exciting. She had slipped away from the convent many times and wandered into Galway, walking up and down and watching all those people trundling past. She loved the excitement she got in going out the small gate in the eastern side of the wall during the last two classes of gym on Wednesdays. She loved the feel of being outside the walled prison of the school with its watching magpie nuns and dull routine. Outside the school she felt the immensity of the world, the huge dizzying variety of it.

"Once," she whispered, "I even took the train to Dublin. You'd love trains, Sean. I'll take you on trains when you're better. You'll see."

She had sat by the window and watched the country unrolling before her in the morning light like a canvas of mountains, lakes, rivers, and fields. Everything delighted her, the little stations with single lines of men and women on the platforms, the suitcases bumped onto the narrow rack overhead, the men with their newspapers, the women who talked over knitting, the boy in black pants and white shirt who pushed a trolley down the aisle of the carriage and asked did she want tea or coffee. It seemed a never-ending journey; how long the rails were, how they stretched and curved and how the train beat in that soft musical rhythm across the magical country. She wanted never to arrive. She wanted it to go on and on, clickening clackening, whooshing into tunnels and out again, racing on past the fields where men stopped to look and sometimes wave. She waved back against the glass.

The nuns of course were beside themselves. A flock of them set out into Galway to find her. Some of the other island girls were brought to the Mother Superior's and asked if they knew where she had gone. With each hour her awaiting punishment grew greater. When Sister Agnes suggested aloud that the girl should be thrown out of the school, Sister Mary for a moment took the suggestion literally. She couldn't understand the sheer boldness of the girl, how she intentionally did things to upset and annoy them. There was a bad streak in her, she believed, like rashers, and only kept quiet when the feeble slow steps of Mother Superior sounded in the corridor and the door opened with the enquiry as to had the girl been found. This has happened with this girl before, said the Mother Superior, addressing the nuns in a slow soft way and letting her words rise like birds off the greatly ridged field of her brow. The Sisters listed the girl's failings and then waited for the small humped woman in white to answer, looking across the golden mellowness of the autumnal light in that room only to see her nod, place her hands together in front of her, and say: we must pray for her. Sisters, Hail Mary . . .

Returning, Isabel got off the train in a dream. She walked out of the railway station into the polished cold of the Galway afternoon and made her way back out along the road to the convent. The journey was still with her when she reached the gates and felt the tight white fingers of Sister Concepta grab onto the top of her arm and walk her, one arm angled up high in the nun's grasp, the other low like a broken doll, to the front door. At first, she told Sean, none of them knew what to say to her. They led her to a room and left her there, to wander over to the great window that looked out on the grounds, the chestnut trees unleafing with the high wall behind. Now her imagination could take her beyond that wall whenever she wanted. And when, after almost an hour, Sister Agnes walked in, biting the inside of her right cheek and clutching her hands too tightly in front of her as she listed the various punishments and suspensions that they had settled on, Isabel felt no anger or shame or remorse. What she felt was the exhilaration of freedom. "Like dancing," she whispered.

She had been gone from the island only three months.

1 3

To Sean, Isabel told everything. He became a part of her, and in the following few years it was for Sean that Isabel most often wished to come home. He made a few sudden movements of his head or his fingers, and small choked sounds low in his throat. He was recovering, her mother had told her. One day he'd have everything back, she said, and for that Margaret Gore kept a spiralling stairway of prayers ascending to the heavens from her nightly place on her knees by the fire.

One afternoon in the week after Christmas, as she sat in the room, Isabel took up Sean's old whistle and turned it in her hands. She held it out before him and watched his eyes. They flew beyond and back through it like hooks drawing it across the air. Up to his lopsided grin then, and the little reddened sore place at the corner of his mouth where saliva ran out, she placed the bright mouthpiece.

"Blow, Sean," she said.

She waited and felt the effort build in him, the incredible suspense of his whole being balanced there on the lip of the instrument, a moment beyond music. "Blow, Sean, blow," she said, and fell sideways off the chair as her brother's arm swung round wildly in an attempt to find the fingering and crashed against her face. He moaned and slumped over in the bed.

"It's all right, Sean, I'm all right," she said, getting up and moving him back against the pillows. His head was on his chest, his eyes not rising. Isabel waited a moment; the wind picked up the rain and threw it against the window. The sister stood there in the small damp bedroom and then started again, taking her brother's head in her two hands and holding it so she could meet his eyes and read the pleading there, placing the whistle in his mouth once more, and this time guiding and placing both hands as well. For an instant Sean clutched on to the whistle like a railing or a rope, keeping his hands from falling. He was curved into it, falling forward and sideways, bent up and around, gripping so hard he was forcing the mouthpiece against his gum and bringing blood. He nearly toppled from the chair. Isabel held him. "Try and blow, Sean," she said. He tried to blow and the whistle fell.

He tried ten or eleven times that afternoon. But once, when the early-night darkness had shut in the island and the view beyond the bedroom window was nothing but a seamless sheet of deepest blue, he clutched the whistle and threw his breath forward and raised the index finger of his right hand to play a single wavering note that climbed the air with the majesty and wonderment of miraculous hosannas.

So there is a God, thought Isabel Gore as she sailed back into Galway after Christmas, feeling the glimmering of hope for her brother and the easing of the burden of guilt.

14

Wives create their husbands. They begin with that rough raw material, that blundering, well-meaning, and handsome youthfulness they have fallen in love with, and then commence the forty years of unstinting labour it takes to make the man with whom they can live.

The husband my mother made in the early years of her marriage was founded solidly on two principles: that a man should provide and a woman clean. While he kissed her cheek and went to work, she stayed in the little two-bedroom house on Sycamore Road that for six months or so was to be in her later memory the single happiest place of her adult life. She wore a yellow apron and sang to songs on the radio, dusting and scrubbing the clean house for an hour or so before brushing back her hair and walking to the shops with such a simple and buoyant happiness that to her new neighbours she seemed a girl glowing with love. She acted, she thought, the proper way his wife should act, and when he returned in the evenings, travelling from the office in those days by bicycle and unclipping the flaps of his trouser legs before coming cold-cheeked to embrace her in the immaculate hall, she was dressed in a different frock and smelled of eucalyptus. She laid his meals on the small Formica-topped table in the kitchen and listened earnestly as he told her the few minor and trivial anecdotes of office life. She was suddenly serious for him now. She was a wife, and no longer a girl, and by the end of her first year of marriage had folded and put away the teasing, playful manner she had had when they first met.

She encouraged him in his career. When the first traces of his headaches and the alarming thinning of his hair began, she imagined them to be the necessary badge of any successful man in the country's civil service. He looked like an executive, she told him, denying to herself the gathering evidence of his frustration and the growing yet silent rage that rumbled inside this thin man in the bed next to her. She made the world even tidier for him, one memorable day and afternoon changing every pair of curtains in the house and wallpapering by herself the tiny bathroom in a tone of pale pink that she thought more soothing than anything. He failed to notice, of course, entering the small neat living room with its matching brown sofa and armchairs with their lace head-and armrests and sitting into the deep weariness of his life while his hair fell out in silver strands she would vacuum and brush up in the morning.

They had no children. They spent money on the house, and for five years it went through an elaborate series of new looks, each one more ambitiously designed than the next, until to scratch the wall in the bathroom was to reveal a rainbow of pastel shades in which could be read my mother's hopeless biannual efforts to sustain her domestic dream. She did not, naturally, think of it that way. She was making their home, and in the process grooming into being the imaginary husband she could live with. She bought his clothes, she threw out the worn Saturday trousers he felt most comfortable in, urged him to shave on weekends too, to abandon his habit of the bicycle and to buy instead their first car, an impossibly small black Volkswagen in whose front seat they journeyed into Wicklow on Sunday afternoons, my father hunched, craning forward, with his knees bumping the steering wheel; my mother alongside him, regally erect and beautiful as a queen.

By the time my father had been three times promoted, I imagine my mother believed her work with him was over. He no longer squeezed toothpaste from the middle, never came from the garden onto the cream-coloured carpet she had bought for the hall without removing his shoes, never attempted to wear the same socks or underpants two days running, bathe less than four times a week, nor leave the toilet seat up after urinating. His career was a marvel; he was clever and quick, and if now there seemed to Flannery no sign of that lanky lovesick boy who had whiled the week like a terrible purgatory until Friday nights, it was a small loss for such success, he admitted.

There was a summer holiday then, a packed new Ford leaving the new house on Mulberry Lane and racing off into the countryside. I was happy, yes I was so happy, my mother would later tell the wallpaper and the curtains. How I was happy! My father did sketches of fields and mountains. They had all-afternoon picnics in sun-warm meadows; briefly my mother let go of the tight grasp she held on their lives and let the immensity of the blue sky and the chorus of the birdsong sweep down on her. Nine months later I was born.

This story came to me, like all the rest, in fragments. By May once more my father was gone and my mother came downstairs. We cleaned the house of all traces of him, and a week after he had disappeared not even the faintest smell of him was left. My mother talked as she worked. At first it was a kind of clipped crossness, a thrown phrase at the grime that collected in the sink, the tea leaves that swirled and clogged in their haste around the plughole. I paid it no attention and carried on, brushing for her the ever accumulating but unseeable dirt of life.

While she talked I stayed with her, pretending to clean and following in her wake and listening. Only in the late afternoons would she stop. Then the house was set, poised for a moment on that precipice of perfect cleanliness, and my mother would be almost happy, standing there in that fragile instant of stillness before the next particle of dust arose and softly fell.

15

By the first week of September my father had still not returned. I couldn't go to school and leave my mother until he did, and sat at the end of the season in the small front room watching the bend in the road for his gangling figure. I would not forgive him so easily now, I told myself. The summer had been an agony of coming-and-going light; briefly the sun had shone. One day my mother seemed perfectly ordinary, pottering through the chores and cooking the half-tin meals she fed me, singing Gilbert and Sullivan; the next day she was arguing with the radio, shouting off her head off at the gardening program while the sudden showers lashed like dementia against the window.

I had lived three months in the half-light of the house without my father, and each day after the next I had found myself gathering a few more of the stones of anger. How dare he do this to us? What gave him the right to walk from the house one late spring day and abandon us to this? I blew up in furies of silence, staring out the window. I forswore him; I promised myself to ignore him when he returned, then decided to attack instead, to beat my fists against the thin selfishness of him. I went out the front door and stood in the September evening, anticipating him at any moment, my hopeless anger cocked and unholstered for some Wild West schoolboy showdown in the sunset. Had any boy ever such a father as this? With my mother's face gazing blankly from the upstairs bedroom window I stood by the front gate watching the fathers and husbands of ordinary households turn their cars in their driveways and step out, clunking the door, shaking out a hall-door key and walking in their every evening doors with a briefcase or newspaper in hand and a Hello, I'm home on their lips.

"Hello, Nicholas."

His hand was on my shoulder even as I turned to see him and we were walking in home, this gaunt striding man in a long, open raincoat and I, his son, suddenly swallowing the inflated lumps of confusion and uncried tears.

He had lost his key. I unclenched the fist that held mine so tightly and he took it.

"Good lad," he said, smiling briefly down at me and in a single easy movement letting himself back into our lives. The feel, the smell, the sense of him was back. Even the hall as he stood in it seemed to fill with his presence and air; there was the stiff strong tang of the oils on his clothes, his fingers with their tapering reach into the emptiness around him seemed ready to touch and take up everything. A sea and mountains swept from him and settled in the hall, airs and winds of bogs and hillsides, blackthorn hedges, the prickle of furze, the breezes of early morning over uncut meadows of high hay were all about him. For a moment he looked at me. He actually looked, and for the first time in my life, shaking under his scrutiny without the slightest idea of what he might say or do, I glanced up and saw something like pride burning in his eyes.

"Nicholas," he said again, as if testing my name like an old key, and seeing if he could re-enter the world of his family. "How are you?"

The anger had flown out of me and was replaced by the feeling of wanting desperately to be touched, to be held by my father.

"I'm fine," I said, and looked at the edge of his coat, studying a frayed place where wire or briars had cut into it.

"Of course you are." His hand was upon my head, and I was

pressed close to his chest. Whether he held me there or I myself was the one who could not step away, it was a long moment. I closed my eyes and held on to him, too close to see the tears I imagine filled his eyes or the grief and regret that crashed over him, tumbling him about in the hopelessness of loss that each return home must have signalled to his mind. God had taken him away, and each time he returned there was a little less of us left. It was an age before he spoke, and when he did I felt he had already decided something; he was sorry and was going to try to put things right.

"Is your mother upstairs?" he said. And then, a hand disappearing in the ancient coat, and five pounds suddenly showing. "Here, go down the road and get us a cake."

I went outside, he went upstairs. I had five pounds in my hand, we were rich. I ran as fast as I could through the streaming archways of falling leaves, the coming-down kingdom of banished summer that I kicked and leapt through, footballing clumps as I went, giddy again with the child's dream of the perfect world, the endless light, and God come home once more.

16

I imagined my father had come back to love my mother. God, I imagined, had briefly freed him from his vocation and decreed instead that this was the time to save our family. Perhaps He had gone to live with someone else, wreaking havoc on their life even as He was about to restore ours. Where exactly I got this notion I am not sure. In the five pounds in my fist perhaps I had dreamed or hoped into happening a fresh start, in the look of my father's eyes perhaps I gleaned a flash of that man under the trees and the streetlight asking his girl to marry him. Coming back along the still suburban streets with the cake in my hands, I thought I was hurrying back into the settled and cosy nest of ordinary life.

I remember everything of that short evening journey, the cool smells of leaf-embedded grass rising into the pink and grey air, the shut houses behind their gardens, rose scents, the feel of a stone wall I let my fingers rub along as I went, warming to burn, the evening bus from the city pulling in, Mr. Dawson with his *Evening Herald* rolled stepping into my running and giving a little quick playful swipe at my head. It was one of those moments that seem held in sharpest focus, as if the world had quietly slipped into a brighter intensity and everything was lifted up, clear, radiant, remarkably there. The clouds were majestic, the people on the far side of the street clothed in a dazzling luminousness. Even Mrs. Heffernan, bending down into her chins to examine and unfold the five-pound note, looking at it on the counter, pressing it out as if it might turn unreal before her eyes, had the air of an angel. As she handed me the cake, I knew the world was starting over. In the crinkle of the cellophane I felt it. I wanted to laugh out loud. Everything in our lives was going to be all right now. I was going home from the shops to my mother and father. I was going to step inside the hall door to the miracle of ordinariness, the kettle on the boil, the tea leaves being spooned from the caddy and the table set for chocolate cake.

But nothing was that simple.

Between my leaving and returning the world turned. My father ascended the stairs two at a time, rustling in his raincoat past the place where I had sat on the evening of his decision. On the upstairs landing his great boots thumped on the bare floorboards, the centers of which were already vaguely embrowned with the footsteps of our days. Dirt fell out of the lift of his heels. The thick smells of him rose ahead into the upstairs of the house and he crossed the space to my mother's closed door. His eyes, I think, were brimming at last with the warm recognition of who she was in his life. He had come back this time for her, to that white bosom on the bed, the blissful forgiving feeling there was, the sheer surrendering peace in holding her, in laying his head down and saying, I'm sorry, and feeling her hand on the back of his head absolving him even as she witnessed the dirt of ruined dreams all around her.

It was for her that he came back. Wasn't it? Wasn't it? For the woman who had seen him crash out through the wallpaper-world of pastel shades and pressed shirts that was her way of loving, for the woman whose eyes no longer shone and whose back curved with the weight of failed hope and lost love, measuring her day in sleeping tablets?

Wasn't it for my mother that he had at last come back? To explain the brutal selfishness of God, taking him away into the private agonies of his yet unknowable talent, leaving her, alone, with me? Wasn't that it? Wasn't that what shook in the hand that reached for the handle of the bedroom door, that brought him shaking and weeping hot tears for the first time in his married life as he stood there at the shut doorway, feeling momentarily that he was doing the will of man not God, that his decision to paint and go away had all been a monstrous error, that he had never heard the Voice and for two years had blundered in a waste of spirit and love?

My father's hand found the door locked. His calls to my mother went unanswered. He beat with his fists and called out her name, again and again, tears burning from his eyes. By the time I had come in the front door, the cake in my arms, he had broken his way in and discovered she was dead.

I I

1

When Isabel Gore returned to Galway after Christmas in her final school year, she did not know that she was going to fall in love. Her father had walked with her to the ferry, and standing a moment in soft rain, he held on to her arm and did the hesitant cough and mumble that preceded a major announcement. Feeling his fingers clutch the elbow of her damp gabardine, Isabel knew a warning was coming. But just what the Master Gore was hoping to warn his daughter against neither of them knew. When she looked at him his face was full of rain. He blinked at her. Quick nervous smiles crossed his eyes. The ferry was banging against the tyres along the pier and the engine roaring. The few passengers were aboard and lined up behind the clouded windows of the small open cabin. A boy in a yellow slicker waited to throw the heavy rope off its mooring.

It was something to do with the sea, the Master thought, with waves crashing, yes, and a quality he had noticed in her over the Christmas, that now seemed to make the sea so unbearably vast and great. The waters were churned up. How cold and grey, unforgiving, changed. He gripped his daughter's arm and heard her say, *What is it?* loudly over the engine. Words rushed around in him, swimming on the quick coming going tides of the three whiskeys that had started his morning. He cursed himself for taking them, wished he had another, and all the time stared at his beautiful daughter's face. Had she been a little colder at home that Christmas? As he stood there he felt his eyes tearing up.

"It's all right," she said, "I'll be back again in the summer. Go home, Daddy."

She hugged against him and then was gone, jumping from the last step to the outstretched hand of the ferry's captain. Her hair was around her face as she waved goodbye and the boat sped off, bumping away into the weather and fading into itself like a photograph in reverse development. When it was gone, it was hard to imagine it had been there at all, and the Master turned and walked up from the pier toward the village in the same knot of gloom that had tied itself up inside him since early morning. He still did not know what it was. There was no school, and so he crossed the little arc of white sand and shooed the five donkeys gathered there before going to sit in Coman's and take tea, pulling out a small paperbound copy of Yeats and trying to concentrate on reading until lunchtime. It did no good, doom travelled him like an itch. The poems and three pots of tea fuddled him more.

For the rest of that day and most of the next week he couldn't escape the sense of having been given a warning to pass on to his daughter, and each morning as he came from the house down along the little narrow road that led to the school his eyes rested on the winter sea and then puzzled and squinted at the watery message of his daughter's future that he could not read.

2

Galway city in the winter of Isabel's eighteenth year was racked with the worst Atlantic weather in memory. Storms sailed in the bay and the sea walks were washed with spray. Whistling gales swept round corners of the narrow streets and the people hurried between pub, shop, and home in thick coats, hats, and headscarves. Eyes down, a hand holding the coat tight over their chests, women tilted at an angle into the gusts, bags blown backwards on a trailing arm. The skin of faces was polished clean, ears were bitten off, and Galway eyes watered and blinked at the unbelievable weather that gripped the city for three months. Each day seemed worse than the one before, until a gradual acceptance grew, and every man and woman walking through the city in the January, February, and March of that year knew like a sour neighbour the hurtling chill and wet gales that came with hail and rain off the Atlantic.

It was a time of predictions and long memories. It would clear on the second of February or, when the sleet ripped through that day, on Valentine's Day. In the convent school three nuns died in the same week. The heating was turned up high and the girls moved between the tropical climates of their French, Spanish, and geography classes and the brutal cold of the mathematics room, where Sister Magdalen had turned off the radiators in a particularly errant moment of vision, believing that Our Lord wanted the purity of the girls' souls to warm them from the inside.

And still the skies stayed broken and black. It came like a sickness off the sea, one storm after the next, clattering the loose sash windows where Isabel sat and read over again the last letter from home. Back on the island they were prisoners of the weather now. The school was closed for a couple of weeks. Her father stayed late in bed, rising in the early afternoon, standing in the kitchen and leaning on the deep stone ledge of the window to look out the thirty or so yards of the visible world. The mainland was lost to them, and the freedom there was on a summer's day in seeing the limitless expanse of a blue sky over a blue sea was inversed now, and the stone walls of the houses and the little fields were the still jails of winter.

All along the west of the country the winter raged. The storms, one man said, were from Iceland, taking off the soaking mat of his cap and standing into a doorway with a half-corona of hailstones melting greyly into his beard. From hell more like it, said another, and when will it ever give up, will you tell me that? Pubs steamed and held their crowds in the loud warm complaining company of misery. Doors blew back on their hinges as the wind carried in another. Raking coughs and running noses, red ears and eyes, chilblains, sharp toothaches, and cold toes became the character of the city. Everyone was wrapped into the dream of spring, as if the season of winter were a punishment for the untold sins of those who lived up and down all the remote beautiful places of that coastline. Over the midlands somewhere the storms weakened. In Dublin, said the radio, there were cold showers and some wind.

The nuns, tackling the problem of the weather as if it were a sieging heathen army amassed at the convent doors, had drawn up a plan of campaign. Girls were to have double portions in the mornings, girls were to wear a second vest and school cardigan at all times, girls were to have an orange every day, girls were not permitted to leave the school grounds or go outside during breaktime or Saturdays while the inclement weather held. To divert the attention of those under siege, activities were arranged. Time had to be filled scrupulously; leagues of table tennis, netball, and other indoor games were announced.

To Isabel the harshness of the weather was nothing compared to the frustration of being locked within the great white schoolrooms. She wanted to get out, to walk. She was supposed to be preparing for the last examinations of school and a place in university. But now, sitting in the convent behind the rattling panes of hailstoned windows and looking out into the pale colourlessness of the view, Isabel wanted to escape it all. School subjects seemed to die on her. In the rain-sealed rooms the wind outside was louder than learning. And so, using the changeover moment between classes on a particularly brutal February afternoon when the sky fell in sleet, she pulled on her gabardine and slipped out of the school.

The air was sharp as glass. When the hail hit her face she almost laughed. Her fingers unclenched to feel it, and she walked swiftly across the drenching grass of the playing fields. If she made it as far as the bushes she'd be fine, she told herself, not running or ducking, but striding out into the murderous hard rain, feeling it needle already through the damp hood and shoulders of the green gabardine. She was soaked at once, but stepping onto the path outside the convent for the first time in a month, she was full of a shining exultation. Her hood had blown off and her hair was plastered thickly against her face. Her cheeks stung. The grey school stockings gathered like wet weights around her ankles. Small spouts of rain shot off the toes of her shoes. Such things she would remember later, those weathered moments of feeling the surge of freedom like some fabulous springtime already rising budding and flowering inside her as she walked down the path towards Galway city in the grip of the worst storm of that winter. The weather would always be part of the memory. The smell of rain, the stung pure cleanliness of her face beaten fine and shining with it, the droplets that ran into her eyes as the red car slowed and then pulled over beside her.

At first she thought it was the nuns and kept walking. The car inched alongside her and the passenger window was rolled slightly down. Isabel thought, If I run now I'll have five more minutes, five minutes before they catch up with me and I'm back in the room too dry and too warm and already forgetting how marvellous this is. Then she heard a man's voice.

"Do you want a lift in?"

There was no reason for her to get in the car. She had wanted to be outside in the rain, to feel the freedom of the chill air hurtling against her. But her hand was already opening the door. It was one of those moments when the plot of life jolts forward and understanding and planning vanish in a rash action; she would get farther away from the convent in the car, it was part of the escape, the risk and adventure near the edge.

She was in the car in a moment, the rain pouring off her onto the torn tan leatherette of the seat and the thick scentless breath of the car fan blowing into her face. She didn't look at him right away. She blinked the rainwater from her eyes and peered forward through the slapping of the windscreen wipers. It was an old car and drove with a kind of loose bumping and rattling that made it seem as if various of its collected parts were detaching themselves onto the roadway behind. Upon its back seat were two large rolls of tweed pressed upright into the fabric of the roof; about them was scattered an assortment of odds and ends, pages of newspaper, brochures, a cap, Wellingtons, a raincoat, a pliers, a length of chain, and, pervading everything, a smell of dogs.

"You're mad to be out in it," said the man, giving a little he-he laugh and slowly shaking his head. "Do you know that?"

She thought first of the car more than the weather, and then turned to look at him. He was fair-haired, his eyes were green. He was short and thickset, strong. She noticed his left hand on the gearstick, the swift almost angry action of how he threw the small red car into a little speed and hurtled them forward into the grey miasma of Galway city. He wore a kind of orange country-and-western shirt open at the neck and in the pocket a pack of cigarettes. When they slowed into traffic he thrummed his fingers on the top of the steering wheel to a tune she couldn't quite make out.

In ten minutes in the car with him she didn't say a single word. And then, curving into the centre of the lashed, deserted streets he asked her where she was heading.

"Anywhere'll be fine," she said.

"Jesus." He was laughing more than swearing. "Anywhere, fuck's sake." He shook his head gently and Isabel looked at him for the first time. "Where you going, I'll take ya."

She had no idea where she was going but suddenly wanted to say the farthest place.

"I'm not dangerous, ya know," he said, and chuckled to himself at the thought. "Of course maybe you're out for the walk, were ya?" He laughed and beat the palm of his hand down on the top of the steering wheel and turned and grinned a boyish unconfident grin at her, staring across the width of the car to lose himself completely in those unbelievable eyes that in that first real moment of their beginning first smiled, then laughed too.

3

His name, he said, was Peader O'Luing. His mother ran the wool and tweed shop on Cross Street that his father had started thirty years previously. Prionsias O'Luing had been a well-known tin-whistle player in Galway. He had founded the shop as a way of surviving for his music in the city, and for years while his three sons and three daughters were growing up had established the place as a kind of ramshackle woolly centre for travelling musicians. The back door of the shop let in on the side door of Blake's public house, and through the children's school years the vision of assorted musicians sleeping stretched on the counter or on the wooden floor wrapped one beside the next in great bolts of tweed and other cloth was not an uncommon one. Maire Mor, Big Maire, the wife, was as gifted a musician as her husband, and until the day he died, falling off the unsteady stepladder and smashing his head full of whiskey and music on the ancient mahogany counter, she would play in the evening *seisiuns*, fiddle under her various chins and a pint of stout within reach of her massive right arm. But after the funeral her own health failed. She soured like milk and abandoned music. Two of her daughters were in England nursing, the third was married in Mayo. None of them wished to return to her, and so she drank the bitterness of her misfortune in continuous glasses of vodka, with only the vaguest realisation that she was becoming a monster.

By some curious mechanism that had more to do with the absence rather than the presence of choice, the shop came to Peader, the middle son. He had no idea what to do with it. He was twenty-five and until his father's death had managed to scrupulously dodge the question of supporting himself. He lived at home in the old rooms above the shop, he did some carting of boxes and material and for this occasional duty drew a salary for himself whenever he was able to open the till unseen. What he cared about were his father's three greyhounds. On weekday evenings he took them out. They sat in the back of the car, long and lean, their heads erect and peering forward into the Galway traffic. Northwards out of the city he drove them, heading along the Oughterard road to a place twenty miles away where he stopped and let them out. With their leather leashes wrapped around his fist he walked off the main road down a narrow botharin which he had discovered by accident led a full circle of seven miles back to the car. It was desolate beautiful country, the green and dun colour of the fields scattered with the great jags of rock, the sense of the land stretching endlessly away into the weathers of the sea. The hounds had been his father's passion. Prionsias O'Luing had won money on them, and growing up, Peader had heard various stories and rumours of how the shop had been gambled, lost, and won back on two courses of the greyhounds. He imagined it was true, for the scope and breadth of his father's infatuation with the dogs was such that the single dominant memory he had left his sons was of his moving all three of them into one bedroom for two weeks before a race so that the hounds might benefit from the greater rest and comfort the interior of the house offered over the sheds. They were served stout in wooden bowls when not in training, their potatoes were half-boiled, not soft, soggy, or floury, and taken with a scoop of butter and no salt, broken but never mashed. They must always be walked seven miles when in training, preferably never returning along the same route but circling in an anticlockwise wheel in the last two hours before sunset. Sugar lumps were rationed for them, a sheep's head boiled for a day in the back kitchen made them faster than wind. Such things were the inherited wisdom of the sport in the O'Luing household, and Peader accepted them, adding in turn his own secret methods, singing quiet choruses of country-and-western songs down the long, winding roads in the rain, whispering the words *fast, speed,* and *win* into the cocked delicate shells of the hounds' ears.

Such was his life until the day he stopped the car and saw Isabel Gore for the first time.

4

In the heart of Galway city in the downpour, Isabel told him she was going to the bookshop. To get to it he drove around the one-way traffic system, bringing the car down the narrow curve of Shop Street and pulling up right outside the green door. The moment they arrived there was too soon for both of them. The engine was running, the windscreen wipers sloshing against the heavy rain. There was nothing to say, and in the instant before she reached for the handle, Isabel felt gather inside her a knotted ball of words and feelings. She flushed, wanting to say something, and embarrassed herself for being so foolish. Then, in a single moment that was to last longer than a year's memory of it, she opened the door and it blew sharply outwards off her hand. Rain clattered against it as she took a last quick glance across the car at him, his smiling eyes, his round face, and the something she was never quite able to pin down that seemed so vulnerable in him as he said, Well, goodbye, and, Anytime you'd like to go walking in the rain, and she stood into the terrific wet chill of the wind and hail and leaned in to quickly tell him her name.

It was a week before he arrived at the convent. The weather was still broken and the darkness that fell at four o'clock drummed hail against the high windows of the upstairs room where the girls sat to study. Peader pulled the red Ford up outside the arch of the main doorway and in a new tweed jacket he had taken from the shop rack that afternoon hurried up the four steps to bang the brass knocker of courtship. Almost at once he heard the footsteps coming, and when the door was opened by a plain-faced nun with a pursed mouth and small eyes, the wind, hail, and he entered the long, polished hallway like dangerous emissaries from another world crossing the drawbridge into a hallowed sanctuary. He asked for Isabel. The nun looked at him. She smelled the smell of sex but did not know it. The pursed mouth tightened and over the small eyes her eyebrows curved into question marks. From where her hands were held whitely together in front of her, the nun reached and turned the shone brown knob of the door into the reception room. "Are you family?" she asked.

"Yes," he said.

There was rain and sweat on his brow. As he crossed to the window and looked outside, he wondered what she would think. He opened his top shirt button and stretched his neck, he tapped his fingers nervously on a table and tried hard to hum the beginnings of a tune. When Isabel opened the door he felt his heart surge like electricity. The air went out of him. He had to heave on his lungs to keep himself standing, as the blow of her appearance overtook him and all the words he had prepared that day.

"You?" she said, "it's you?" The nun was still behind her at the door, and so immediately, for her sake, she added, "Sean," and wrapped her arms around him in a quick embrace he was not to forget in all the restless sleeplessness of his next two days. As the nun closed the door, she let him go. She put her hands to her mouth and stepped back towards the door, waiting, listening, holding for another moment on to her laughter until the retreating footsteps died away and she exploded. "You!" she roared, and then shushed herself, whispering and giggling as he grinned at her. "You're very sure of yourself, aren't you?"

He opened his mouth for no words and just stared; how beautiful she looked, the two sleeves of her cardigan were pushed up midway on her arms. She had been drawing a strand of her hair down over her face in studying and it flew loosely in front of her. She blew it to the side. "I've already a week's punishment exercise because of you . . ."

He stepped towards her. "Maybe I came to give ya a hand at it," he said, mastering the weakness inside himself with a show of false bluster and moving closer to the girl in her mother's cardigan whose face and eyes and hair had shot him through with arrows.

"Well, you've great nerve," she said. "Anyway, I can't go out. I'm kept in afternoons, evenings, Saturdays and Sundays."

"But . . . what about with your cousin?"

Standing there across the spotlessly clean room from her, with the hailstones beating outside, Peader O'Luing grinned the round ridiculous grin she would fall in love with, and began the conspiracy of their courtship.

On Sunday he called to take her to her uncle's for dinner. She would be returned by seven in the evening, he told the pursed mouth and small eyes, offering Isabel his hand and telling her a wildly invented stream of family chitchat as they turned their backs on the nun and walked out the doorway of Isabel's prison into the bluster of the weather and down the steps to the car. Out the driveway their laughter bubbled, and as the windscreen wipers worked the rain beyond the gates they were already given to each other. The countryside the small red car swept into was flooded and frozen, grey not green. The shadows of stone walls were white with unmelted hail. Nobody stood about or took walks. The sky was a steamed glass that cracked daily, letting slant through the falling air the shards of that long winter's stay. And yet, to Isabel and Peader, in the purr of the car fan and the smell of hounds, it was the perfected landscape of illicit love.

5

That evening after he left Isabel back in the convent Peader went home, returned the jacket to the shop rack, and stepped next door to Blake's. His mother was there, her eyes rolling a little in drink and her massive chin falling on the wedge of her chest. In the steaming crowd of the brown pub a red ring of faces were nodding over their pints. The music was quick and gay and light, there was jubilation and celebration in it, and as the first mouthful of his drink ran down his throat Peader felt he was hearing it for the first time. Nothing was like this before. His eyes travelled from the bow and fiddle, the stops and quick fingering of the whistle, up and across to the small window of clear glass and the view of rain made briefly golden as it fell across the streetlight. He watched the rain and heard the music and saw only the returning memory of the girl's face.

They had been together for little more than four hours. He had not even kissed her; she had glanced her lips against him as she opened the car door and stepped into the rain. *Thanks, see ya. Slan.* And yet the idea of her had completely overtaken his mind. She was the girl out for a walk in the wildest day in a decade. She was the girl who smelled of rain and wind. Now, sitting at the counter in Blake's hearing music and feeling the alcohol warming inside him, he fell down the steps of what he thought was love, falling ever deeper as he played over, time and again, the image of her face and let himself feel the hollow pain of longing to see her again.

Half an hour after entering the pub, he was more in love with her than he imagined it was possible to be in love with anyone. He wanted to talk, tell about her, shake himself and jump, kick, scream, laugh, roar, throw things and break them; he wanted to let it out, the sudden balloon of beauty that she had inflated below his heart, to express her, to fall back, sigh, sing, and be for as long as forever the sweetness of this happiness; he wanted to be the music.

When they closed the pub and his mother passed him on the way to her bed, she saw it in his face as clear as a rash and thumped up the stairs without a word, already knitting the rows of worry that she was losing her son. Peader said nothing. He went out the side door into the rain, drove the car in a skittery wobble through the midnight downpour as far as the sheds of the hounds. There he unlocked the galvanised door and let himself in under the clattering roof to lie in the incredible clamour of the rain, whispering to the dogs her name.

He did not sleep for two days. He grew red-eyed and wild-looking, already sickened by the fear that she would not, could not care for him. It was the worm in his winter rose. For nothing was as deeply set in the heart and mind of Peader O'Luing than the nagging suspicion that underneath all he was worthless. He took the hounds out for interminable walks, leading them through winds and rains he wouldn't ordinarily walk in himself. One moment, skies clearing, the air clean and fresh with even the slightest tremor of spring, he was ecstatic and light with hope, walking the greyhounds along the rainbow of himself; the next moment, he was overcast, shadowed into a personal darkness where a stone in his hand might have beaten the dogs to death. Isabel, Isabel. He said her name out loud along the road, letting the voices of the rain wind take it into the air so that it went before and after him across the countryside.

Isabel, Isabel.

Tying the leashes of the hounds to the back of the car, he got in alone and sat, letting his wet clothes breathe and closing his eyes in a hopeless search to refind for a moment that smell of Isabel in the rain.

For Isabel it had not been the same. She had thought of him, brought him closer at times, sitting in a dull class of French grammar or Russian history, only to let him go again and switch her mind away to the chalked words and figures on the blackboard and the prospect of her future. She had been a good student, could still get to university, the nuns had told her, telling her too that if she gave up now the world would have nothing for her.

On a Saturday evening in study class the words of the pages suddenly slid away. She couldn't concentrate. She found an hour passing with nothing done. She had turned twenty pages of textbook without the slightest memory of what they contained. She looked up and saw the pursed mouth and small eyes staring down at her from the top of the room. She turned to the window and smiled.

It was the game she loved at first, the comedy of it as he called at the door in his tweeds and respectfulness and the steady pat of Sister's shoes coming down the long corridor to summon her for her cousin. She would hear it coming before the rap on the door, sitting there on the side of her bed or at the desk, where for a week she had been trying to write a letter home. She would hear the footsteps and laugh, putting a hand to her mouth to catch it quickly, throwing back her hair and standing up to get ready, holding off that look in her eyes that was proud and victorious until she was already down the corridor and out through the front door once more, feeling the wind like an embrace and the raw kiss of freedom.

6

They drove west into Connemara. As the car hurtled down the center of narrow roads, racing away into the great emptiness of bog and mountain, Isabel felt the exhilaration of freedom and danger. She loved the madness of it, this Sunday escape with the almost stranger, the giddy speed. Peader was so nervously happy in the seat next to her that words burst against each other in the pipe of his throat, and as he drove, the hummed nasalised fragments of cowboy tunes betrayed his bubbling gladness. He said nothing to her for ten miles, each minute feeling the growing distance from the convent as a gathering proof that she cared for him. It was almost too much to believe, and staring ahead he hardly dared tell himself that it was she next to him. He drove and hummed and followed the road that seemed to go nowhere with nobody on it. The grim loneliness of the winter landscape was beautiful too, and although Peader did not think of it, had not plotted it as another suitor might, nor imagined the effect on an island girl for weeks imprisoned in the rooms of a convent, it was the perfect setting.

An hour out of Galway he asked her where she would like to go.

"Anywhere," she said. And then: "I'd love to get out and walk."

He grinned and laughed. "Jesus but you're mad," and pulled the car over to the side of the road.

"Isn't that why you like me?" she said, and was into the wind with her hair blown forward over her face before he had time to think of an answer.

They walked beside each other along the verge of the road under a great white sky. The mountains were a pale blue in the distance. Water ran in drains or gleamed like fallen bits of sky amidst boggy places that were brown and black with winter. No birds flew. A single car passed them in an hour's walking, so slowly and gradually vanishing down the curving ribbon of the endless road ahead that as they looked after it time and distance seemed recast in a new way and the road became an eternity. It was the stillness Isabel liked, and even the chill of the wind. And while the round squat figure of the man bundled in a thick tweed coat beside her was not the one she might have dreamed in sunlit moments on school afternoons, he was the one who had brought her out to this, and she did not pull back or shiver when he took her hand. Still, they said almost nothing. It was a place without words, that road in Connemara, so steeped in the wind and silence that even the road that ran through it seemed a slow stopless passing on. The world was elsewhere with its motion and noise, here was only loneliness and quiet. The rain had held off in the slopes about them. The wind was behind them, its hundred hands on their backs nudging them onwards, gusting so that they stumbled closer together on the uneven way. His eyes were stinging. He felt the limp weight of her hand in his. The slim wedge of it he was grasping onto as if it were the buoy that kept his soul from floating off over the mountains. It was like holding on to the hand of a doll, and yet even the slightest movement of his fingers within hers, the merest caress spun him like a top and he ached to kiss her. The sound of their footsteps on the road as they walked on, the scent of her that bloomed and hid in the Connemara wind. What was she thinking? What feelings ran from the pale hand into the clutch of his fingers around it? If he let it go would it search the cold air a moment to refind him? The questions loosened the bolts of Peader's nerve, in a moment unhinging his happiness. The sleeplessness of his last few days fell on top of him, his brain thrummed, he felt his legs go weak, and held on to her hand tighter. The unsaid words sickened inside him. Why, why had he said nothing to her? Why hadn't he told her? Why couldn't he bring himself to begin? He couldn't. It was all soured with fear. The silence frightening, not beautiful. The air darkened, the clouds rising and coming down off the mountains like spiteful gods. The stillness of the moment was gone, and as if time itself had returned and beat faster than before, Peader saw Isabel going back inside the convent and another spiral of wakeful dream-swept days and nights beginning. He could not bear it. He raised his head and blew a sigh and squeezed her hand in his. He squeezed it tighter and then tighter, shutting his hand around it so strongly that in a moment he was crushing it within his fingers, as if the bones might shatter and their skins blend. Isabel let out a cry. She turned towards him, a wisp of her hair caught in the corner of his lips, and like a man going down in shattered pieces, Peader O'Luing buckled and sighed, turning and reaching to find her face with his reddened hand and founder at last on the island of her kiss.

7

A chain of Sundays, through the last months of that frozen winter and the final awakening of springtime once more. Saturday evenings Peader cleaned out the interior of the small red car and got it ready for Sunday morning. He told his mother he was going to meet friends, but from the changing habits of his dress and hygiene Maire Mor interpreted the truth, piecing together a girl of sufficient unsuitability for her son for him to want to shield her from his mother's gaze. After morning Masses she pursued and detained the mothers of his friends. Over the course of a month she stood stoutly before each of them in turn with the same delicately oblique line of questioning. She had a mortal horror of admitting that her son kept the girl a secret, and so let drop into the conversations instead a series of semi-references, hints and innuendos whose responses in the eyes and words of her companions she watched like a hawk.

Within a month she had Isabel in her mind's eye. She was a schoolgirl, no less, a thing of seventeen that for weeks now had turned her son into a morose lump of silence and brooding.

He said nothing anymore, took his meals, came and went from the shop within the bittersweet vapours of remembering or anticipating the girl. Monday to Saturday he took the hounds or drove alone back to the places where he and Isabel had walked the Sunday before. When he walked the hounds back over the route of their lovewalks he imagined he noticed in their stride and bearing a sudden quickening and sharpness; he told them her name and they raised their eyes at once to its sound in direct mimic of the response of his own heart. They were the closest things to him now, these slender animals of speed and grace with all their racing coiled and unsprung within them. They knew, he told himself, in the deliberated agony of each walk, the terrible longing to run.

In five weeks of Sunday outings, five seven-hour Sundays with long kisses and cool cousinly goodbyes before the convent doors at their ending, Peader was still unsure of what if anything Isabel felt for him. He had not said he loved her, but was certain she knew, a certainty all the more painful for the uncertainty of her response. She came with that same mixture of pride and rebellion down the corridor and past the pursed mouth to meet him at the convent door every Sunday, every Sunday sitting into the cleaned-up car to go off with him into the more remote corners of the west. For politeness he asked her how her studying was going and she replied: "Dreadful. I'm doing nothing," she said, and in that Peader took his greatest encouragement, briefly letting himself imagine she thought as much of him as he of her. He thought of tender things to tell Isabel about himself, but even as he was about to, the ghost of his father sat into the car between them and it all seemed ridiculous and foolish. In the whirlwind of fear and longing that is the first weeks of love, Peader O'Luing questioned, found, and lost faith in everything. When they got out of the car to walk, if he didn't reach for Isabel's hand, she wouldn't reach for his.

The bleakness of that winter at last let up, and first two then three days came without rain. It was the end of March. From within the grey stone the population of the city reemerged on its streets with the dazed look and cautionary steps of people unused to walking in the light. All skies were watched for thunder, but the clouds that sailed in over the islands from the west were the pale white tossed linen sheets of springtime. They fluttered overhead benignly, travelling the blue air above the city rooftops like God's dreams, glimmering with sunlight. Birds returned from the invisible nowhere of their wintering, darting, flash-flying, alighting in choruses on the ancient stone ledges of the rooms above the shops on Shop Street. Grainne Halloran reopened the florists. The first daffodils of the year she placed in a bucket at the front door and the unreal brilliance of their gleaming brought Peader to her counter within half an hour, handing over ten pounds for a great fistful of the blossoms which he half-hid within his coat going down the street to slip them into the car. It was the first real Saturday of that spring, and buoyed by the flowers and the light, he decided in a single stride down Shop Street that he must advance his courtship to the next stage or go mad. When he thought of it, it was as simple and obvious as a move in draughts: on Spy Wednesday they could tell the nuns the widower uncle was taken ill, Isabel was needed to help out. She could leave the convent that evening and not return until Easter Sunday night. Peader could tell his mother his friends were going away together for a few days until Easter Sunday or even Monday night. He could take Isabel in the car as far as Donegal. By the time they returned a threshold would have been crossed: he would have made love to her and banished forever the uncertainty of her feelings for him.

It was as simple as a move in draughts, or appeared so to Peader O'Luing going down Shop Street in the light-headed and airy excitement of the first sunshine of spring. The following Sunday morning he drove the wilting bundle of the daffodils in the passenger seat to the convent. It was a fine day. The gravel of the long, arcing driveway crunched beneath the car like children's sweets. The tall trees that ringed the playing fields were coming into bud, and what had seemed the grey prison of winter was now a tranquil spreading parkland turning green in the spring. He left the flowers in the front seat and hurried up the steps to the front door. When the pursed mouth and small eyes opened it, the dead air of all the girls' lost time escaped down and out the corridor like a sigh, rushing for the tremoring freedom of the wind and trees. He hadn't to ask for Isabel anymore. He was let into the waiting room in small-eyed silence, standing by the window, idly moving with his fingertips the copies of *The Messenger* on the table. It was only when he heard the footsteps approaching that the momentousness of his plan made itself plain to him and his fingers screwed up with fright.

8

As it happened, there was never a hope of Isabel spending the weekend with him. She came into the waiting room with her hands thrust deep into the pockets of her cardigan and a distant look in her eyes. She was not able to go out with him.

"They're keeping me in."

"Fuck. Why?"

"I failed three of my exams. They found out I've no uncle in Galway. I'm to go home on the ferry on Thursday."

"Shit. They can't tell you what to do," he said angrily, louder than he wanted, speaking out of the immediate shock of seeing collapse even the Sunday drives and their central kisses, the stepping-stones upon which he thought the sanity of his life had come to rely. "Fuck's sake. Come with me now. What are they going to do anyway, expel you? They won't, come on . . ." He had taken hold of her arm and had already pulled her a few steps towards the door before he realised he had heard her say No and Stop it and Let go of my arm, you're hurting me.

The sleeve of Isabel's cardigan had been pulled down over her hand. She stood across from him, rubbing a place on her arm. In a flush of hurt and disappointment and regret, disbelieving he had been so rough with her, Peader blurted out: "I wanted you to come away with me next weekend, I wanted us to go to Donegal . . ."

Isabel looked directly at him, the small thick man with the pained round eyes and crooked nose. It was the first outright expression of his love. She was amazed, not by what he felt, but that there in the waiting room he had brought himself to declare it.

"I can't," she said, and heard the small quick rap that preceded by a moment the opening of the door and the appearance in the entrance of the small-eyed nun. "Excuse me, Isabel, I think Sister Magdalen is waiting for you." The nun stood there behind a smile and waited, waited until the silent weight of the awkwardness pressed so forcibly on Peader's shoulders that he feared he was stooping, facedown, as he hurried past both of them and out the doorway into the spring-light air of that ruined Sunday.

Thinking of it later, Isabel realised that by that Sunday afternoon in the week before Holy Week she had still not fallen in love. It was true that her studies had fallen away, shelves of her mind tottering into a mire of indolent daydreams. Her brain had become soft, she thought, stretching back her neck in the silent studyroom, where two hours had passed without her learning anything. There was no sharpness, no perception of all that moved in paragraphs past her fixed gaze. She knew the pen marks, the grain and knots in her wooden desk more than the textbooks, could tell blindly by her fingertips the place where years of idling pens and rulers had scarred the timber. It was useless, the hours went by. Isabel herself could not understand it. Over the course of her school years she had not made any true friend in the convent, for although there were many girls who liked her, there was a difference about her that kept them from coming closer. Now, as she found herself regressing through the class and simply unable to study, she had no one to whom she could really speak. It wasn't Peader, she told herself, marking a slow blue curve of ink on a page of the poetry book. She wasn't madly in love, or anything like what she imagined madly in love would be. She liked him, and the pattern of their Sundays in the small red car. It was a kind of island, she thought, that car with the two of them moving with so few words through all the fabulous scenery of field, bog, and mountain. There was something in Peader that was like herself, he too was a little adrift, cut off and separated from the ordinary. She liked his awkwardness as much as anything else, she smiled, arcing the slow blue line into a circle on the page and beginning to retrace it, moving the pen over and over along the same line and looking down at it as if for clues to an answer. No, she wasn't madly in love, and that Sunday afternoon when she walked down the corridor towards Peader with her hands deep in the pockets of her cardigan knowing that she would no longer be able to slip out the convent door into the freedom of the car, it had been the drive more than the driver she regretted. But then, only minutes later, returning from the waiting room through the dead air, hearing the soft footsteps of Sister Assumpta coming behind her and then fading into the side room where she calculated the convent budget and waited to answer the front door, everything had changed. He had declared himself, and in the aftershocks of Peader's anger Isabel could feel the measure of his longing for her. She was shaken. Her hand held the banister going up the stairs to the studyroom. Her head felt light, and in the following hours of that Sunday afternoon her mind flew like a kite in the strong breeze of her going with him to Donegal. What would it have been like, full days and nights together in a place she had never been? She could think of nothing else, and that night she was the one who didn't sleep, turning to face the moon in the window with the wide eyes and pale excitement of a girl feeling loosen the string that held her.

9

Until Thursday she lived with the buffeting, the tugging, toing and froing, rising and falling emotions in the quick winds of her heart. He had wanted to take her to Donegal, and the romance of that idea as Isabel thought of it over and over again began to take on the dimensions of love. For four days there was room for nothing else in Isabel's mind, and on Holy Thursday afternoon when the minibus called at the convent doors to take her and three other island girls to the ferry, she knew that she couldn't leave the mainland without speaking to him. Once the bus was outside the convent gates she moved across and sat next to Eibhlin Ni Domhnaill, asking her in a half-whisper to meet the Master at the pier and tell him his daughter had taken sick on the bus and was going to wait and come home on the next day's ferry.

She had asked it without even knowing what she intended to do. When the bus pulled over and she stepped out with her bag into the sharp salt tang of the sea air, it struck her with the force of old memories and she almost wanted to go home at once. But she didn't, and out of sight of the bus driver she slipped behind parked cars and a fish van and made her way back alone into the city centre.

There was a familiar feeling to these moments now, the same thrumming quickening heartbeat that pulsed through her as she broke the rules and headed off in her own direction. This time, though, it was not her freedom she was seeking, and as she walked amidst the shopping streets of the old city, losing herself in the bright Easter-week crowds, she was ever more firmly closing the doors behind her into the prison of the relationship. She had to speak to him. The light breeze and buoyancy in the afternoon made blooms of her cheeks. Her eyes glittered in the falling ladders of sudden sunlight between streets. Everywhere there was a mood of holiday, and the narrow paths trickled a constant file of women, children, and a few men going about the business of getting ready. Twice Isabel passed the shop where Peader worked, twice she moved past its window without looking in, holding her breath the six paces while wondering if chance would have him look up and see her. As the ferry had already sailed and she was without the money to stay the night in a hotel, the size of the risk she had taken was a fat ball lodged in the base of her throat. She passed the shop a second time, walking by, every step loaded with waiting and longing for his voice at her back calling her to stop. No voice came and she passed by. She crossed down and up the street on the far side once more, this time turning in the green door to the old bookshop where he had first left her. A genteel elderly lady with half-moon glasses and silver hair smiled at her across the counter as she came in. "Nice today, isn't it?" she said. Isabel nodded and looked around. Peader wasn't there. Why she had imagined he might be she didn't know. She was waiting for help, a sign, something to reveal that it wouldn't be all her doing and that love had its own volition and will outside and beyond her. She faced the walls of books and put her bag on the floor. From off the front room two archways led down a small slope in the floor into another room of books. They were stacked from floor to ceiling, old and new, the greens and blues and reds of their bindings keeping hushed and stilled the million voices of words, all the vocabulary of grief and love and wisdom just beyond hearing. In an hour there within the green door bookshop in the heart of the city Isabel looked at books and fell within a quietened spell of peace, for a time hearing each of the voices of the books she took down and opened. As the afternoon grew later and the light outside was swiftly withdrawn across the western sky, the lady with the half-moon glasses came from behind the counter and returned books to their shelves. She had watched the girl coming and going through the shop, climbing the creaking stairs to Irish Literature, returning and ending up in Poetry, and now standing beside her she drew out a new edition of the love poems of Yeats. "This is beautifully done, I think, don't you?" she said, handing Isabel the poems and looking into her face with eyes of such radiance and understanding that for a moment they might have been the eyes of Love itself.

Ten minutes later, Isabel left the shop with the book in her bag and crossed up the street to O'Luing's Wool and Tweed Shop. She opened the door to the jangle of a small bell above her head and stepped across the wooden floor of the empty shop, whose smell was already familiar to her. There was an instant, a moment of absolute emptiness, then Maire Mor swept through the door on a wave of alcohol. She saw the girl in the gabardine, recognised her from the two times she had walked so slowly past the shop earlier in the afternoon, and knew at once that it was she.

"Hello. Is Peader here?"

"He's not."

"Will he be coming back soon?"

"He won't. What do you want him for?"

"He knows me, I'm a friend . . ."

"Are you in trouble?" The mother shot the question like an arrow. With plump hands on ample hips she aimed it directly into the girl's face and let the four blunt words cover the multitude of myriad stupidities and mistakes of which she imagined her son capable. Isabel was taken aback, she glared at the small round woman.

"No, I'm not. I'd just like to see him."

"Well, he's not here. He's above in Carmody's," she said, and then hissed, "drinking himself sick over some"—she paused, wet her lip, and spat—"bitch."

10

Later, Isabel was to realise that the walk to Carmody's lounge was the shortest walk of her life, the distance between liking a man and loving him abbreviated into the few minutes it took her to go up the street and change her life forever. Later, she was to understand the route better, to know that as she wandered up the narrow path with her head full of defiance and the spring night sky dusted with stars, she was already within a spell. Already she had crossed the chasm of her hesitations. The night lent her its mood, and by the time she stepped inside the door of Carmody's to the low smoky light and dull thudding of music her eyes were shining with the shock of feeling for the first time that now she was at last in love.

She moved through the lounge as if it were littered with the outrageous obstacles that lovers imagine are the world trying to thwart them. Then she saw him, sitting there, drowning slowly in the bittersweet seas of his unrequited feelings. She stopped, but only for an instant. For the defiance and daring and danger were all connected now, charging her past the bends of hesitation and doubt, and with a hopeless inevitability carrying her footsteps across the lounge until she sat down beside him to reach and take his hand. Peader laughed and cried in the same moment; he choked his words out.

"How the . . . ? O Jesus, Issy."

When they walked outside in the Galway streets Isabel leaned her head against his arm. Her eyes shut with the charge of sweetness, the warmth of him, and she walked blindly, taking his kisses on her neck up the street, bumping against him and moving on, two figures beneath the starlight, hand-locked, electric with desire.

III

1

After my mother died, thick grey drapes of silence were drawn inside our house. For the six months of winter my father stayed at home and in that time spoke barely ten words. He became a thinner version of himself, fine and flakelike, with only the incandescent brilliance of his eyes betraying the presence of any feeling at all. He paced the glaring brightening darkening fury of his feelings through the empty rooms of the house in such ways that I grew to interpret anger, bitterness, and failure from the sounds of his shoeless feet on the bare floors. He did not speak about my mother or the manner of her death. As far as I knew he did not paint. I began to think that that episode of our life had ended, that it had been some satanic prompting that had maddened him into going away often and long enough until at last without kicking or screaming love sank into madness and died.

Now our days and nights took on a new pattern. I went back to school. I sat in the high-ceilinged warm rooms where the rain beat all day outside in another world and I could forget everything but history and geography, Caesar's Gallic Wars, and the puzzling poetry of Yeats. My bicycle had collapsed on the brutal hill of Trees Road, and having jammed the mudguards in place, banged the buckled wheel, and hung the brake blocks tentatively in position, I managed to sell it for ten pounds. I saved this and any other money I came across, pocketing it against the prospect of some calamity I felt certain would befall us next. I walked to school, leaving the house in the lightening blue and coming home in the swift-falling dark past all the happy homes of the city's southern suburbs. I loved the chill of that winter, the dampness drying off the wrinkled back knees of my trousers all day, the hood of my duffle coat blown back going home and the plastering of hair to my head. I felt I had escaped everything walking in wind and rain. That winter I left the house every morning expecting to return and find it empty. But somewhere, rumbling through the emptiness, my father was always there.

Months passed. We moved into a trembling spring, as if against our will. My studies had improved dramatically, and as Masters and Brothers alike changed their tone, moving like whispering statues around the knowledge of my tragedy, the schooldays passed more easily. The thrilling promise of the season, all the light flickering noons and afternoons of April and May gave way to an uncertain summer. The wildflower meadow sprung up again in front of our house. Each morning, lying late in bed awake, I listened into the silence for the slightest muffled sounds of bare feet that meant my father was still there. Some days I could feel the restlessness in him filling the house. He came up and down the stairs five times in an hour, settling nowhere, going and returning from his studio like some demented creature trapped within his longing to be away. His hair was long and thinning and wispy, a white veil that fell back off the shining dome of his forehead and made him look like some grave figure of the Old Testament waiting for a sign. If he was, that summer it never came. I began to imagine he was searching through the house for something, or trying to enter one of the bare rooms quickly enough to catch the fading presence of someone he had heard from below. As June and July swept past on a misted screen of light rain and broken cloud, my father struggled against going. I knew it. And by August realised I was witnessing a man in mortal combat with himself. The same Voice that had prompted him to leave his job and family and go away to paint was absolutely silent now. Was he supposed to give up now, paint no more, surrender himself to the truth that he was a less than brilliant artist, or had mishandled the inspiration given him from God?

At the beginning of summer he blundered about the empty house in search of the answer. The kitchen had long since become the main living room and by summer had taken on the look and smell of a dump. All the dishes had been used, first filling the sink and then piling over along the counter in a sprawling souvenir of our months of boiled or burned dinners. Pots were universally blackened, their inside bottoms developing a thick rind of burn that soapless cold water failed to remove and which in turn thickened into the soup or sauce of the next day's dinner, building up like sins on the bottom of a soul. You dove your hand for cutlery, fishing it up out of the cold odoriferous mess of the sink and rinsing what could be rinsed. The drip stains of tomato and other vaguer things had hardened into the paintwork. Without decree or any conversation, it seemed that after my mother's death the notion of cleaning died with her. We took out of the mess what we needed and put it back afterwards. The crumbs collected on my father's bare feet, the broom grew cobwebs.

But then, by late summer, as the windless humid mist of weather settled over the countryside, the smells of the kitchen climbed the stairs, and one morning at eight o'clock my mother woke both of us from sleep. She rapped on our doors with a kind of urgent knuckling and brought my father and me out of our beds to the upstairs landing as surely as if she had called our names. We looked across the empty space at one another. Sleep on my father turned him into a grandfather. His eyes were small, lost in beds of wrinkles, his hair ridiculous and wild. He looked at me, I looked at him. He didn't have to ask if I had knocked on his door. We knew it was she and stood transfixed in amazement, breathing softly on the emptiness, until at the same moment we heard the small clattering of two dishes against one another in the sink downstairs.

Very slowly, his long stride somewhat uncertain and his toes cocked up carefully off the floorboards, my father walked past me to the top of the stairs. There it was again, the same noise of the dishes.

By the time we reached the kitchen that morning my mother had gone. But some trace of her was left behind. Standing there in the curtainless kitchen with the summer morning streaming in the big window, my father turned to me and smiled the way he hadn't smiled since before she died.

"Go and buy some washing up," he said, "will you?" digging out a ragged pound note from the secrecy of his trouser pocket and pressing it into my hand.

I flew to the shops, racing through the warm beginnings of the day until I had outdistanced sleep and weariness and even fear itself, rushing past the nightmare that maybe, just maybe he would be dead or gone when I got back. He was not. He was standing in the same place where I had left him, the sunlight striking the whitened chest hairs that spiralled up out of the hoop of his vest and the traces of smiles still circling about his mouth. His eyes were sparkling, his back was straight, and his hair was combed in a way that to his son made him look like a king come out of exile. I held up the plastic bottle of the washing-up liquid and we started.

If you passed along the back of our row of houses and peered in over the low garden wall, you might have imagined it an ordinary scene of domestic life, a father and son washing and drying and putting away the dishes while their mother rested. There might have been another like it over another wall in another house farther down the road. But in our kitchen that summer's morning, even as we passed the houseware to and from each other, unpiling pots, pans, cups and saucers and stacking them along the counter for slow washing in the warm soap of my mother's memory, it was not dirt, grime, or oil we were washing off, but grief. I swept it from the kitchen as my father dried. Together we rubbed the sun-warm windows over the sink where so often my mother had stood, peeling, paring, or polishing while she stared the dream of her married life away down the little tangle of garden and across the wall to the back of another house's dream. Tears fell from my father's eyes into the sink and were lost in the suds. My mother had died into the deep sleep of a whole jarful of tablets, but as we stood in her kitchen now it seemed it had been grief itself that was sleeping and was only now waking. The more my father washed, the more his tears flowed, and mine with them, both of us standing there, father and son, unable to speak and washing dishes like the loudest declarations of love.

After the kitchen we moved into the hall. My father found a broom and paddled the dust towards the door in clouds. When I opened it the house sighed, birds flickered up out of the meadow. The sunlight lanced in. My father meanwhile had opened the door into his studio and for the first time in over six months I followed him in. He had let the broom fall to the floor just inside the door and was moving along the far wall gathering paintings. There were more of them than I had expected. Dozens of canvases. He bent down and looked at each of them, stacking some carefully while pushing others backwards into a heap in the centre of the room.

"Take all those out, will you, Nicholas? Good man. Leave them in the hall."

I counted twenty-four, great squares and rectangles of angry colour in which I could see no image or picture, nothing but the effort and the paint. The others, the ones he left in the room, were different. In two or three I thought I saw my mother, just a glimpse of a figure moving on the edge of a canvas that was thickly covered in blues and greens and purples. There was something warm in them, something new for him. I could see skies and hills, and again that figure of a woman, just there, a reminder, a shape to which the paintings seemed to come and try to leave at the same moment. Gently my father ushered me out. "Those are not finished," he said.

"I like them," I said quickly.

"Well," he answered me over his shoulder, and then handing me a brush, "you can help." And then, with a half bemused laugh at the irony of his life, "They're all shite."

We laid the twenty-four canvases on the hall floor, and in tones of grey and mauve spent the early noontime painting over each of them. We had large brushes, and as we bent over to do the work I could feel the desperation and hope of the paintings vanishing under the long, slow strokes. They were the works of my father's first trip away, that first calling which had come to seem so intentionally malevolent and black, God's own little joke on our family, the foolish vanity of talent. By the time we had finished, my father seemed less burdened. He took the canvases one by one, holding them carefully between the flat palms of his hands like great tablets and laying them around the walls of the studio in the very places they had been once before. My mother was watching from the last step of the swept stairs. She could see them through the doorway, the semicircle of erased paintings waiting to be begun once again, and she smiled. Or so it seemed, the momentary wave of her warmth floating through all the downstairs rooms of our house, the ineffable memory of her touch and kiss alighting on the sides of our faces, rustling the little hairs at the backs of our necks and turning us around, father and son, to look at each other helplessly in the cleaned-up everywhere of the house to which she had returned.

2

At six o'clock we went out for tea. It seemed a remarkable thing. I remember it as a great voyaging forth, my leg flying out at full stretch to try and keep up with my father and the summer evening full of yellow shimmering and birdsong. It might rain or drizzle all day, but summer returned for the evenings, suburban evenings of men and dogs out walking, football games on hard, beaten greens, girls at bus stops, boys with golf bags or tennis rackets stooping forward on bicycles as they pushed up the homeward hills or hung about on grass verges talking about nothing, kicking at daisies, and waiting, waiting for the unbelievable long-lasting light to lower and fade. It was the holidays, the air buzzed. My father led the way out of the estate and past the gaze of our neighbours out towards the upper roads and the countryside. "There was a small village up here once," he said, "now it's a bloody town.

Still . . ." He talked straight ahead and walked past the moment of ill humour. "We'll get our tea there, right?" he said. "Right," I said.

It was a small café, a bright empty place with four plastic-topped tables with sugar bowls and milk jugs. The chairs were green plastic. At a counter in the back a girl with sprinkles of pimples served tea and pies.

"Cottage pie, fish pie, shepherd's pie, or chicken pie," she said.

The pies took five minutes. My father brought down the teas and set them on the table. His legs were too long, when he sat on the green chair his knees rose above the tabletop, so he sat back towards the middle of the room and held his teacup and saucer balanced on the centre of his chest. He took slow sips and smiled a lot. Smiles kept breaking out on him, and without knowing why I kept smiling back. It just seemed right, as if a great enormous cloud had been shifted out of our life and we were in the clean new beginning, although of what I had no idea.

"You're a good son, Nicholas," my father said.

I smiled into my tea. The pies came. Small oval-shaped things under brown pastry. I cracked the top with my fork and watched the swirl of steam and smelled the smell of the stewed meat as my father bit into his. We were never more father and son, I thought, at any moment in our life. I was never more happy than in the brief instants of just sitting there in that small plain place with the smells of meat and the sounds of cars going by in the summer evening. I took a bite of my pie and it burned me. As I turned the food quickly around in the inside of my mouth, my father told me he had to go away again.

"I don't want to leave you, but you'll be all right for a week, won't you? I'll only go for a week," he said. "In a week I'll make enough progress to bring back a half dozen canvases and finish them here. Ten days maybe."

I said nothing. I rolled the meat around in my mouth, felt the burn travelling through the roof into my head. He was going away? He was going to leave me? I felt a headache starting.

"It's not going to rain for six days," he announced, "and you're big enough now to mind yourself for a week, aren't you?"

I spat out the meat. "Why can't I come?" I couldn't believe I had said it. I was staring at him.

"I can't afford nice places, Nicholas, I sleep out, I find barns. It could be cold and damp." He paused and met my eyes across the table. "Will I get somebody to mind you? Do you . . ."

"No."

"Later," he said, "when you're older you can come." The girl with the pimples came down with the bill. She was closing soon, she said, and looked at us with our half-eaten pies and went away.

"Why?" I said.

"Why what?" my father said.

"Why do you have to go? Why can't you stay at home, why can't you be . . ."

The summer evening stopped, drew in like a held breath. The silence swelled, thickened. My father dug at the pie crust. He looked down at the fork in his hand, showing me the shiny, sun-freckled dome of his forehead, where suddenly the wrinkles seemed deeper than I had noticed. His head was cracked with them, the chiselled furrows of unfound answers to that same question. He laid down the fork and let his hand find them, his fingers moving back and forth feelingly.

"Nicholas," he said.

The room was exploding, the airlessness, the closeness, the burn in my mouth, the smell of the pies, the girl at the counter all conspired into my headache. At once I knew what was coming. I had an instant flash, a forehearing of those calamitous words that had already destroyed our family once. I knew before he said anything that there was no other answer. I didn't want him to answer. But he did. And sitting there in that small cramped restaurant in the built-up tremulous stillness of the summer evening, I heard my father say the same words I had heard him tell my mother in the kitchen.

"I have to paint. I believe it's what I'm supposed to do. I don't expect you to understand. But it's what God wants me to do." He said it and stopped. The girl at the counter had heard him. She stifled a gasp that might have been a giggle, and when my father looked around at her she rubbed the clean counter busily. She had a maniac in her shop, she was thinking, a long tall baldy fellow with bits of wispy white hair. When she got him out she'd have to call her friend and tell her. "You won't believe it, wait'll I tell you, it's what God wants me to do, he said. God, no less," she'd say again, and giggle into the mouthpiece, looking down at the vacated tables and the locked door where the madness had been let out safely onto the street.

I wanted to hate him. I walked a foot behind his giraffe-like stride and watched the people watching us. Did they all know he was off again? Did the urgency of his vocation leave traces in the very air he loped through? What kind of father would leave his son like this? After all that had happened, how could he think that God still gave a damn? I wondered and walked on. We took a circle route home, rounding farther than we needed to pass along the hilltop roads that opened broad views down to the bay. The sea looked shallow and silver in sunlight, buildings glistened, and we seemed to be walking along a high rim of the summered city. Into my father's step came a lightness and ease I had almost forgotten; he was away, or nearly. Belief was flooding back into him. Birds in hiding made leafsong overhead, and for all I wanted to, I could not hate him. When we turned the final bend and came in home, my mother was waiting. She was there in the cleaned-up house for no one to see but us, sitting on the swept stairway, smiling in the shine on the cups or moving lightly in the creak of the floorboards upstairs. She had waited for us to come back, waited to see if he had told me.

That night as I tidied my room she was standing in the doorway. She did not have to tell me anything. I knew her message without hearing it, knew the thing she had come back to say, sweeping her way across the limitless blue and gold horizons of heaven, past the cold glass windows of the million stars to stand in my doorway and tell me: that my father was right, that it *was* what God wanted him to do.

3

In the morning my father outlined his itinerary. He was going to Clare, to the sea. He would take the train as far as Ennis and make his way from there to the coastline. I had enough food in the house, and for milk or anything else I was to use the ten-pound note that was rolled in the jam jar of bills on the kitchen windowsill. He had gotten ready before I woke and a bundle of canvases was tied together in the hall. There was a tang of oil and spirits, smells of adventure. The front-hall door was opened on the morning and the delicate balance of the day, caught between sunlight and showers, trembled like my faith. My father in his shirtsleeves was a silver of energy, a thin quickness moving up and down the stairs and in and out of the studio in a bustle of preparation. When he looked at me I looked at his wrinkles. "You'll be back in a week," I said, standing by my mother in the hallway. "Right," he said, reaching his hand to my shoulder and giving a short warm squeeze, letting the wrinkles unfurrow for a moment and his eyes smile.

When it was time for him to go, he stood in the doorway, loaded with canvases, brushes, and paint, and held out his hand. I held out mine and he grabbed it, sending a shock of love through my arm so forcefully that tears shot into my eyes.

"A week," he said.

"A week," I said, and felt the coolness of the air rush against the palm of the hand he had let go. He headed out the driveway and, with a flying wave of the great flag of his hand, was gone.

It took me two minutes to decide. And another ten to take the money from the jam jar, put it with what I had saved, take my coat, a small carrier bag with a jumper, socks, and underpants, and head for the train station. My father was walking, hitching an improbable lift from any car whose driver was bemused or curious enough to pull over for him. I took the bus, reasoning the expense against the necessity of catching the same train as he. I sat upstairs in the front seat and peered down into the slow morning traffic for any sight of the long, thin figure carrying his bundle like a ragman along the paths that led into the city. But there was no sign of him. At the quays the bus pulled over and I stepped out into the tremendous flux of colour and noise that was Dublin in the summertime. High clouds sailed across the sun, moving green shadows along the river. My heart was racing. What if he was already ahead of me, already in his seat on the train watching the platform going slowly backwards? I stood off the crowded path and began running.

The train left at ten to ten. I sat in the back carriage on the side farthest from the platform and watched the last stragglers flapping awkwardly past with plastic bags, rucksacks, and small cases. By ten to ten my father had not passed the window. There was an announcement: This was the train for Nenagh, Limerick, and Ennis. And then the shutting of doors all along the train, a call, a whistling, a ticket collector joking to someone out the open window of the door, and the first three jolts, the quick stiff shudders that were the releasing of the brakes and the kicking of the engine as we shook then rattled then rolled past the end of the platform out of the station and away on a curving rhythmic beating into the countryside. We slid into country I had never seen, past old trackside houses with their washing lines and small gardens, places printed with the noise and life of trains, the clockwork regularity of the whoosh throughout their days and nights. Children didn't look up or wave. Beyond them, the newer suburbs of the city, the white blocks of life neither villages nor towns, just rows upon rows of houses, attached, detached, and semidetached. It was half an hour before we were past them, before the green outmeasured the grey and the banks beyond the windows ran up into the tangled briars and ditches of the fields of Kildare, then Laois. The ticket collector came through the carriages, swaying over the punching of paper holes and telling Spanish students to take their feet down off seats. There was no smoking, he said, pacing through wafting screens of smoke and banging the flat of his fist against a back window to let in the louder rush of the wind and the tracks and the smells of woodbine and hay. It was all new to me. I sat beside a small woman in a big coat who kept her hand on her handbag at all times, nodding into the drumming rhythms to dream of thieves, suddenly jolting upright with a cry until she looked down and found the bag was safe in the sweat of her hands and she could close her eyes and be robbed in peace again. She said nothing to me. I was too excited to sleep. I was too afraid that my father was not on the train, and too afraid that he was. What I intended to do in either case I am not certain. The magic of the train would resolve it, I imagined, the newness and innocence of arrival, the fresh beginning, all that. I sat back and stared out the window. We moved into the middle of the country, a great green immensity rolling into hills and mountains that wore the shadows of the sky. Cows were still shapes in the landscape. The sense of space was incredible, the largeness, the openness of it all, the distance that stretched across the fields drawing me out, longing to be there, running or sitting or lying down into the infinitesimal sweetness of the summer grass. As the train sped on, ever farther westwards, the landscape became more extravagantly remote, the sky bigger. The rattle of the tracks was a trance, and after a while the flashing of the countryside past the window slowed into a steady rolling, a sweeping panorama that ten carriages ahead, on a southside window, I could imagine my father staring into. For two hours we moved in the same dream. Then, at Limerick, we changed for Ennis. "Change here," boomed the ticket collector, big-footing his way down through the smoke and banging open the window two cold priests had closed.

Delaying, peering from the doorway the length of the platform, I was last off the train. Clutching my bag I hurried down and stood beside a pillar that cried out in alarm as the small woman in the big coat popped out from its other side and held her handbag to her chest. I apologised and hid myself.

There were less than forty passengers for Ennis, a little clustering of country people standing expectantly. I looked for my father and couldn't see him. Then, slowly, from the far end of the station came an old engine pulling three wooden carriages. It heaved and squealed and soured the air with the smell of oil. From the engine window the begrimed and toothy face of the driver grinned out at us as he performed his miracle and brought the train to a stop. "He looks a hundred and ninety," muttered the handbag lady, raising her belongings chest-high and sweeping forward for her seat. I moved out from the pillar and was on the step into the carriage when I saw him, a flash of white hair, a tall figure with the underarm bundle of his things as he came out of the waiting room and climbed onto the train. He was there. My father. He was so intent on not missing the connection that he didn't look once to his right or left. He got on the train, moved into the first carriage, and sat down. A moment later and we were rattling in a new rhythm into the west.

4

My father was on the train; I stood in the corridor between cars and felt the slopping of an oily sickness in the barrel of my stomach. My feet were rising and falling softly. I couldn't think, or couldn't think just one thing at a time, rushing instead through the myriad runaway thoughts of panic. What was I going to do? What would he do, what would he say? Would I go up to him once we arrived? Would he send me straight back? And what was he thinking now, sitting not forty steps in front of me in a train travelling the full width of the island from where he imagined he had left alone his only child in a house with his mother's ghost? I slid down against the door until I was sitting. Was he not thinking back at all? Had he already crossed over, left all thoughts of that other life and now sat anticipating only the week he had given himself to cover the canvases in the images of the west? I didn't know, but for two hours sat there on the floor of the train and let the tides of doubt and nausea wash first one way and then the other across my insides until the engine whistled when I looked up and at last we had come to Clare.

The station was small. A train arrived there only once a week, clanking nervously in next to the rings and pens of the cattle mart. The passengers got off with some relief, hastening away to cars or buses and the bustle of the country town down the road. From the rear of the train I watched my father stepping down. He crossed the small platform in the gusting of a summer breeze, a lift to the air that made him pause and steady his canvases, before heading away along the back road behind the town. I waited three minutes and then followed him. He seemed to know exactly where he was going and marched away with that same certain purposefulness that had carried him in and out of the several crises of his life.

The road ran along by a row of houses and then past a high wall that offered no shelter and caused me to let a half-mile open up between us. He was the flicker of white hair in the distance, a ruffle of coattail. The afternoon was quick and breezy, clouds flew past, the very air was different. We were still miles from the sea, but already I could feel it, out there, somewhere ahead of us, the ocean I had never seen. From time to time my father put out his thumb to the cars going past, but none took the chance of stopping for him and he never broke the steady beat of his stride to look out at them in hope. He walked out of Ennis, and I followed. He walked on the side of the road that went northwards to the sea, moving always a bend or so ahead of me until I realised he was not going to get lifts and could let him pull away by as much as a mile as long as I made it up before the next town. Throughout that afternoon, then, we paced towards the coast. He stopped once. At a low garden wall where the bushes grew at frantic angles inland away from the burning of winter storms he took off his boots and rubbed the soles of his feet. Little bits of cardboard stuffing fell out on the ground, and he tore and shaped a new insole from more he carried in his sack and then walked on. I gained ground on him then, stopped at the same place, and ate the first three biscuits of a pack I had bought at a shop along the road. It was on a rise looking west, and only as I sat there gazing down the road at the thin figure of my father moving away did I realise that on the rim of the horizon, there beyond a little curve of grass dotted with white caravans, was the sea.

It was another two hours before we had reached it. By then the afternoon sky had surrendered to the evening clouds; the wind was blustering, cracking the sheets on washing lines behind the caravans. The sea was in the wind, my sweat tasted salt. As I walked my eyes kept leaving my father and swimming out into the waves and the islands in the distance. I like to think there was something already drawing me then, something that was nothing to do with him, but a feeling the hours of walking, the sea air, and sounds themselves had already instilled in me, touching me with a sense of the freshening wildness of those western places that was not to leave me for the rest of my life. I like to think I loved it as soon as I saw it, that I knew the end of our journey was in sight the moment I looked up from that rise in the road. Whatever the case, when my father stepped in over two lines of barbed wire and made his way down to a small strand in the dimming evening, I came carefully behind and did the same, sneaking down across the tufted grass of the sand hills.

By the time I had come to the edge my father was already naked. And even in the moments I watched him walking that high thin walk of his into the thunderous crashing of the first waves, taking them across his midriff in white embraces of chill spray, yelling out in what might have been elation or anger and shaking his hair, I was already stripping and running down, screaming and shouting, leaping the waves to save him from drowning himself in the sea.

5

My father was neither happy nor angry to see me. At least not in any way I can describe. Later I told myself he may have been both, for although a thin man he was capable of the broadest range of emotions. Over the roaring of the waves and his own shouting he didn't hear me calling, and turned as I reached him only to stagger sideways into the foam, both of us going down into the broken surge of the chest-high waters with the same gasp in our mouths and amazement in our eyes. We came up spitting. As we did, grimacing the water out of our eyes, the tide sucked at my legs, pulling with such swift undertow that I was lifted off the sand and swept at once ten feet from him out to sea. I kicked and thrashed, remembering as a second wave lowered itself into my screams that I couldn't quite swim. I was thirty feet from him in an instant, sailing and sinking away on the amazement of the swift sea, my foot and ankle poking up ridiculously into the sky, falling back, plunging down like some tremendous anchor until the water ran across the bridge of my nose and I breathed horror through my screaming eyes. My father appeared and disappeared in the scene. I saw him. He saw me, or the naked white body of what he took at first to be certainly my ghost. At first I think he imagined that as such I didn't need rescuing, I needed wrestling. He put his hands together and dove like a prayer. He vanished and I went under. The world bubbled out of me. I felt hands grappling me and my body glistening and slipping through them. He couldn't hold me, my legs were up, my head was down. The sky rolled round and round in my eyes in the last gasp moments of my life, and then I sank a final time, plummetting through the swirling foam down down beyond the frantic waters to the still clear cold sea floor, where at last my father's fingers found my hair and jerked me up.

I burst into daylight, lifted, wild-eyed, into the air and spewing the sea back into itself. We were far out in the tide now, ebbing away so that for the first time I saw the marvel of the little strand, how perfectly cupped and secluded it was back there across the combs of the breakers, how tiny and sad the little tossed bundles of our separate clothes. My father's arms were about me. I kicked my legs and they flopped uselessly, making a small splashing that the waves carried away. I think I shouted or screamed, gulping more water, gasping and sucking at the air for it to fill me, falling out of my father's arms once more, going down, coming up, thrashing and flailing until a hand crashed into my jaw and for just a moment the sea stopped. Silver stars flew up out of the water, sound was switched off, and then my chin was cupped in the great vice of my father's hand as he swam dragging me out. When he was within his depth he stood and carried me, our two naked figures emerging into the suddenly chill air with the sea running from both of us. On the sand he laid me down. I was still coughing and spluttering, my eyes rolling, when he stood the full width of the sky over me and looking down said:

"Well, God wants you to live, Nicholas."

6

It was the beginning of a week of surprises. If I had surprised my father in suddenly appearing naked alongside him in mid tide when he expected me to be on the other side of the country, that was nothing compared to what lay ahead in that week in the west of Clare. It began quietly. My father, it seemed, had had no intention of drowning himself. It had instead been a kind of western baptism, a dousing in renewal.

At first I hardly noticed that he was a different man, that he was released now from the prisons of his life into doing what he sometimes believed without doubt was the Will of God. He dried me with his shirt until the chattering of my teeth stopped and I could put on my clothes and tell how I had followed him. He looked down into the sand and laughed. Then he got up and wandered off, leaving me sitting by the canvases and bags, hugging my knees and staring out at the extraordinary seductive power of the crashing ocean. How could the fierce collapse of its thunderous waves, time after time on the dark-sand shore, seem so full of softness and ease? How could such force seem so peaceful? The very waters that had frightened the life all but out of me were in the slowly fading evening like the invitations of dreams. I might have walked down into them, so fabulous and wild did they seem, but for the sounds of my father's footsteps as he came back, armed with rubbish and sticks for the small and brief fire he lit in the shelter of the dunes. It was our first evening's camp. We ate biscuits and dry bread and cheese. My father had milk he shared. We grew hungry and cold again, of course, but to me at least it didn't matter. Wrapped in every piece of clothing I had brought, I huddled down in the hollow of the dune. It was a boy's dream, a night under the summer stars with his father, within the ever-falling sighing of the night sea and the marvelous knowledge that life was real and that God didn't want me to die just yet.

The following morning I woke at five and found my father gone. The tide had come in and the waves grown louder. Gulls were screaming in the blue sky, and the sea wind blew in the cove with a soft whispering emptiness, running round the sand hills and out again, smoothing out footprints until the morning strand looked again like the first place in the world. I got up quickly. My father's bags were still where he had left them, and imagining that somehow in nightmare we had changed places and he was the one now being swept out to sea, I hurried to the high tideline, peering out into the waves. For a while I thought he was certainly drowned. I paced up and down along the wet sand, sinking and staring outwards, shouting out his name as the water rushed in joyously across my shoes and the sound of my voice was made small by the sea. Where was he? Was he drowned? Was that dark half-shape in the distant waves his body, that flash of white his head? I squinted and stared, was sure it was, was certain it wasn't, and might have stripped again and dove in, tempting God to save me once more, were it not for the chance flight of a low gull catching my eye and turning me round to see where, forty feet above the dunes in the sloping grass, my father had set up his folding easel and was busily painting.

I sank onto the sand. He must have seen me, must have heard me calling, I thought. Why hadn't he let me know? For five minutes I sat there on the wet sand. No wave of his hand, no call, no acknowledgement of any kind, just his long figure stopped crazily to the canvas and his hand moving with the brush in quick, sudden movements. I went back up to the camp and lay down. It was five o'clock in the morning, my feet were wet, my eyes stung, and I had just learned the first lesson of that week's education in art: once you begin, nothing else matters, not love, not grief, not anything.

When my father painted, the world beyond his view vanished into nothing. Day after day, wherever we were all along that beautiful coastline, he established the same pattern, rising while I slept, setting up his canvas in view of the sea, painting for four hours in mixed tones of yellow and red and blue and green, turbulent images of spilled colour that on the third day I realised in a sudden flash were in fact nothing more than the sea itself. Everything he painted was the sea; but it was never blue or green. The sky was never the soft and limpid overhanging I saw when I looked west. For him, in his paintings, sea and sky were the expressions of something else, they were the constant and yet ever-changing monologue of God Himself, the swirling language of creation, the closest thing to the beginning of life itself. He painted for four hours and came back to where I was waking, his face drawn and exhausted, the crazy long hairs of his eyebrows flying out at the edges like wings and his eyes puffy and small and streaming tears from the wind. He lay down when I got up. He gave me money to walk to the shops to buy the day's food, and when I was gone he slept. Later, by midday, he was awake again. And if the field we were in was close enough, he stripped and went down to swim, taking me with him sometimes to tech me how to breathe in water. The days were full of uncertain weather. Rain kept threatening but never falling, holding off in huge pale continents of cloud, slow-moving shapes that above my lying-down head joined one onto the next, sliding together all afternoon until the sky itself was one immensity of whiteness and the fragments of blue were tiny gaps unreachable and high as heaven. After bread and biscuits, or cheese, or sometimes ham, and the shared pint of milk, if we were not moving on, he went back to work, starting the day's second painting, never touching the morning canvas until the following dawn, by which time, if the wind had been blowing, myriad grains of sand would have found their way onto the paint and the brush would work them deeper into the picture's texture.

While my father worked I went off walking, moving down to the popular beach or into the holiday town, where everything was hopeful and bright. There were families everywhere, loose loud chains of them wandering down the streets, in and out of shops, young children with rings of ice cream round their mouths and saddles of freckles across their noses. Sometimes I tailed along behind them, the unknown brother, the last of the family, for a while just on the edge of ordinary life.

When I got back my father would still be painting. The afternoon canvases were different from those of the morning. At first I thought it was his tiredness and the pressure into which he had stoked his brain that made the second paintings of every day seem so much more desperate and urgent. A flat grey ribboned into black in all of them, the tones of everything deepened, the yellows and blues that sparkled and raced into the morning works were here half-hidden, disappearing flickers of light into the churning swirl of darker shades. After he had painted four or five of them, I relaxed, realising that they were not the works of personal anger or grief but simply the pictures of what my father saw, God's changing humour in the afternoons and early evenings, the sky in the sea like a face aging.

Most days he painted through until eight o'clock. I watched him from a distance, looking up from whatever seashore we had stopped at to see his tall figure perched and stooping over a canvas that was buffeted like a sail in the sea breeze. There were stones around its base, anchoring him for the day at whatever site he had chosen, keeping him there under broad western skies whose swift majesty and change seemed to mock all effort to capture or tame it. Sometimes a car stopped on the road behind and tourists, Germans or Americans, made their way slowly down across the tufted grass to see. They approached uncertainly, not quite sure if this man with the long white hair was someone they ought to know or run from. When my father never turned or looked at them, mixing the colours and applying them without the slightest show of recognition, they walked away as uncertain as before, driving along the high road and out of my childish dream that they might see the paintings and be astonished, offer great sums of money, and herald my father a genius.

Our evenings were cold and quiet. Even the warmest day became a chill night. The sea wind forced us back into the sand hills. I had no books, no radio, and sat hunched on the sand staring out at the humped shapes of the islands for hours at a time. Generally, my father fell asleep early. But sometimes after we ate and before he curled into his coat on the sand, he sang a piece of a song, or rather spoke the words in the verse rhythm. I had never heard him sing and felt ever more strongly the realisation that this was a different man from the one at home in the sitting room. Here everything about him seemed released, and I could only imagine how silently he had rattled for so long in the jails of his office career. On one of the first nights he asked me, offhandedly, what I knew to sing or say, and in a faltering half-whisper that mixed into the whoosh of the night waves, I said some school poems I had learned by heart, and then, without thinking, began the slow intricate fabulations of a learned passage of Ovid, then Virgil.

"Dine hunc ardorem mentibus addunt, Euryale, an sua cuique deus fit dira cupido."

They were sounds so soft and full in my mouth that the very saying of them was a kind of magic, a kind of disappearing, upwards and outwards beyond the breaking of the surf and the distant shining of the lights on the islands. I sounded the Latin and the words floated on the wind. I said a remembered line, and another. My father's eyes were closed, but he was listening too, as if it were a fine music that the wind played off the stars.

When I finished, he slept. The sea pounded on the ancient shore.

7

I said the Latin every night after that. He sang something poorly, stopped, and then I started, skipping the school poems and beginning, following a silent accord such as two lovers might share and conjuring magic with sounds of Latin. I was as surprised by it as he was, and found myself anticipating the nights as I wandered through the seaside towns. Looking back, I realise that I had found the beginnings of my own identity, the first quivering emergence of my own shape out of the great shadow cast by my father. In the Latin I had something. That it seemed at once absolutely foreign and at the same time strangely fitting to the wild open night spaces of the west made it all the better. We lay holed up in the corner of a dune with the wind rushing over our heads, and I said words in Latin. Of course it didn't strike me then that there was any other reason for my having turned to the Virgil or Ovid after the school poems ran out. I wasn't thinking of anything other than the flash of panic I had felt to have something to say for my father as he had asked. I didn't know then that the sounds seemed a symbol to him, that they came that first night like heraldic angels trumpeting in his ears, and through his own son's mouth, the confirmation if any was needed that God had come to the west coast of Clare and that in the sudden sweetness of the holy language was the revelatory message that yes, those paintings of the sea were the very things that He Himself had brought William Coughlan there to paint.

8

On the last day of the week we walked south and east again in the direction of the train station. Every canvas my father had brought with him had now been worked on. Seen all together they were remarkable; there was a style running through all of them, the same underlying vision of mornings and evenings, light struggling to spread out or stay against the onrush of dark, the shimmering and answering reflections of air and water that seemed in these paintings to have aspired to the condition of fire. The two latest pictures, not yet dry, I carried back-to-back and separate from the others in a kind of drawstring carrier that seemed ready-made to fit them. They were, like all the others, silvers of the sea we were leaving behind.

There was a sadness in returning as well as a sense of victory. My father had done what he came to do and was eager now to be back in his studio. But even as we tramped quietly along the road homeward, I could feel the memories of the summer sea already shifting and sighing inside both of us. There was something that was impossible to leave about that western coast, and moving as we were with our backs to the blue horizon and the stacked canvases flapping a little in the wind, every footstep was a triumph over the temptation to stop and go back.

In the pie café my father had said it wouldn't rain for six days. It was the first time I had known him to make any prediction and had at first taken it only as some rash expression of hope not fact. It was the kind of thing you might say setting off, I told myself later, he meant nothing more by it. The skies we slept under were too uncertain for forecasts. They came and went on the moody gusts of the Atlantic, bringing half a dozen different weathers in an afternoon and playing all four movements of a wind symphony, allegro, andante, scherzo, and adagio, on the broken backs of the white waves. Clouds, thumping bass notes or brilliant wild arpeggios, were never long in coming. It had seemed it was going to rain all the time, but never did. My father did not look concerned, and on the fifth day as I woke and found myself instinctively searching the sky for the weather note, I realised that to him his prediction had not been hope but fact. It wasn't going to rain for six days, it was as simple as that. Our trip, though, was seven, and on the morning of the day we were to walk back toward the station my father drew out of his bag sheets of clear plastic with which we carefully wrapped the paintings. The two in the drawstring carrier he handled separately. "When it rains, Nicholas," he said, "we'll have to mind these two carefully. I'll give you my coat for over them as well."

The sky under which we set off that morning was pale and unremarkable. The air had a coolish lift to it, a freshness that was the forebreeze of another month, the quivering note of September. We marched out of the field, stepped over three lines of barbed wire, and headed up the softly rising hill away from the sea. Cars slipped past us. My father took no notice of them and kept his eyes straight ahead, slowing his stride sometimes to let me catch up or standing on a small crest to pause and look back, measuring in the long ribboning grey of the road how far we had come. The train was not until early the following morning, we had one more night to camp inland somewhere near the station, and it was to there we were heading, the pictures hung on our backs like the huge strange stamps of a far-off country and the rising wind pressing us forward. By noon we had left our last glimpse of the sea. By early afternoon in a place called Kilnamona it began to rain.

My father took off his coat for the two most recent paintings, bundling them tightly as the landscape all around us closed in, its colours fading into the drizzle. How quickly everything changed. The clouds sat down, the light left the day, and the pastoral greenness of all the stone-walled fields surrendered to a grey and desolate emptiness. For miles it was raining. At the edges of the sky you could see the fraying of clouds and the water spilling, like so many downstrokes of a sable brush. The lift and energy of the day were washed away. We tramped on without talking and the holiday cars swept by. My right shoe was holed and took in water, the legs of my trousers thickened and weighed, but after a while I grew used to it, for there was a kind of calmness and peace in walking through that rain. You imagined you were heading for the other side of it and moved one foot after the other in a kind of silent trance, the miles disappearing beneath you and the rain still falling into your face. My father didn't say a word. He had a soft hat in his coat pocket and wore it as his only protection, the long strands of his hair gathering and releasing little streamlets down the back of his shirt. I could see the tips of his shoulder blades pressing out through the wet fabric, their high angles jutting into the air as if at any moment they might stretch and expand, feather into wings, and take him flying off down the road ahead of me. Such things I imagined walking behind him in the rain. Everything about him had come to seem almost mythical to me, his long bent-forward figure, his great forehead, the eyes that blinked away the beating weather and gazed relentlessly forward down the road. I loved him now in a way I hadn't before, and bore the increasing water-logged weight of the coated and wrapped paintings on my shoulders as evidence or proof. Whenever my father stopped for me to catch up and come alongside him was a moment of such satisfaction and happiness, a swelling instant of love and pride that I had come with him, that he had let me, that I had seen the other side of him and was now helping him bring home the greatest paintings he had ever done, that I wanted to laugh there on the roadside. He put his hand on my shoulder, straightened the straps of the bag.

"Do you want to rest?" he asked.

"I'm fine."

"We'll go beyond the next rise, all right?"

"All right."

And on again, the rain still falling, the road winding down through a closed village of quietness, my father pacing a few yards in front of me, unable to keep his stride short or his eyes off the horizon. By mid-afternoon he looked like he had gone swimming in the sky. The clouds had thickened and lowered. Potholes in the rough road filled into grey pools which cars plashed through on their way away, anywhere out of the rain. Under the dripping of a great green chestnut tree we stopped to eat. Our biscuits and bread were damp. The trunk of the tree had a thick sweet smell of autumn, and we sat upon the base of it looking out at the dark trail our footsteps had brushed out of the silvered grass. It was a thing I remembered, years later, going back to try and find the same tree. That brief marking of our joint trail off the road and under the chestnut, that place where everything was momentarily perfect, where we sat under the light pattering of the leaves, father and son, and ate quietly, where my father put his face down into the paint-stained cup of his two palms, rubbing away the rain before lifting those eyes free to look across the little space at me and say: "You're a great help to me, Nicholas. I'm glad you came."

As simple as that, that moment at the end of the trail through the grass and under the dripping boughs of the chestnut tree. If we could have been lifted up, gathered into cloud then, I would have been happy forever. If we could have lain down there or burrowed like animals into the sweet brown smell of the tree itself, screened from the world in veils of rain and the scents of autumn, everything would have stayed the way it was. There could have been peace.

9

When we finished eating we sat on for a while, saying nothing, listening, looking out. It was as if neither of us wanted to move out of that moment, its green and glistening haven, its drizzling serenity.

Then, at last, my father shifted his legs and said: "I suppose we'll get colds if we stay too long. Come on. We'll have some hot tea somewhere along the way."

We moved out of the field and left the tree behind, marching down the road once more, bringing only the memory. The rain felt colder and our progress was slower, but by evening we could see the rooftops of the town squatting under the clouds in the distance. We stopped on the last hill, then took a turn off the main road along a small boreen. Cows were grazing in the stubbled white fields where late hay had been cut. Blackbirds flew up and down, moving a little ahead of them.

"There's an old barn down this way," my father said, leading us forward between the hedgerows to a place where new hay was stacked high under a red corrugated roof. The old cottage next to it was a disused ruin, its thatch fallen in like a gaping mouth. The barn was used now by a neighboring farmer, but with the hay in and the evening drawing on it would give us the night's shelter and a sleep in out of the weather. Besides, there was nothing better than dreaming on a bed of hay, my father told me, swinging off the burden of his art and letting his long frame sigh back onto the harvest. I looked down at him. His eyes were closed. He lay so still that for a moment I thought he was already sleeping, that somewhere between his lying back and his landing on the hay dreams had already overtaken him and he was asleep. I took off the drawstring bag carefully and laid the paintings down still wrapped in his coat. A minute passed. My father didn't move. Rain ran off the roof of the barn. Another minute. I looked down at him. He was asleep. As quietly as possible I moved to sit down and wait, when My father sat up.

"Nicholas," he said, "come on, we have to go."

"What?"

"Tea."

He stood out of the two-minute dream with wide-awake eyes and stretched the wings of his arms before grabbing me by the shoulder and guiding me out into the rain once more. "Leave everything," he said. "There's a place near here, we won't be long."

He swept me along with him at a quick pace. It was, I thought, as if we were fleeing the scene of a crime, almost running down the narrow road together to arrive wet and breathless in the door of a small pub and grocery shop. We stepped inside onto a stone floor and let ourselves drip in the brown light. There were no other customers. A round woman in a blue apron coat came through a curtain from the other side of the house.

"Yahs," she said slowly.

"We'd like a pot of tea," said my father, printing the wet shapes of his shoes across the floor to stand towering over the bar.

The woman looked up at him, and then quickly across at me. "Yahs," she said, and turned roundly out back through the curtain.

My father and I sat down at the only table. He had woken from the dream with such a sense of urgency that at first I thought it was simply because he had almost forgotten his promise to me of tea. But now, sitting across from each other a week since our evening in the small café, I knew it was something more. I was beginning to be able to read the signs now, the messages coming through in the deepening wrinkles on his forehead, the look in his eyes. My father faced the door and when the tea came drank from a brown-stained mug the dusty flavored liquid without taking his eyes off the entrance. He tapped his fingers or twisted them into looping awkward knots that cracked and released into the empty air. He swallowed the tea in a gulp. It was too hot and he tilted back his head with his mouth open, blowing the burning away, and then staring across at the door once more. What or whom he expected I had no idea. I was used to my father's abrupt moods, used to the surprise and mystery that so informed and magnified his character that they seemed as much a part of him as his arms or legs. He had a reason of his own, I knew that, and sat there with his face gazing past my shoulder just waiting to find out what it was he must do next.

He waited until I had finished. He was eager to be gone, I knew, he wanted to be on the other side of that door, but controlled himself enough to ask me if I'd like more. Then he asked how much we owed, took the wet money from his trouser pocket, paid the woman, and swept us out into the rain once again. I was expecting him to tell me something as I hurried along by his galloping legs, the skies opening and my heart thumping. What was it? What was happening? The water soaked the shoulders of my father's shirt. I could see his skin showing through in a way that made it seem more exposed and vulnerable than if he were naked. The rain blew over the tops of the hedges. We were walking fast, then suddenly we were running, running so frantically fast with long slapping sploshing wet strides that I knew it was not the weather we were hurrying from now but back to the paintings.

The paintings, the paintings.

I couldn't keep up with him. He was two then three yards ahead of me, plashing down the puddled boreen like a wild animal, his arms flying out now and his elbows pumping furiously. We were still a hundred yards away when he started shouting. It was a yell, a long panting running roar that went ahead of us down the empty road in the rain, a crying out against fear and doubt and God Himself as we rounded the last part of the bend, past the ruined cottage and up to the edge of the hay barn itself. My father stopped as if struck. He froze there in the rain, tall and white, staring at the six cattle that had broken out of the field, that had rucked the hay, pulled and nosed at the plastic coverings on the paintings until at last in brute chance they had sunk hoofs through the stack of them, ruining beyond recovery all but the two pictures I had carried in the drawstring bag.

My father stopped when he saw them. He stood there until I caught up and was alongside him, stood there without moving even as I herded the cattle off back up through the gap in the wire they had come down. He stood in the rain in the same spot, like a man waiting to be struck down. When he wasn't he crossed in under the shelter of the hay barn. He was sitting down on the hay, holding the broken pieces of the holed pictures when I returned. My tears were streaming into the rain.

"Sit down, Nicholas," he said, so softly that the words were almost lost under the hammering on the roof. "Sit down," he said. There was a pause; it was less a pause than a great hole in the belly of our life. It bled everywhere into the wordless falling of the rain. Then my father muttered under his breath. "It's a test," he said, "it's a test." And then, letting go the paintings and lying back into the hay, closing his eyes against the unbelievable and outrageous ways of God in his life, he whispered, "Say the Latin, Nicholas, say the Latin."

The rain fell. I spoke the words I did not think he understood, and let their sounds blow away about the barn, mysterious and secret and somehow soothing, expressing as they did through the quivering of my voice something of the unknowable puzzle of love. My father closed his eyes, but could not keep back the tears.

10

Margaret Looney knew what love was. She had discovered it by chance on a bright-lit spring day in Killybegs many years earlier. Muiris had been in the town only a week, substituting for the ill Master McGinley. On a sun-lifted Tuesday he came along the harbour and into Doherty's for a newspaper. Margaret was the girl at the counter holding three apples and falling headlong into his life. They exchanged a few words, nothing more, but in the moment each of them walked away they already carried with them like a spore the beginnings of their life together. Each time Margaret saw him after that her heart filled like a pool. She imagined when she closed her eyes that her insides were overflowing with happiness and that it wasn't possible to feel still more. When she did, when he took her arm a week later and walked her past the harbour where the high hulls of blue and red boats spilled the heady perfume of fish into the air, she thought she would simply burst. She was a Donegal girl, he was a schoolteacher and poet, he was from an island. He told her the lines of poems as they walked by the sea's side. For a low-sized man he moved with an unusual sense of purpose and a kind of feckless gallantry that made him seem to her lovesick eyes a part of poetry itself. She loved him more each day, she told the mirror in her bedroom, coming in late and sitting in starlight to stare in amazement at what was happening to her life. The sea stirred outside the window, the curtain blew in like a bridal veil. Margaret hugged her arms about herself in the half-darkness and went into dreamy sleeps in which Muiris appeared and disappeared like moonlight under cloud. In the mornings when she opened her eyes her heart was in her mouth. Her fingers trembled doing up the buttons of her dress. God, what was she going to do?

The very ordinariness of a simple day was beyond her. She touched her fingers against her arm, imagining for a moment they were his. *O God.* Sitting inside the upstairs window of the seaward house where she had grown up she picked up a pen to try to say something to him. All his words, his sayings were so interesting and colourful and wonderful, and she was so plain, so ordinary to herself. What could she say to a man like him? She drew circles and spirals on the corners of the page. The wind gusted and she held down the paper as if about to compose. What was it she wanted to say? Suddenly the wind dropped and in a moment that she would remember with a giggle and a blush for the rest of her days, she wrote Muiris Gore the only love letter of her life:

Dear Muiris dear, dear, dear,
* Take me away with you.*

Your love,
Margaret

Taking a basket that lay by the kitchen table, she swept out of the house and down the morning town, wearing the deep flush of her feeling and the smiles that kept breaking around her lips. The sea of that spring day was to stay with her always, its constant sighing day and night like a passionate accompaniment, and even the thick scents of the gleaming and flapping fish basins, the silver life of the ocean caught, exposed, and thrown out on the briny pier, was to inform the memory of courtship. Love was to change everything. It moved through the town where she had grown up and made it seem remarkable, charged with life. She left the note in an envelope at the house where he was staying and hurried home to await his call.

He arrived an hour after the afternoon school bell. Muiris held her hand and walked her past the schooners and trawlers in the Donegal harbour as if their sides of rusting and creaking iron were the red-and-black timbers of Venetian gondolas bobbing in the sunset.

Margaret Looney knew what love was. Right away she knew her heart was balanced like a wafer on her tongue. And when she kissed the schoolteacher by the back wall of O'Donnell's in the drizzling rain, she knew he had all but taken her life. At the end of that evening when he asked her to marry him, she knew there was no other possible answer but yes, and when, three weeks later, he began to talk excitedly about teaching on an island, she heard the words with a mixture of familiarity and bemusement, as if they were being read to her like the back chapters of the story of her own life.

When they sailed for the island to take up his job, Margaret had not yet set foot there, had never seen its million stones, nor felt press down on the top of her head the absolute grey hush of its wet winter stillness. It was the quiet not the storms that was frightening, the sense that the island had slipped its moorings and was slowly adrift on a tide of forgetfulness. At that time Muiris hadn't started drinking yet, or at least not in the way he did later, after Isabel and Sean were born and he woke one morning to realise that poetry was behind him. In the book of her marriage Margaret would have many pages of remembering, there would be the before and after, the Donegal and then the island days. She would remember and wonder, think how at first her husband had dreamed into the Atlantic island air a kind of Greek life of art and culture, had founded a writing group in the school, brought out on gusting wintery Thursday evenings almost the entire walking population of the island, sitting with their pens in hand over free copybooks, waiting to compose while the gales unroofed their houses. When, two years later, the first slim paperback of their work was published in Galway, there was nothing included by Muiris Gore but a short foreword in Irish, which seemed to the few reviewers who read or understood it an outright vitriolic against the mainland government and its meagre support of the islanders. When Margaret read it, sitting up in bed under a thick layering of quilts and blankets, it was more than that, for in its anger she read the story of her life, and wondered how the loving and courtship of the Donegal town had been transformed into the chapters of this. Now, she knew, they would never be leaving, that the island was to stay their home, and that to her husband, in his disappointment over the swift and terrible death of the poetry inside him, its very bleakness was apt, the rock in the sea part paradise and part jail.

It was then, lying there in the bed beside her sleeping husband, that Margaret Looney realised there was to be an emptying as much as a filling of her heart with love, and that as much as her heart had expanded and grown in the first girlish weeks of love in Donegal, filling her until bursting, now, in the years left, there was to be the slow drop by drop bleeding back of it all. It would all have to be given back, and day after day, as the hardship of their life dulled into routine—windowpanes that rattled under the lash of the wind for months on end, rain that leaked beneath the doors, her husband out and drinking, electricity cut off and the radio shut down, the boredom, the quiet and incredible loneliness—Margaret Looney would remember when she first discovered love and wonder at how immense it must have been to be lasting so long.

11

When Isabel returned home on the Easter ferry her father brought her from the pier to the house on his arm, squeezing her hand in relief that she had returned safely and that his grim unease and foreboding of months earlier had proved to be nothing. His lunchtime whiskeys were holding at bay the world, and he brought his daughter up across the sunken stones of the path as if she were the trophy of some fabulous victory. But when the front door opened and Margaret Gore saw Isabel, she knew at once what had happened. With a flick of her hand she swept away the tears that shot into her eyes and hurried across the kitchen to wrap the girl in her arms.

That evening, every man, woman, and child on the island gathered in the small stone church that sat in off the sea under the shadow of a grey hill. It was Holy Week, and under the glowering of clouds and the coming-and-going rain the church hummed with prayer. Isabel sat with Sean beside her mother and father. She said the prayers and stared at the stations, but she thought only of Peader and the warm rushing feeling that rose from her toes when she remembered his touch. If she stared at the candles too long they danced and made her sick. Suddenly she felt hot and unwell. The pews were too packed, the heat had been turned up too high. The air was pale and grey with prayers and the smells of people's bodies. Swiftly the colour drained out of Isabel's face and she felt herself toppling forward. She sat up out of the prayers and caught her mother's quick and concerned glance, a moment in which there pierced Isabel's soul like an arrow the sudden insight that already Margaret knew. The daughter flushed, and then in a slow fading way fell forward, until her mother caught the shoulder of her coat and saved her.

Through Easter Sunday and Monday, Isabel stayed in bed. Sean sat in at the edge of her bed and dozed in his chair next to her. Her father came and went, enquiring how she was feeling. Was it something that was going around in Galway? Margaret Gore didn't ask. She boiled soup and made stews, and then, daring the secret language of her own love, fed her daughter every kind of fish. For four days Isabel couldn't get out of the bed. Fear was like a palm pressed on the clammy slab of her forehead holding her down. She imagined she was pregnant, that there was a certain look or ex-pression to her face that mothers could read in their daughter's features. She turned over and pressed her face into the pillow. Then, the faith and fever of love boiling up in her again, she saw Peader's face and remade her future until it all came out right: how she would leave the convent and get married, how the child would be a girl and grow up a dancer in the house over the shop in Galway. All this at last she told to Sean. She told him in breathless whispers in the bedroom when the rain was beating outside and her mother was frying fish. She told him so urgently and passion-ately that the very whitewashed walls of the little room shimmered and her heart seemed laid out, quivering with life on the blankets of the bed. Whenever she stopped telling she wanted to start again. She couldn't keep herself from going back into it, retracing time and again in the exact same way as did her mother in the kitchen the steps along the way, the day by day mystery of how she had fallen in love.

Sean sat and listened, and when Isabel took his hand and squeezed it, he squeezed back. When she lay back on the pillows in the dark wave of her hair, sighing and sleeping, tossing and turning in memories and dreams, he sat in his chair by the window on the sea and sometimes, without a sound, wept for the loss of his sister.

On the Tuesday ferry a letter came from the convent. When it arrived Margaret Gore realised she had been expecting it and took it from the kitchen door into the privacy of the damp bathroom while her husband was still asleep. Her hands shook while she read it: Isabel's concentration poor, very weak results in the mock examinations, the visits on weekends by her cousin, the certainty that she would not get to university with such results in the June exams.

She folded the letter carefully back into the envelope. It was the proof where none was needed that her own intuition had been right, that it was love after all. Margaret stood there. Out the open window seagulls arced and screamed in the grey view of stone and sea. One of them flew past, carrying in its beak some rubbish from the back door of a neighbouring house. With her eyes on the window, the sea air, and the harsh sounds of the seabirds filling the room with her Donegal memories, Isabel's mother tore the letter slowly in two, then in four and in eight, posting the fragments out into the wind so that truth might perish and love survive.

Margaret Gore said nothing to her daughter or her husband, and Isabel returned to the convent after the Easter holidays on the smooth sea of relief. She was not pregnant. Her mother embraced her with tears at the doorway, Sean stayed in his bed and took her goodbye kiss with a shiver and pleading eyes, and the Master marched her down to the ferry once more. He thought she had been ill and was now better, perhaps it was nerves before the big exams. At the pier he pressed the white stubble of his cheek hard against her and said, with the fierce gleaming of his islander's pride, that the next time they'd see her she'd be bound for the university.

He waved from the pier as Isabel sailed back into the port of love once more. When she got off in Galway, Peader was waiting for her. He took her bag and swung open the car door. The engine was running and as Isabel sat into the passenger seat the smells of old tweed and greyhounds struck her memory like a blow, overcoming in a single instant her anxiety and fear. She was back. Nothing had changed. Her heart still sprung into her mouth when she saw him and she had to raise a hand to her lips to hold in the smile. Peader swung down into the seat next to her, clanking the gears, smiling too, neither he nor Isabel yet able even to ask how the other had been, or offer the slightest compliment or joke so beside themselves were they with what they thought was the charge of their attraction.

But something had changed. If Margaret Gore had spoken to her daughter she could have told her. In love everything changes, and continues changing all the time. There is no stillness, no stopped clock of the heart in which the moment of happiness holds forever, but only the constant whirring forward motion of desire and need, rising and falling, falling and rising, full of doubts then certainties that moment by moment change and become doubts again.

The moment Isabel saw Peader she felt nothing had changed. She wanted to touch him to be sure, but folded her hands in the lap of her green dress and threw back her hair, smiling out the side window of the car and breathing softly the strange breath of this love into which she had so deeply fallen.

Peader took her past the convent and out of the city. He pulled the car sharply over on a side road and switched off the engine. He could bear it no longer. For ten days he had turned on the spit of desire, hot, sleepless, taunted with the taste of her kisses and the memory of her skin. If before he had longed only to be near her, to be walking by her side down those long, silent desolate roads of the western rain, now the feeling had changed to something more urgent and demanding. For the ten days of Easter he had blundered about the shop and the city, humping great rolls of cloth around, banging into things, thumping up the stairs as his mother entered the shop, suffocating in the smell of her powders and creams and opening the rooftop windows on the streaming rain.

He ate nothing and drank everything. There hadn't been a night that he had not returned from walking the hounds to sit up to the counter of the pub and begin the downing of the black pints of forgetfulness and peace. Not that he could sleep. His skin was still alive with her. He couldn't escape the memory of feelings, which already he was discovering were stronger than feelings themselves. For the ten days of Easter Peader's life had been a hell called Isabel. Now, pulling over the car at a place where the great rocks that lay strewn around the grass made Isabel think of the broken pieces of ancient hearts, he turned to the girl who had taken his life and, with one hand tangling around the back of her hair, drew her to him with the force of anger.

His love was rougher this time. This time there was more need than tenderness, and when Isabel was sitting later in her room in the convent she felt as if she had crossed another threshold, broken into a new place of danger and excitement from which she would not find it easy to leave. When the lights went out she lay in bed under the starless sky; she closed her eyes and felt the first bruises of his mouth coming on her breasts.

12

It was to be a hot summer. In June Isabel sat her exams, walking out of the examination hall as if it were the shell of a life she had already discarded. How could they matter now, all those questions and answers? She was in love. She walked boldly on Peader's arm, drove away into the summer evenings in the small red car, maddening the nuns into silent furies of spite and anger as they watched the last schooldays run by and felt their power fading. Still, they had warned her. She was told she would not be allowed to finish sitting the exams if she didn't stay in her seat writing until the bell. But she couldn't, she told Sister Magdalen, standing before her in the front hall and letting the sweet breath of a new perfume blow in on the draught from the hall door. It was so beautiful outside, wasn't it, Sister? Didn't God want us all to be outside in the glory of His creation? The nun turned on her heel at the girl's insolence. At the top of the stairs there was a rushing clatter and whispering as listening girls vanished to their rooms. Sister Magdalen would have liked to strike her, but paced down the shining corridor with the blows all unstruck and the rage boiling. She marched out of Isabel's sight through the heavy door that led to the chapel, there to kneel and pray, offering it up and finding relief at last in the serene faith that He Himself would take care to punish this girl over whom they had now so completely lost control.

Galway boiled pink in the sun. The June mornings rose dazzling and blue over the stone city, and down by the seafront boats sailed on the rippleless mirror of the stilled Atlantic. It was a time to be in love. The summer air itself seemed to conspire in it, and once the examinations had finished, Isabel wrote to her parents telling them she had taken a job in the city in one of the best wool and tweed shops, a place called O'Luing's.

(When the letter arrived on the island, it was again Margaret who opened and read it. Her husband had gone out with fishermen on an early boat and she sat alone inside the open door of the kitchen holding the single page in her hand long after she had finished reading it. Now she knew who the boy was. She had simply to go shopping on the mainland to see him for herself. But what would she tell Muiris, she wondered. She folded the letter into the pocket of her apron and stood in the doorway of the cottage, looking across the shoulder-high wall of stones to another door where Maire Conaire, whose daughter had just come home from the convent, was looking directly across at her.)

It had been Isabel's idea more than Peader's. With each day's examinations she had felt the sense of an ending. A part of her life had finished and for the first time she did not want to return to the island, to see the summer students arrive in their ferryloads and hear the flat and broken accents of their childish Irish floating across the strand. She wanted a new life to begin, and clung suddenly to the unlikely saviour of Peader O'Luing. (Love, her mother might have told her, was part imagination, its web spun as much in the dark lonely separated evenings of longing as in the shared times together. It would not have weakened love if Isabel had come home, but perhaps the opposite. But Margaret did not write this to her daughter. She sat with pen poised over paper for two hours, thought a dozen different letters, and then wrote only that they would miss her and that she hoped Isabel would continue to write often.)

They were parked in the car on the road above Oughterard when she asked him. Peader, she said, I'm not going back for the summer. I want to stay in Galway. He knew of course what was coming, and found himself for the first time feeling truly superior to her. She was only just beyond a schoolgirl after all. He felt her move close against him in the car and a shiver ran down his neck. A month earlier he had worried about the summer; if the ten days of Easter had been so brutal for him, what would the summer hold? But now, with Isabel here beside him, kissing the side of his face and asking for a job in his father's shop, Peader was suddenly striken with unease. Even as he listened to her telling him how they might need an extra hand during the busy tourist season, and even as he agreed to give her a job, knowing there would be no need and less than ten tourists stepping shyly into the dim shop to order suits or buy wool, he felt torn between feelings he didn't understand. Something in him had changed the evening Isabel arrived in the bar. Yes, he still thought her the most beautiful girl he had ever seen, she was a flame inside him and he could not be ten minutes in the car beside her without longing to touch her face. But still, it was as if, he told his greyhounds later, lying beside them on a blanket in their shed and realising with a shock the sickening mystery of his own heart, the moment Isabel had fallen in love with him he had fallen out of love with her.

13

Peader O'Luing gave Isabel Gore a job and woke the next morning with the task of telling his mother. Almost at once she hit the roof or, rather, the low ceiling above the narrow stairs upon which he told her and where she forgot to duck, yelling *Christ!* and springing three inches of amazement off the step and into the air, falling upwards to crash her head on the roof before rolling down the entire stairwell and bowling over her son, to arrive in a whimpering tangle on the shop floor. She had broken her leg. She would be unable to work in the shop for eight weeks, the aged and deaf Dr. Hegarty told her, roaring in her face.

So it was that when Isabel arrived in the shop downstairs Maire Mor was bedridden in the fetid atmosphere of the room above, lying on each side half-hours at a time and sucking dates. (Once, when she was a girl, a visiting sailor had let her eat a date from his lips. It was the forbidden fruit, he had told her, pursuing it around her mouth with his tongue and knocking them both to the floor in a fit of squirming and giggles. Dates were the taste of sex for her after that. There was something about them, and yet for all the time she had been married to Peader's father she had only ever eaten them on a few occasions; they were dates with dates: the times she ate the fruit and their nine-month anniversaries later when each of her children had been born.)

"My son's in love," she hissed to the dead air, sneering at the ridiculous notion, spitting a fragment of the dates at invisible harpies. She could hear them talking downstairs, woke when they laughed, gummed off another corner of the dates when her mind ran lewdly away from her down the stairs and in the door, where she imagined she saw them making love on the floor. Maire Mor mashed the dates around in her mouth, swallowing back the sweetness like wine; day by day her leg healing as the secret cancer in her colon grew.

14

After the first day Isabel did not again visit Peader's mother in her room. She tidied and dusted, took a half-warm kiss from Peader as he hurried through the shop, grabbed a bolt of tweed, and disappeared. In the silence and dust of the stilled shop, Isabel waited for the bell above the door to jangle and shook herself into work whenever she found herself staring listlessly at the people passing outside. The light of the fine morning faded and vanished. Peader did not return and Isabel did not know whether to close the shop for lunch or stay and leave it open. She imagined Peader coming back at any moment and ran a cloth up and down the clean counter, trying in vain to rub away the dust of disappointment that had already settled in her heart.

That first day Peader did not return by six o'clock, and when Isabel left the shop and locked the door behind her, going up the street light with hunger and turning down by the cathedral to the house where she was staying, she was no longer the girl in the yellow dress passing like a perfume with first love. In eight hours in the shop she had sold nothing and spoken to no one. She had hardly seen the man she had stayed in Galway to be near. That evening, while she waited for him to call, she wrote a letter home: She had just finished her first day's work, it was exciting and exhausting, serving the customers, choosing wool, measuring cloth . . . Her imagination failed her halfway through, and she filled the remainder of the letter with a detailed description of her room. Isabel read the letter back and added a footnoted special hello for Sean, then she slipped it in the envelope which her mother would open two days later, reading the words aloud for her husband and son but seeing in the space between them the shadows of the truth.

For Isabel it was to be the first summer after childhood, the summer whose long, empty blue days passed by the shop window as on a screen, the summer in which she first realised the complex dimensions of her heart. Peader came and went through her days and nights like sudden sun or moonlight. The requiting of love had sent a deep shock through him, stirring sudden moods of restlessness and rage he didn't understand. When Isabel said she loved him he didn't want to believe her, when she crossed the room smiling he wanted to escape. And yet still, he loved her. He did, he told his mother, arguing at the doorway into her room before thundering down the stairs in a mute rage, unable to speak, his fingers clenching and freeing as he stood in the middle of the shop floor staring at the girl whose eyes lit for him like no one's ever had. He looked at Isabel as if she were a mystery, and she crossed the floor to him, smiling, reaching out a hand that made him shiver when it touched. What was it? What had happened? He couldn't bear her wrapping herself onto him and moved impatiently away, hurrying out of the shop with a sudden goodbye and leaving Isabel lost for hours in the hopeless conundrum of love.

Day after day Peader O'Luing drove the car out of Galway as if it were a posse and sped into the airy emptiness of northern Connacht to wrestle with the monsters of his feelings. Did he not love her after all? It was too impossible to believe. Upstairs in his mother's room, he argued like a man who would lose his life if he lost Isabel. And yet the moment he came down and saw her there in the dull light of the shop, something in the intricate machinery clicked and wheeled inside him and he was repulsed. He didn't understand yet that it was in fact her loving him he hated, that the moment Isabel gave herself to him she fell from the high place in the stars where Peader had first put her, that somewhere inside him was a mocking voice out of his childhood instilling the unshakeable creed that he was an idiot and useless and that loving him was a useless idiotic thing to do. Peader understood none of that yet. It would be three years and sixty-eight days later before that thought would fully strike him and he would realise on a rush of Power's whiskey the inescapable misery of the rest of his life. That day he thought it was something else, he didn't blame his father, but looked at Isabel, his wild island beauty, and saw only a shop girl; she was plain, she was ordinary, she was a girl like his mother must have been, and immediately, even as Isabel's face brightened at the vaguely comic air in which he stood there,

Peader felt the need to hurry from her, get away, and breathe by himself. He parked the car and idled the day, staring out the opened window at the purple shapes of the mountains while Isabel stood amidst the sun-struck beams of dust, shining the frown of her face into the counter and waiting, waiting for him to come back.

When he did, driving out of the winding roads of the mountains, he outraced the monsters in himself and roared back into the summer evening city with rekindled dreams of the girl's beauty. He came from the car then, storming down the streets of Galway with the old rage to be near her, to kiss the lips, to touch the face that he did not notice was already turning pale. He opened the door and the bell jangled. Isabel did not look up. She was too proud and hurt, but her fingers shook as she folded for the fifteenth time the same length of brown tweed.

"I'm sorry," he said. "Christ, Isabel, I'm sorry."

They stood across the shop floor from each other in the stilled moment that was to become a familiar episode of their relationship, the moment between pain and forgiveness, the ticked seconds of the stopped heart before Isabel surrendered pride and looked across at him.

"I'm an idiot," he said, and grinned, holding out his hands on the line that brought Isabel to him, smiling and forgiving in the sudden relief that her heart had not yet been broken. They went out the door and let it lock behind them, their hands clasped and their footsteps skipping quickly along the emptied streets. The sun was still shining over Galway. The air had the lift and spring of the sea. There was fiddle music coming from a stone alley and to its lively reel Isabel and Peader danced a few steps, breaking apart and coming together again, hurrying on past the musician, down the alleyway, and farther still from the gloom of the day.

"I should have bought flowers."

"You should."

"I mean it."

"So do I."

"I will, then, I'll get you flowers."

"And where will you get them now, at this time?"

"Here, sit down, wait here."

He was gone ten minutes, no more. Leaving Isabel by the Long Walk, looking out across the stilled waters of the Claddagh, where a blue boat lay on the mirror of its own hull and made her imagine a sea so calm she might have walked home across the water, Peader turned back into the city. He needed to do something to win her back, he had thought. It was a feeling with which he was comfortable, the feeling of needing to impress himself back into her heart, and he hurried back through the streets plundering fistfuls of late marigolds, lobelia, and petunias from shop-window boxes and the street-end half-barrels of the Galway City Council. In ten minutes he was back with a wilting display. He gave it to Isabel and she laughed, smelling the flowers once and then throwing them onto the gold and silver rippling of the water.

"Why did you do that?"

Isabel bit her bottom lip, and then turned her eyes up to where he stood over her. She was the girl from the island again now, the girl who would come and go through Peader's heart with the flash and brilliance of a knife, the girl who was not in love with him but with whom he was madly, desperately in love, the girl with the streak of wildness running through her as she answered him: "To see if you'd get them if I asked."

When Peader dove, minutes later, the golden road of sunlight to the island shattered on the surface of the water. The flowers bobbed on his waves, and Isabel stood and clapped and laughed, forgetting for a while, blushing deeply down the length of her neck as one by one she saw gathered in a bouquet the watery blossoms of proof that they were, after all, in love.

15

It was August when the letter came. Margaret Gore was watching for it and took its brown envelope from the pier like a bitter medicine she knew was needed. She did not walk home but carried the letter unopened around the northern shore, making her way out onto the black crags of rock that jutted into the softest foam of the blue sea. The spray skirted her bare legs where she stood and read that Isabel had failed two subjects in her examinations. She read down through the marks, threw into the tide the nuns' note of explanation that Isabel had not worked since Christmas, and wondered how to tell her husband.

It was the bluest day, clear and cloudless. Beyond the curve of white sand the sea was dotted with children swimming, and against the black bottom of an upturned currach, Muiris Gore was watching them. When his wife saw him she still had not decided how to tell him. She came slowly along by the pier and down onto the sand. It spilled inside her shoes and she took them off, walking barefoot across the cool dampness of that shoreline which had become her prison. It was going to be a blow, she thought. He is going to hear me tell him and feel in one instant the final collapse of his last dream, the end of his hope and belief that somehow in Isabel he had managed the thing his life had missed. I'm going to knock the last love out of him, she thought, holding the letter by her side and coming nearer to him, although he still did not see her. His eyes were fixed on the children in the sea. He was wearing the old tweed jacket she had already repaired a dozen times, a coat he preferred over better ones and whose feel and fabric his wife had come to imagine were part of himself. As Margaret Gore stepped the last yards through the sand, she felt a sudden wish to cry out, to have him turn in surprise and find her there by his side with no other reason for her coming than to sit down into the brown and whiskeyed smell of the jacket and wait for his arm to come around her. She wished away the letter in the last steps, walked through the simpler world where the children swam forever in summer seas under blue skies and she and Muiris Gore were the parents only of dreams.

Her husband turned when he stopped hearing her. She was a yard from him, standing motionless on the sand. She could not move. I won't tell him, she thought, no I won't tell him.

"Tell me," he said.

Three weeks later, Margaret went to Galway to see for herself the face of the man who had stolen her daughter's heart and sealed her husband's soul inside the pale and shallow gold of a bottle. She had received no letter from Isabel since the examinations, no reply to any of three requests for her to come home, and as she stepped off the ferry in the high-buttoned coat that raised her chin like pride, she strode into the bustle and noise of the city intending nothing less than to tell her daughter she had broken her father's heart.

She was not used to the excitements of the city. Its constant traffic unsettled her; she felt the cars nudged her side if she walked along the outside of the narrow path and so she kept instead in by the shop windows, hardly allowing herself the luxury of looking at the things of which love had so ruthlessly deprived her and marching on with her head at a side angle searching out above her the name of the O'Luing shop. She was a woman torn in two. Her daughter was in love, and from the memory and understanding of her own Donegal courtship she knew Isabel was aswim perhaps in the most important and passionate moments of her life. These were what mattered, these days of summer in Galway when the mother knew her daughter's heart was thrumming fast and that the grey stone of the island was already sinking like childhood into the far-off parts of her mind, there to wait and shimmer until Isabel was an old woman and her memory longer than her life. The girl was in love, she had thoughts for nothing else, said the mother to herself. And yet.

Margaret Gore crossed Shop Street. Wasn't it somewhere down here?

And yet for three weeks she had daily witnessed the slow and agonising crumble of her husband's heart. On the day of the results, she had taken a wife's gamble on the seashore and told Muiris Isabel was in love. If the memories so stirred her, Margaret had imagined that by necessity the same snatched fragments of the sweetness of the past must move and lodge, shift, fly, and land too in the great empty spaces of her husband's soul. Against them, what mattered, she had asked herself, and answered: Nothing. What if Isabel was no longer bound for the university, what if she was in love and was going to marry a Galway shopkeeper? If she is happy, Muiris, if she's happy? The gamble had failed. Margaret had underestimated the weight of hope that for seventeen years on the island her husband had placed on his daughter's shoulders, doubling that when Sean had his first fit and was thought beyond ever moving out of the house.

(Muiris did not remember love the way his wife did. Until the moment on the shore he had not surrendered vanity or ambition, had not stopped looking forward across the oncoming waves of his life. But then, out of the memorable brilliance of that blue sky, came the blow. Pieces of him fell off. He had been a complete fool. His wife fingered the mended hem of his jacket, she spoke so softly he thought of the image of her voice as the sound of the sea. It was the sea telling him, and the sea he went to that August evening, already fired with whiskey, stumbling over the rocks to the place Isabel had danced for Sean and the world had first started to go wrong. He had missed the message then, he realised, holding the neck of a bottle flashing with moonlight. He was a vain and bloody fool, and was found there in the morning, sleeping on the rocks, by a child of the Hallorans'. For a week he could not face the islanders. The other island girls at the convent had passed their examinations, three of them looked likely to be accepted in university. But the Master's girl had failed. He stayed in the house where his wife could see him and feel as much as he the swing and thump of the sledge of life on the falling-down walls of his foolish heart.)

All this, then, ran through Margaret's mind as she moved down Shop Street with her head to one side and her chin out. The way she saw it, it all came down to this man, this O'Luing, this fellow who had moved into her family's life like a slow-gathering storm. She imagined him as strong and romantic, a Galway man with black curls and a barrel chest, a musical voice perhaps, sensual mouth, deep blue eyes. The better he looked, the easier became the struggle within her, and by the time Margaret passed Peader on the path ten yards from the shop it is doubtful if any of the city's inhabitants would have met the measure of her imagination. She strode by him without blinking, and it was he who took a second look, glancing over his shoulder before hurrying on and pondering all morning while he drove away from Isabel and the shop just whose mother or aunt she was.

It was a surprise visit. When Margaret found the shop she was surprised. When she stood back from it and crossed the street to see if in fact it was not derelict and that her eyes had not imagined the O'Luing name over the ancient gloomy brown shop, she was surprised. It was a surprise there were no customers. Then again, it was a surprise there had been any in the previous decade. The strange and sour scent that engulfed her as she opened the door, the shrill bell, the sudden dimness, the neatness and polish of the dull interior so contrasting with the outside, the opened but untouched look of the rolls of fabric as ready as flypaper, the dustless wooden floor beneath air thick with swirling flying falling dust which, after an argument, had just been furiously swept into rising were surprising, but most of all it was the look on her daughter's face that astonished her.

Within the first half-minute, Margaret knew two things: her daughter was in love, and her daughter was not happy. She crossed the wooden floor still undecided, still torn in two. But by the time Isabel had rushed into her arms and pressed her face tightly against the rough tweed of her mother's coat, Margaret knew which side she had chosen. She unbuttoned the big green button at the top of her coat and her chin came down. She felt the girl thrust against her, and in the moment before Isabel stood back, her mother understood everything. It only remained for Isabel to give her the details.

"Tell me," she said.

As mother and daughter, Margaret and Isabel Gore had never been particularly close. There had been between them always the islands of two men, Muiris and Sean, about whose needs and presence they had come and gone like silent seas. When Isabel left for Galway it was her father and brother, not her mother she missed. She needed to be needed. For Margaret, the thing she missed was the dreamy and hopeful part of her husband that had gone with their daughter. Now, in the grim downstairs of O'Luing's Wool and Tweed Shop, mother and daughter met for the first time as women. They sat on hard wooden chairs behind the counter, and while the cool autumnal light came and went from behind the clouds of the western sky, Isabel told her mother she was in love. She could not explain it, she said. He was nothing like the man she had imagined for herself, and yet she couldn't help herself. Sometimes, when she was angry with him, when he disappeared from the shop and didn't return in the evenings and she went home to the house without seeing him, she could not imagine ever seeing him again. Then something happened. Something always happened. He showed up. She looked at him, she loved him. What could she do? He was marvellous and funny and would do anything for her. While Isabel talked on, sounding for the first time the months of unsaid feelings, her mother listened and nodded and tried not to show signs of the sadness filling up in her. She hoped her daughter would run out of things to say before the tears started welling in her eyes, for in the hour or so in which Isabel poured out her heart to her mother in a way she was never to repeat for the rest of her life, Margaret knew without doubt that the love would end in unhappiness. She listened and said nothing, even as in the upstairs bedroom Maire Mor hung her head over the edge of the bed and listened and said nothing also.

"You're very young still, Isabel," she said at last. "You should . . . Well, does he say he loves you?"

It was hopeless, and the mother knew it, and still could not warn her daughter of what lay ahead. Later, walking back to the ferry and feeling a noticeable chill in the streets, Margaret would tell herself she had failed in her duty as a mother, been too much a friend and not enough of a counsel, should have urged Isabel to be more careful, to hold back, to save that part of her heart which Margaret knew had already been given away. But it was hopeless, so hopeless. How could she, sitting there before the very picture of herself, tell herself not to feel the one thing in her life that had meant more than anything, the miracle days of first love?

The light had cooled and Margaret had listened. Before she rose and rebuttoned the top coat button, she had realised that she was not going to talk about the Master. Isabel was not thinking about university and examinations now, she was thinking about a kind of play-marriage, about working in the shop indefinitely, about changing this and that, repainting it, new shelving, and as she talked, her mother saw the stream of constant customers entering along the innocent and hopeful rims of her eyes. She stood up and they embraced. She asked Isabel to write a letter home, and then, with her coat shut tightly across her chest, Margaret Gore walked out of the shop for what she imagined would be the last time in her life. She heard the jingling bell ring as the door shut behind her and cried her tears openly as she followed her chin up the street. Isabel stood in the shop and reached for the sweeping brush.

She had told her mother so much, but not the one secret thing, not the knotted connection in her mind between Peader and a vivid moment in her past; for when Peader turned his love cold and walked out of the shop, Isabel felt it was what she deserved; it was the inescapable payback for what she had caused her brother all those years earlier; it was the judgement of God.

When her mother left, she lowered her eyes to the floor beneath the weight of that guilt, swept hard with the brush, and watched as it lifted into the air the inexorable dust of her life, which would still be falling three years and twenty-eight days later when the stranger would arrive at the door.

IV

1

There is no such thing as chance. Of this my father seemed more or less certain, choosing to view the haphazard chaos of his life simply as order of a different kind. If you believed in God you did not believe in chance, he told me. The cattle that had broken through the fence and ruined all but two of the paintings were not the instruments of misfortune or coincidence. They were signposts, message bearers, and it was only a matter of time before my father figured out just what they had been sent to say. Similarly, the arrival of my Uncle John at the house three weeks after our return from the west was no mere luck either. First of all, he was not my Uncle John. He was Mr. John Flannery, my father's old colleague from the civil service, and when he stepped inside the clean but empty hallway of our house in the crisp beginning of that autumn I doubt if even he knew the part he was about to play.

It was, in my interpretation, a stroke of good luck, but to my father it was simply the next revelation of divine order. When Mr. Flannery sat in one of the hard wooden straight-backed chairs in the studio and listened to what had happened to the paintings, he could hardly believe it. He was at once struck by two things: that the accident, as he thought it, was the coincidence of a lifetime, and that my father had believed in the paintings with such a passion and faith that he was now either entirely mad or a certain genius.

He sat back and sipped the strong milkless tea I brought him, staring across the studio at my father and waiting to ask a question.

Due to my father's belief, it did not occur to him to question the sudden appearance of his old friend at the hall door. He had welcomed mr. Flannery, as he had done on one or two occasions before, without the slightest hesitation or questioning of what the purpose of his visit might be. He expected grander, greater designs of order to be more mysteriously revealed and was somewhat taken aback when Flannery said: "Actually I was hoping to buy a painting."

My father said nothing. mr. Flannery explained. He was a member of a national organization for the promotion of Irish culture and had been commissioned to buy a painting to be given as a prize. I listened at the door. I was waiting for a new calamity when out of a long, still pause I heard my father answer: "There are only two, they are over here, look."

mr. Flannery looked. I could hear him looking. I could feel in the quiet the slow magic of those fabulous pictures working on his mind, sense and smell the sea that was churning in them, the restlessness and beauty that my father believed were the restlessness and beauty of God Himself.   mr. Flannery was overcome. I knew he would be, for in the weeks since we had returned and I had come and gone from school and seen the work that my father did on finishing them, I knew they were at the very least extraordinary. Perhaps they did not amount to any fixed notion of art, but there was an undeniable something the raging of those colours. My father knew it too. He had already felt the sensation in his hand as he held the brush. He already knew that the rest of his painting life he would have no other subject than these sea views which he would paint time and again, trying to refind in each canvas the moments on the western shore of Clare when he had believed his brush moved with the presence of God. When mr. Flannery spoke there were lumps in his throat.

"Well, they're something," he said.

My father did not reply. I imagined he was looking at them with amazement too.

134

"How much are they?"

I could feel my mother rush down the stairs to listen for the answer. I could see the sudden brilliant end of all misery right there in front of me, the final vanquishing of poverty and doubt and hardship and the beginning of God's reward. Then my father answered.

"They're free," he said.

"No, no, William, how much are they?"

"They are free, or they are not for sale."

My heart sank. I knew the tone in his voice. My mother knew the tone in his voice, and even mr. Flannery knew enough not to object more than twice. My father's sole concession was to agree to hand over only one of the paintings, insisting that his old friend choose which one and making an invisible inner grimace when the man immediately pointed to his favorite. He smiled at the blow and picked up the canvas. He didn't wish to hear any more about it, was standing in the bare centre of the studio on a slim thread of faith when mr. Flannery tempted him a final time.

"You're sure, William?" he said. "It doesn't feel right. I have the money; here, will you take it? Or listen, give me something else, will you?"

A pause, my ear pressed against the wooden door almost hearing the rumble of that distant sea, then:

"No."

The painting left the house moments later. I watched from my bedroom window as mr. Flannery carried it wrapped in brown paper to his car. My father shut the hall door and went back into his studio. He sat on the chair, looked at the last painting, and laughed.

2

Muiris Gore had not expected it. It was like a wink from above, he told two men in the pub where he went to celebrate. When the letter arrived it was his wife, as usual, who read it. It was one of her pleasures, her husband knew, to be the first to open and read their post, to sit there before him knowing he was waiting and watching her face for the smiles or frowns that she let him interpret, saying nothing until she had finished and he said "Well?" and she said "Here" and handed it to him. While he read then, his wife let the news run around inside her. If it was bad, it went deep and quiet and quick to an unreachable place, and even when her husband stopped reading she would say nothing, swallowing the lumps of grief and getting up from the table to wash her hands. If it was good, as it was this time, the news would pop and bubble inside her mouth; she'd start a kind of captured giggle, trying to hold it between her lips until Muiris had finished reading and would look up with the smile that warmed her from her toes and freed the lightness of her laughter.

But this time Muiris did not smile, he frowned. It was the frown of mystery and puzzlement that cleared to wonder as he held down the sheet of paper and looked across at his wife and understood for the first time that she was, quite simply, an angel.

How otherwise could he explain it? To a national competition for poetry in Irish she had submitted one of his old poems, and he had won. He was to go to Dublin to be presented with his prize.

When Muiris left on the ferry two weeks later, sitting carefully inside the open cabin in his good suit and noticing how the salt air was already dulling the shine off his shoes, he resigned himself to not visiting his daughter in the shop. This was not the time to talk to Isabel, he told himself, and sat in a smokers' carriage, where the journey across the country passed in a thick white cloud of oblivion. That evening he attended the presentation dinner. He heard his poem read by the Cathaorlach, Sean O'Flannaire, and thought of his wife back on the island with the rainbow smiles in her eyes. He swallowed hard and stood up to bow, falling in love again with young Margaret Looney as he reached out his hand and took his prize of a painting of the western sea by Mr. William Coughlan.

The following morning Muiris Gore boarded the return train in Dublin, sat by the window with the painting wrapped in brown paper at his side, and on the back side of a bill of sale from Nesbit and O'Mahony's Hardware and Household began his first poem in thirteen years.

3

Time does not pass, but pain grows; this is the condition of life, my father maintained. Time only exists if you have a clock. In our house the batteries in the clock on the kitchen windowsill had long since leaked the acid of Time, and so my father and I lived on in a kind of spell, marked by the dead rattle of leaves at the door or the sudden gaiety of spring showers at the window. After our trip together to the west, he seemed to abandon thoughts of returning there. It was as if he was certain the greatest of any paintings he might achieve would still be trampled and holed by God. Instead, he retreated to his room and in the switched-off light worked over the brutal knowledge of his failure. I imagine my mother visited him there. He did not bring out paintings to show me. His pain grew.

Sometimes when we sat to tea and the evenings were brightening, he invited me by a look of his brilliant eyes towards the door, to go walking with him. And we did. Always hastening along, always without the possibility of any real conversation. My father made statements, not talk.

"Life is a mystery, we cannot understand it. Once you accept that, it hurts less." A pause, and then. "Or should do."

We raced along with our own hurts, energetic and silent, walking them around the edge of those outer suburbs as if the miles might act as a salve and everything look better if we were exhausted. But it didn't, and my father, who looked old when I was twelve, returned to the house each time like a great-grandfather. He went into his room and sat down; his breath wheezed through his paper-thin chest and he stared at paintings he could not paint. Where was God now?

Six seasons flew past us, I got school holidays a final time, but we went nowhere. In the mornings we lay in our beds and waited for a sign.

But it never came.

How I came to join the civil service I am not sure. It may have been Flannery's fault. It may have been my father's. It was the end of school. Teachers stood before the class and took turns warning us about Life. I read the notice about the exams and sent in an application. To an interview in the city I wore my grey pants and an old school blazer with the crest on the pocket cut off. I think my father thought I was going to a party. Have a good time, he said, from within the studio, not coming out to look as I didn't go in to show. Vaguely I knew it was not something to tell him. Two months after leaving school, he still had no idea of what I intended to do, nor did it seem to bother him. He never said Get out of bed, or Get a job, or Do something with your life. He just let me be, and in that way perhaps deployed the secret and most powerful weapon he had. He let Life come at me when I wasn't expecting it, and I woke up on the morning of the interview with the sudden sense that it was mine and not his life that was out of control. I had to do something. And as my father brushed and scumbled in the studio, intent on brushing out the beginnings of yesterday's painting and failing again, I was setting out the door into the labyrinthine mystery whose forks and bends he had already negotiated.

It was a brilliant morning in late summer, a day so suffused with light and hope that even as the sun shone it seemed to burn its place into memory. The day I began the rest of my life, the day whose sunlight held the city glimmering and brilliant like the castellated and shining towers of a medieval dream, a place whose twin cathedrals and green-capped public buildings stood out along the coil of the river below me with all the promise and excitement of new discovery. I sat on the upstairs front seat of the bus and was carried forward through the changing reflections and brilliance of the sunlight, imagining for more than a moment that something extraordinary was happening. Something had begun, and was being heralded with blueness. I remember my hope as the sunlight of that morning. I didn't notice the lost or fixed expressions of those around me, how thickly the traffic came together at junctions and made the whole slow progression slower still, all centering, closing like a funeral on the city, or how something somewhere shut tightly behind us with a soft click as we came down the stairs and hurried through the light, slipping through office doors of reflected sunshine that left childhood and innocence behind forever. I was aware only of the new beginning which had been scripted for me, and moved into the building and out of the great and frightening vacuum of those end-of-summer days with my heart as full of hope and expectation as it was ever to be again.

When I was offered a job one month later, I did not imagine there had been any room for doubt. It was what I was going to do. I was going to work in the civil service and make some money and fix up the house and pay the bills and keep my father and me warm and fed while he finished the paintings that were the paintings he had been born to do. It all fit together neatly, and only the business of telling my father posed any difficulty at all.

I decided it was best to break the news over tea. Each evening around what I imagined was six o'clock my father stopped working or not working when I knocked on the studio door. He came out slowly into the kitchen, raising his head on his long neck and screwing up his eyes. I met him there as if by prearrangement, and we sat to our bread and butter and jam sighing like workmen, buttering through the silence and looking out through the curtainless kitchen window at the house across the back garden. My father dipped his bread in his tea, a habit he had taken up since finding two teeth on his toast earlier in the summer. He looked across the way and chewed the mush slowly. First I had to tell him I had applied.

"I have news," I said.

"You've been offered a job, Nicholas," he said. "Take it if you think you should. Do what you think best."

And that was that. His tone was so quiet and matter-of-fact, so full of a calm and gentle understanding that I took it to be wisdom itself. I didn't question how he knew. My father was not a man to question, and that evening when I wrote accepting the job I realised his hand might have been on my shoulder all the way.

I began work on a Monday. I had one side of a large mahogany desk, MacMahon had the other. We were Junior Executives, wore cheap navy suits, stiff-collared white shirts with one of three ties, butter-stained by Tuesday with canteen crumbs. In a great long rectangle of a room sixteen of us sat at opposite ends of the same mahogany tables. Our aftershaves mingled. We opened files in green cardboard covers and read for hours the unreadable tedium of government. The clock ticked. Beyond the high windows at the end of the room the light came and went. Coughs and cough drops began the autumn. Every morning it rained. I cycled, and arrived in the centre of the city streaked with black splashes and water running down my face. From the large mat inside the hall door a slickering black trail of the stamp of wet galoshes led to the stairs. The morning's weather dried off halfway up, and when you slipped through the heavy door into the long pale-green office nothing was left of it, no trace of wind or rain and only the quiet two-minute jump of the clock and the opening of the first file to move you forward through the passing of time itself. Tea break, lunch hour, three o'clock walk down to the file room, cigarette butts floating on unflushed urine in the men's toilet, back upstairs, carrying the file you didn't need, sitting into the pain in your bottom again, until the first daring one rose to put on his coat at a minute to five o'clock.

Autumn passed in that long room like a single moment out of my life. It was wet, damp feet smelled. Meagre highlights were Friday noons and liquid lunches of stout, sending the sixteen of us back late into the dozy dull rectangle of the afternoon to hold up files before our reddened faces and wait for the end of the day.

McCarthy was our supervisor. He did not share a desk but sat at his own at the top of the room. His suit, it was said, came from Italy. He called us Mister, and sometimes looked down upon us with such frozen beatitude carved on his face that it seemed the scribbling and blotting of our pens beneath his gaze was to him the secret inner workings of the state itself. He could watch us forever, and while he did we moved our pens ever faster, miming intricate penmanship of the highest order and turning sheets of nothing over and back as if searching their blankness for the runes of time. On no particular schedule, mr. McCarthy rose and swept from the office, moving behind the largeness of his lapels with borrowed importance and heading out the door on the business of state. It was six months or so before we understood he was most frequently going nowhere but the toilet, and that his coming and going from the room was his own invented activity to keep the dust from settling on his suit. As it was, the moment he left us we pushed back our chairs, loosened the grip of Life on the crossbeams of our shoulders, and waited, watching the door with pens ready for his return.

All autumns were damp or wet. Leaves clogged in the gutters or danced with ghostly footsteps at the back door while my father and I sat to our tea. The winters came up quickly. They iced the roads under my bicycle, and I pedalled so slowly into the city on January mornings that each turn of the wheel under me seemed to trim another unmeasureable shaving off my life and bring me to the office weeks older and more tired than the bright gelid hour when I had set out. The days vanished, the dark evenings were thick with coal smoke, brumous clouds that swirled beneath the yellow of the streetlights and screened the stars. When spring came I hardly noticed. There was no dripping trail on the office stairs, the sky that scudded past the high unopened windows above Mc-

Carthy's head moved like brushstrokes with the racing colors of the days. For a moment the blue was deep and still and cloudless, and it was summer. We stared up at it, that patch of perfect promise poised in the window, then we lowered our heads, dipped our pens, and it was autumn once more.

One morning McCarthy summoned me to him. He was a meticulous man. To stand next to him was to be aware of the cleanness of his shave, the neatness of his hair, the smoothness of his suit. He sat without crushing the creases of his pants, leaving only the merest inch of his bottom resting on the seat and angling himself forward to his desk, as if all the more ready to get at the work or spring to his feet and take off on one of his sudden marches down the room and out the door, unwrinkled, creased just right. He was a man who had found his place, and had ironed everything of the jumbled and frenzied chaos that life had thrown at him into the one perfect crease of his work. He looked at me and lowered his voice to a whisper.

"I have had a word about you," he said, and edged even farther forward on his seat until his knees were touching mine. "From above."

In the steady beaming of his brown eyes I could see him taking my life and folding it, pressing it into shape and giving it back to me.

"An enquiry," he whispered, putting his hands together between his legs and holding them there, nodding, just nodding and looking into the heart of the boy who was about to rise like a star into the ordered and perfect constellations of government.

"An encouraging enquiry, Mr. Coughlan," he whispered, suddenly looking down to supervise the bowed heads at their penmanship. "Very encouraging," he said, out of the crease of his mouth while his eyes freewheeled around the room.

Afterwards, I sat down at my desk, looked up at the clock, lifted my pen, and held it there. The light faded at the window, I looked at the file in front of me, and when I looked up again suddenly realised that three years of my life seemed to have passed.

4

At the beginning of the week in which Isabel was to receive Peader O'Luing's proposal of marriage, she found herself standing with a sweeping brush in the centre of the shop floor listening not for the first time to the voice of doubt. Three years had passed. Maire Mor was dead and the running of the shop had fallen more or less entirely into Isabel's hands. She had cleaned and smartened it, changed the shelving, aired the stock, and thrown out into the back yard the older bolts of tweed which fell with a powdery *pffump*, releasing the moths of time. But still, from Monday through Saturday, the O'Luing Wool and Tweed Shop was empty of customers; whatever business it had was largely carried out by Peader from the back seat of the red Ford, and the premises remained the brown and voiceless limbo of the O'Luing family ghosts.

In three years Isabel had grown used to it. Love, she discovered, was like anything else. It was a habit of the heart. You gave yourself to it, and then followed on day after day, tracing ever deeper the unchangeable track of emotions. Every morning she rose in the flat and walked through Galway, letting herself into the shop with the expectation of only the briefest kiss as Peader came down the stairs and mildly embraced her before going out the door. It was the way of this love. It was what she deserved. There was a pattern their feelings had shaped for them, the early-morning coolness, then the evening and nighttime loving that brought both of them like strangers together and left them hours later in the back seat of the car breathing each other beneath the exhausted moon of early morning. Peader did not want her to move in with him. When his mother died, Isabel had watched the guilt ooze like an oil over him. For a month he was beside himself with rage. He blamed his mother for dying, as if it was a last-ditch effort to force her will on him, to push herself into the place of the girl. The night of the wake he drank eleven pints of stout, seven Jamesons, and two tumblers of vodka, leading a jigging party in from the pub only to fall in a spewing faint on the shop floor. Isabel washed his face in the morning. She saw him as a broken-winged and wounded bird she might restore to flight, and imagined that without his mother they could at last rise into the clouds of a more settled happiness. For a week after the funeral, Peader seemed lighter and happier than she had ever known him. He pressed her hand in his before he left in the morning. He took her dancing under the first blue evening canopies of the June sky.

Then, in the middle of the summer, the guilt burst through. She asked him a question in the morning and he shouted back at her. She said he wasn't being fair and he hit her with his open palm across the side of her face.

The red blaze of the pain stayed with her all day. She sat behind the counter and cried, rubbing her fingers on the spreading heat of the blow and trying to find hate. No, she could not truly hate him, her anger kept bursting too soon, and over the course of the six hours of silence, in which she moved back and forth in the trap of love, she understood only that it was beyond understanding. That she had fallen into it and now could not get out. As reckless as it had been for the schoolgirl to slip through the door into his life, it was as reckless now for her not to slip out. But she had to stay, she told herself; then abruptly decided to leave him. She turned over the weather-faded cardboard sign in the front door and stood for a moment looking out over the CLOSED with a dismal, ephemeral triumph as no one noticed. She turned and looked around at the bolts of cloth, their buff and dun tones suddenly suffocating. At first she only meant to pull one of them down, to release her anger on something. But within a moment she had dragged down a half dozen and was unrolling the great tweeds across the counter, down around the shop; she took the cash register and shoved it free-falling with a pathetic clinking of small change and broken bell onto the floor. Still, there was no triumph. No release. The place was simply topsy-turvy now, not so dissimilar or wrecked that it yet mirrored the distraught shape of Isabel's heart. It wasn't enough; taking her coat she went out into the street. What could she do? What could she do to show him? To tear down the terrible gaol that her heart had built for her? He was not what she wanted. He was not so many things, and yet. She walked down Shop Street, unsure of where she was going or if she intended ever to return. She reached the bridge and felt the freshening of the sea. She walked on out the sea road, feeling how hopelessly far she had come from all the sea walks on the childhood island. What could she do? A car pulled over and a man with a German accent asked her for the road to Spiddal. She sat in beside him. There was whistle-music playing on the radio.

It was playing two days later when he drove her back again into Galway, his body still warm and charged from her, as he asked one last time would she not come with him to Donegal.

Isabel walked back to the shop knowing that she was unable to free herself from Peader O'Luing; that her loving him was a thick knot of contradictions and guilt, but that she would never let him strike her again.

His car was in the street outside the shop. The CLOSED sign was still on the door. She was letting herself in with a key when Peader opened the door for her. The dull smell and dim air of the shop smote her like a blow. The cloths had not been tidied. He stood there with the hopeless regret of his character rolling in his eyes and mutely gestured to the dying clutch of tulips that he had bought her two days earlier. Trophies of his repentence, he offered them now like witnesses. Isabel took them from his hand and, looking straight into the expectation of his eyes, dropped them in a heap on the shop floor.

"What do you think I am?" she asked him very calmly.

"I love you."

"What do you think I am?" she asked again.

"I'm sorry."

"You hit me."

"Jesus, Issy."

"You hit me because you hated me."

"I'm so sorry. I'm so fucking sorry, Issy. Jesus."

"What am I supposed to feel?" she asked the side of his turned-away face. "Am I supposed to feel fabulous because of these?" She picked up the dead flowers and held them to his face. "Am I supposed to feel that it's all right? Peader, is that what I'm supposed to feel?"

Peader waited a moment in a dazzle of pain. His father was standing behind him, laughing. Peader felt his face burn scarlet, then his hands shot up his eyes and he cried out with rage against the ghost and fell to his knees.

"O Jesus!"

It was not what she expected; there was a click within the machine of love, a reverse whirring there in the ruined shop on the summer noon that sent Isabel back towards him at the very moment she might have been free to step away from this flawed love.

"Do you hate me?" he asked her.

It was a moment that was to return again and again, play and replay in the chambers of her mind. *Do you hate me?*; the manner in which he stood there, his fractured and thick-lipped expression as far as Arabia from the prince of girls' dreams; yet how, only moments later, she was holding him in her arms, renewing the world with a kind of terrible tenderness that depended on grief, and falling into desperate kisses that burned with an urgency to repair heaven.

5

Isabel let Peader's marriage proposal hang in the air for a week. She wrote a letter to her mother, deciding to declare for the first time in writing some of her feelings for Peader. Wrongly, she did not think Margaret Gore would understand the contrariness of the relationship and wrote only of the loving side of it. It was a way to prepare the ground, she reasoned, to woo in the gradual idea of marriage that she already knew would shatter her father. Besides, it might be soon; she was afraid she might be pregnant.

When Margaret received the letter she read its true meaning at once and knew that a wedding might be imminent. Muiris was in the room reading over the ninth draft of a new poem when she stood at the doorway to the sea pondering how she might tell him. She feared to snap the fine thread of happiness he had now found in his work and tucked the letter into her housecoat until she could decide what to do. Later that evening, when her husband had gone out, she sat beside Sean in the room watching television. He had grown into a thin pale man, his childhood lost like a bottle in the sea and with it his love for music. Nothing seemed to spark in him now, and he lived on mute as an island in the vast unmappable seas of his incomprehension. He would never leave home, and his mother cared for him without regret, seeing in the hopeless mystery of his condition some further evidence of the rocks in the road of love. She was unsure of whether Sean followed the television programmes or not, but they at least seemed to bring a kind of peace to him, and so nightly he lounged there, his head to one side staring at the images of other worlds. That evening, not quite sure why, Margaret opened the letter and told him it was from his sister. While Sean gazed ahead at the television she read him the letter.

He didn't react, and Margaret supposed it had meant nothing to him. But the following day Dr. Connell visited and said Sean had taken a turn for the worse. Muiris and Margaret stood in the kitchen and looked down at their son under the blanket in his chair, both of them seeing as if plainly visible the intricate and entangling web into which he was spinning himself. He wouldn't take his food but lay curled in a ball with his eyes fixed on the faraway place of grief. Not for the first time his parents were advised to send him to the mainland for caring, and not for the first time did they refuse. It didn't seem right, Margaret said, sending him away like a shame. He was their child and he would stay with them on the island for as long as they lived there. Muiris moved outside to the little front garden when the neighbours called to see the patient. He couldn't easily tolerate the circle of sympathisers and the little hopeless audience of tea drinkers and prayers, and he stood instead outside in the drizzle letting his despair fragment into the first words and phrases of a new poem. He watched the sea and the rain make the mainland disappear and threw out the line of his prayer that something might happen, that the world was not random and an infinite and divine majesty might respond.

A week later Sean was no better. He seemed if anything to be vanishing further into an unseen world and his mother decided to write to Isabel and tell her. The letter arrived on the shop floor on the morning Isabel was to give her final answer to the proposal of marriage. She opened it, closed the shop, and caught the ferry home.

When her father met her, clasping her hand to help her onto the pier, he was moved to sudden tears that he coughed and choked away into hiding. She walked by his side, this beautiful and dazzling woman, her head high and her uncovered hair blowing every which way. "How is he?" she asked him, and when he told her he saw her face on the afternoon she had first brought Sean home from the cliffs. His mind strained, the lives of his children flapping like sheets on his line. And now this was to bring them together, he thought. It was something like a family secret, a strange bond, for although neither Muiris nor Margaret had ever again spoken with their daughter of the day of the accident, it was there every time the four of them sat together.

Father and daughter walked home, each of them swaying slightly under the different burdens of their lives and neither of them speaking. Muiris rehearsed entire speeches, opening sentences, slow approaches to the boggy ground of Isabel's other life on the mainland, but he could not quite bring himself to speak. But why not, he thought; why can I not just say it to her, make a beginning. He turned over a phrase, prepared it, but let the air take it away. It was hopeless, he couldn't risk whatever this warm yet wordless glowing was between them, and as they came near the house and Margaret opened the door, he knew that what passed in an instant between them was never to be his.

Isabel hugged onto her mother, fitting tightly like a piece in a puzzle.

"He's not well, Isabel," Margaret said, standing back a little while Isabel went into Sean's room. With Muiris standing alongside, witnessing the deep tenderness Isabel showed to her brother, Margaret Gore could not yet tell her daughter that she feared she was wrong to have read her son Isabel's letter. Now she couldn't explain, and the mother and father stood there mutely gazing as Isabel cradled her brother's head and whispered greetings that she could not be sure he received.

The wind whistled about the windows, the night fell. When Isabel came into to the kitchen for her supper and Muiris disappeared out the gale-swept door, sailing swiftly starboard to the pub, Margaret asked her for the first time how she was.

"I'm fine."

"Is it so hard to tell me?"

"Tell you what?"

"That you might marry him."

Isabel spooned the soup in front of her; her mother's voice was low so that Sean mightn't hear in the next room.

"He's asked me."

"I know that. I know that. And what have you said to him?"

"Nothing."

"I see."

"I said I'd tell him in a week."

"And when's that?"

"Today."

"So you're not sure?"

Margaret knew as soon as she had said it that she had crossed into a place she had not meant to, that her own desperate longing for her daughter was sweeping through the room and about to wail like a demon at the advent of grief and error. Why, why, all that time ago, had she not stifled this love when she had a chance?

"I'm never sure about anything," Isabel said simply. "Sometimes I am, and then the next day I'm lost. Then I say to myself, are you ever sure about anything?"

"You can be sure what you feel for him." Again Margaret felt her insistence like a metallic ring.

"Can you? I can't."

"Then you shouldn't marry him."

There, she had said it; she had released the words that risked turning her daughter from her; she could feel herself already the man's mother-in-law, that disapproving figure out there on the island he would never want to visit. She was already his enemy now, and should her daughter choose him, there seemed no way back; for the part of Isabel that loved Peader must surely hate her. She was foundering in the knowledge of how hopeless was her situation when Isabel answered her with a question.

"Were you sure?"

"Yes," she said quickly, flying back to Donegal and being the girl carrying the basket with the letter down the street, remembering with bittersweet pain the fleetness like wings in her feet coming back from seeing him.

"Yes, yes, I was," she said, "and you need to feel that sureness, Isabel, for all the things that'll be ahead of you. You need that. Because there'll be trials, and you'll need to know that you were sure he was the one when you face them."

Sean moaned from the room, the sound small as dust, but Isabel stood up to go to him.

"I don't know," she said, and moved away.

6

The rain lifted the following morning and Isabel brought Sean outside in his battered and rough wheelchair. The roads on the island were more like ancient pathways and bumped him jerkily as they moved away from the house and out into the broader gusting of the sea. He sat silently at an angle and Isabel felt the dead weight of him as she pushed, struggling almost at once, even as they were only heading out from the village. Still, she drove him on, moving him away from their home as much for her own sake as for his. When she awoke that morning the air in the house had been suddenly tight with the echoing questions of the night before. She had lain in her childhood bed and opened her window on the voices of the night sea. There had been no stars and the coming and going darknesses of the clouds above drifted like brooding ghosts. Her sleep was ragged, and at breakfast the feeling that she had arrived at a precipice in her life at once translated itself into a desire to take Sean to the sea.

They moved out beyond the houses and the morning greetings and were a pair of hushed figures, brother and sister, retracing the journey of years earlier when the accident had happened and Isabel had first begun to believe that hers was to be an inheritance of damaged dreams. She was angry with herself for not knowing what to do about Peader, and then despised herself for the littleness of her worries when she looked down at her brother in the wheelchair. Life, she thought, was a reasonless mess clotting around her, and all the excitement and wonder of her girlhood on the island was now gone on the tide: Sean had not returned to health, Peader was like a brightly painted liner, half-sunken in the water, leaking an ugly spillage that it seemed she had to repair. The two seemed intimately connected in her mind.

They moved along slowly towards the precipice and the edge of the island. Isabel was not sure if Sean could even remember the accident. Certainly he had not been back in years, and although his sister could not quite explain why, she desperately wanted that morning to return both of them there. The gulls flew up from underneath the edge and made a raucous laughing overhead as Isabel struggled hard now to get the wheelchair over the stones. The sky was broken with clouds and the wind made the air glassy. The seabirds hovered and fell, rising again through marvellous curves as if following along the invisible tracks of God's heart.

Breathless and flushed, Isabel clicked the brakes on the wheelchair and sat down on the rocks, her hair gagging her mouth before she tossed her head free and looked across at her brother.

"Do you know where we are?" she asked him. "This is the place we came that day after school." She looked out to sea. "That was the day everything started to go wrong." Sean moved to one side in the chair and fixed his eyes on the faraway horizon.

"Nothing was ever right for me after that. No more than it was for you. I just wish you were all right again, you know? Just that you got better and stood up and said, 'Howya, girl' or something and we could walk back home and I could tell you about Peader and you would help me. I know you would."

She let her words trail off into the wind, and sat there a while suddenly realising that she had come expecting a miracle. That was what she was waiting for, waiting for the moment God was passing by the cliffs once more and gave the nod of recovery to Sean. For in that moment the crack in her world could heal and marriage to Peader would be the dreamsweet heaven she had once imagined. It would be the sign she was waiting for.

"You know he's asked me to marry him," she said. "I know you know that. Mother thinks that's why you're so unwell now. Is it, Sean? Because I don't know that I will marry him. I haven't decided. I don't know if I ever will. In some ways I love him and in others I don't. Not at all. So I guess that means I shouldn't marry him. What do you think?"

Sean made no movement and Isabel said nothing more, waiting in the slow-moving morning and gazing out at the changeless horizon on that western sea for any sign of God coming. Since she had left the island she had abandoned the habit of going to church and never said any formal prayers. Still, she believed God was somewhere out there in the uncharted skies, visiting even now the life of some unsuspecting innocent. It was superstition as much as faith that kept her on the cliff edge, hoping for a sign, something to resolve this clot of her life. An hour passed. And another. They grew cold. Even the gulls gave up and flew away. Come on, come on, come on, Isabel urged in a mute pleading that willed the heavens to crack and let down mercy. *Come on, come on.*

Nothing came but the afternoon and hunger, and the ghosts of despair. Sean made no sound and sat without moving, his eyes fixed with a kind of entranced rapture at the empty air, as if all the time encircled by angels.

7

Isabel gave God every chance. She pulled the wheelchair home behind her that afternoon, Sean travelling backwards from the scene, and swore that if the day was fine tomorrow she'd take him back there.

And she did.

It was a kind of vigil: each morning of that week Isabel stayed at home, her mother watched her wrap Sean in the blanket and push off out the front door. Margaret imagined what was happening and grieved silently at the desperate loving and hope that was scalding her daughter's heart. She knew that this too was part of the wretched puzzle of life, the insoluble mystery of why things are as they are and why we seek to match and pair events into the thinnest fabric of meaning. She packed biscuits underneath the blanket and said nothing, knowing that it was something that Isabel had to do and that the human need to feel one can cure another is more powerful than fire. She watched them go off into the midmorning and knelt by the range and said her own prayer.

When Isabel and Sean passed along by the schoolhouse, Muiris put the students at an exercise and watched out the window. The sight of them lacerated his heart, for he felt Isabel's pitiful hope with the freshness of his own years earlier when the accident had first slashed open his life and he had wornout the knees of his trousers with beseeching. He was wounded all the more now for knowing that her wishes and prayers were hopeless and that each day's vigil at the cliffside was tearing another rent in the innocence of her heart. For her now, as much as for Sean, he wished something might happen, and while they were away he taught his classes with his mind floating on half-formulated prayers that he might be struck dead and his son get up and walk.

The students finished their exercises while the Master was away in his mind. They marked their desks or fired inky paper pellets, some of which fell with a small splat against the painting on the back wall that Isabel called *The Treasure*, that great hurly-burly seascape framed in oak and painted by William Coughlan.

Muiris allowed a minor riot to fill the classroom before he brought his attention back from his son and daughter. He snapped the air with his eyes as if with a strap and over the bowed heads considered all kinds of divine bargains. The day was interminable, the clouds matting in a slow foreboding and the sea endlessly churning about. There was no escaping it, and in such moments Muiris thought it was far worse to be on an island. It was as if the all-surrounding sea was the implacable and unfathomable heart of Life itself into which his questions fell and sunk like stones. He wished he could see away into another vista and suddenly told the class to put down their pens and listen to the fable of Moses and the Red Sea. While he told the story—even though he had told it to the older pupils once before—he could himself momentarily imagine the sea to the mainland parting open; he could imagine the fabulous need and prayer that might cut and spread the waters like a knife; he could see Isabel and Sean on the cliffside, the wheelchair glistening in the windy light and her asking for a sign, and then suddenly the majesty, the moment, *Think of it*, he said. *Think of it*, he said again, leaning forward on his high chair and sweeping an arm out to the Atlantic that ringed their lives, holding his hand there so that Cronin and O'Flaherty stood in their seats to look out the high window with expectation.

"The instant when"—he grimaced at the awful faith required—"when, against all the odds, when it seemed more hopeless than hopelessness itself, when the world seemed most a godless blackness into which there would be nothing but bloodshed and horror, right then, the sea, boys and girls, the sea opened and they were saved.''

He let the school off early and sat alone in the empty building, hearing the vanishing cries of the excited children and looking out on the deepening grey of the sea. It was a cooler afternoon than the one before and yet he hadn't seen Isabel and Sean return from the cliffs. He sat in his place feeling a reasonless fear creep over him that something dreadful had happened. He had a locked cupboard beneath the window and went across to it now, took out a bottle, and poured himself a half-tumbler of whiskey. He drank it standing beside the painting that was a reminder of his wife's love and tried to wash away the fear. Why was it, he wondered, that he seemed to be awaiting tragedy? He could not quite pin down the feeling, and instead of helping him reach any closer definition of it, the whiskey blurred the premonition into various shapes and closer, none of which came close to the truth. For, not that afternoon, nor the one after, nor any of the days or nights of that week did Muiris know that his daughter was on the cusp of a new life, and that the thing he was dreading was nothing but that. He waited until the sky was growing darker to decide to go to the cliffs and bring his children home. Yes, he would go out and get them; he was their father, he could steer them safely in out of the danger. Right then, he said to himself, shambling down the classroom. Right then. When he opened the schoolhouse door to step out, a flock of gulls screamed overhead and the whiskey lit suddenly inside him, making momentarily a glittering and glassy resolve out of the shards of disappointment. He stumbled and was sharp with himself to stand upright and not act the fool. Anything could have happened. Something had; he knew it had. Damnit in Christ, he knew. He knew something had happened, and started with a jerky and uncertain haste towards the far shore, for all the world imagining that he was about to encounter the dreadful and awkward hand of God in his life once more.

They could both be dead, he thought. They could be already drowned and I sitting there in the bloody classroom. They could have jumped. She could have done anything, she seems so. So. Hurt.

He had walked four hundred yards on the flame of whiskey, in the full expectation of meeting disaster. He felt so lit that he imagined as he hurried that he might pull down the very angels that bore his drowned children away into the sky, pull them down and wrestle free from any far and glowing heaven their wild island-made souls. If they were taken, he thought, if they were taken he would; he would.

Then there they were, returning along the stony ground, as if from the Kingdom of the Dead. Isabel was pulling the wheelchair behind her and Sean, cheek-burned from the day's wind, was leaning to one side, only his head visible, so that at first it seemed his sister carried an infant on her back. There had been no tragedy. Nothing of the marvelous or the doomed had parted the sea and changed the world, and as Muiris came to a stop before them he burst into tears. He put his arms out around the awkward grouping of them and hugged on, unable to ring his children within his embrace as he once had, unable to make the inviolable fort of his arms that hooped them to his heart, but holding on nonetheless. He held and wept against them without speaking. He bent and kissed his son's face and held it in his two hands and shook it slightly with the charge of his emotion. God, I love you, he thought, the simplest words and the feeling running through him sharply, parting him between the force of loving and the hopeless inadequacy of his ever truly expressing it. Muiris hugged onto both of them. He pressed his forehead down on the crown of his daughter's lowered head, hoping to leave there like laurel leaves his gratitude for her and his understanding of her taking Sean to the cliffside. The whiskey sweetly raging, Muiris held his children on the stony path in the late bluster of the island afternoon, full of a sense of apology and love and grief, his eyes running, his limbs shaking, and feeling closer to both of them than he would ever feel again for the rest of his life.

8

The following day Margaret Gore told her husband about the wedding proposal. Muiris went to school and said nothing, and Nora Liathain, throwing a handful of breadcrumbs to her clutch of hens as he passed, hardly noticed he was snapped like a wafer.

9

Isabel stayed on the island for a week. She spoke to Sean and waited for the miracle until at last she no longer believed it was coming. Still, she took her brother to their place each day and tied more tightly the knot of her life with the pain of his. Of all the bargains she could coin in those hours on the cliffs one stood out: If You don't want me to marry him, then make Sean all right. On the Sunday, after Mass in the small crowded church, she decided to wait one more day and then go back to Galway. If something was to happen it would happen now wherever Sean was; she didn't have to bring him to the cliffside, and so instead she went to her bedroom and packed her case. From the small white chest of drawers with the broken metal handles her father had promised often to fix she took out clothes that were pieces of her girlhood, skirts and dresses that released into the bedroom air her own self of years earlier. There she was, Isabel at twelve years old sitting on the bed in that ancient patterned crosswork of green and red. There were books and photographs and scraps of the kind of things that were stored away in drawers for the dust of their memory to accumulate and be blown gently now into that Sunday afternoon.

Within an hour she was surrounded by herself. She took things from the drawers as if they were the lost treasures of a shipwreck and laid them on the bed, on the hard chair, and finally on the floor itself, the room transforming into a collage of her life. The more she emptied the drawers, the more apparent did it seem to her that she was that afternoon marking an ending; that the girl summoned by the old clothes was no longer her and that already she was able to look back as if at a stranger. She got a plastic bag and began to fill it with her past. She wanted to keep nothing and made jumble of the old essay copies and spelling tests and favorite cardigans her mother had stored away for some fond time in the future. When she had cleaned the place of everything and the bedroom was like a levelled site with the black plastic heap to one side, Isabel lay on the bed exhausted.

So, she thought, that's the end of that.

It had begun to rain for the first time that week, falling as it always fell at half past three on Sunday afternoons and wrapping the island in a dark shawl. From the mainland it would look now as if the heavens had descended on the small hump of sea-lashed rock, softly releasing behind grey veils whatever secrets and mysteries only islanders learned. The wind kept the rain at the front of the house. Margaret finished washing the dinner dishes and crossed the small kitchen to wring out the soaked towel that was wedged in at the back of the front door. Then, seeing her husband slip into the deep warm contentment of his Sunday nap, she went to knock on Isabel's door.

"Isabel?"

She stepped inside the room and saw at once, with a sharp blow of dismay, the packed suitcase and the plastic bags.

"Are you all right? What are you doing?"

"I'm going back tomorrow."

"Are you?"

"I put a lot of old things in those bags; you can give the clothes away, and the other one is just stuff for burning."

Margaret looked across at the two bags and nodded her agreement, even as she knew that within two days of Isabel's leaving she would be unpacking them again, turning over the memories of her girl and then hiding the stuff away in the garret room that served as the attic. She sat down on the end of the bed.

"Did you tell Dad?"

"I did. I thought it was only right. And he's delighted for you."

"He didn't say anything."

"You know him. I mean he'll need time. That's all. It was a bit of a surprise, I suppose, and anyway, I told him that you weren't sure." Margaret looked at the sprawled figure of her daughter on the bed she had outgrown. "Are you?"

"I don't know. I miss seeing him," she said.

"Yes."

Isabel did not say that it seemed inevitable now, that there was no way to turn back, and that a long, fateful road seemed to have led her from the cliffside years earlier to the moment she was deciding to give her life to Peader O'Luing.

The light in the room was dim and growing dimmer still between them, with all Margaret's unsayable warnings and wisdoms lying heavily in the air and Isabel's mind sluggish with the weight of the week's failed expectations. There was nothing more to say. No miracle had come, no answers. They left the room together to make tea and see to Sean, passing the remainder of the rained-in evening moving carefully around the possibility of arguments.

Isabel went to bed that night before her parents, and silently asked one last time for a sign before she took the boat back in the morning. It had seemed to her more likely that answers and signs might come to her there on the island rather than in the moil of the city; she wanted to feel more clearly what to do and so lay in the bed awake, hearing the slippered movement of her mother going to her room and the latch's click on the door an hour later when her father returned from the pub. The house fell silent, and then fluttered with snores and sleep sounds and the softest muffle of the sighing sea. She lay still. The plastic bags had been left by the door and her own ghost had slipped from them to sit waiting at the end of her feet. In the morning it would reoccupy the room, keeping her girlhood strangely imprisoned in the tidy, empty space, like a sea-whisper within a stone-walled island field.

The night was like an ache, and in the morning when the light broke Isabel rose feeling battered. She moved with an automatic numbness and kissed her father goodbye as he left for the school-house, neither of them mentioning what was uppermost in their minds. She went to Sean in his room and spoke to him for a last time, telling him that she would be back in a few weeks and they would go again to the cliffs together. She looked at the side of his face and felt as she always did the sharp pang of her grief for him. Why? Why did it have to happen? Why wasn't it her? He made no movement in response, but lay drowsily gazing past her at the unspooling of his mind.

"Well," said Margaret.

"Yes, I'd better go."

"You'll be all right?"

"I will, yes."

They were standing at the front door letting in the wind. Margaret spoke hurriedly: "If there's anything you want to talk to me about and not tell your father, send it in a letter." She looked at her daughter and waited an instant to see the message alight there, then hugged her to her breast. "Put a little star on the back of the envelope," she said, "I'll know then."

And then Isabel was back on the boat sailing to Galway, eight days after asking for the first time for a sign from the heavens. She sat out on the deck in the constant spray, travelling in the slap and sway of the water and turning over in her mind questions about marriage. She had reached a dull hopelessness by the time the boat was docking and had stood up with her case to reenter the un-certain maze of her life when she saw Peader O'Luing standing waiting for her. He had a clutch of flowers in his left hand, holding them so tightly that their sweetness was almost running down his fingers.

Isabel could hardly move. How was he there? How of all the days had he chosen this one, this boat to meet? The thought that her mother had phoned him flapped across her mind and was dis-missed. No, it had to be something else. She took a step onto the mainland and felt rising out of her on wings the dark birds of gloom. She was smiling. The smile breaking on her lips with the knowledge that here at last was the sign she had been waiting for, here he was, thrusting the flowers towards her and grinning the broken grin of embarrassment and relief. She did not think then that he was a desperate man, that since the day she had left him he had floundered amidst the echoes of his father's taunts, and that nothing could hush the inner voices of mockery but the return of this girl. She did not think he could be so desperate as to have gone daily to the docks to await the incoming ferry with his flowers and see if she had come back. Isabel thought only that here was a man who had been guided into her life like a fall of light every bit as sudden and dazzling as the one which had landed in her brother's mind on the day they had played at the cliffs. She thought this flawed love was something she could not deny, was what was meant for her, and knew before he spoke that yes, by that evening as they lay naked together in the room above the shop, their bodies hungering for each other and their mouths escaping in kisses from the need for words, she would already have answered his week-old proposal and said, yes, Peader, yes, I will marry you.

10

It was a Friday afternoon late in August when God spoke to my father for the second time. He came in a fiery chariot with trumpeting angels down the streets of Dublin. His winged steeds beat the golden air with silvered hoofs, and hosannas rang thunderous with rapture into the cloudless sky. The majesty of His mantle stilled the motion of the earth itself as He swept forward to enter our house and tell my father that his life's work was done. The ordinariness of the day was transformed. There was singing in the air, and invisible choirs poured forth Glorias in excelsis like the emanations of God's own soul. The hallway inside our front door was a burnished gold as He passed it. There were flights of doves, conjured like white blessings in the air and alighting on my father's astonished shoulders as he sat unsuspecting and immensely weary in the room where he had found himself no longer able to paint any pictures. The door opened the way light falls into a dark place, and my father stood up and let it touch him. He didn't speak; the tall white thinness of him like a sheet of paper waiting for the Word, as the room thronged with angels and the heraldic music of their trumpeting rose in crescendoes to deafen his ears. The house itself was illuminated and seemed to rise in the air, its glowing radiance visible from as far as the Dublin mountains and the choiring spirits making the afternoon air ambrosial even in the shopping streets and malls where people paused in the majesty of the moment, sweetly unaware of what was happening.

From the moment God entered our house my father recognized Him like his own father, and as he stood up in the dazzling moment he realized he had been expecting this all along. He had been waiting in fact from the moment months earlier when he had sat in the room unable to paint anymore. Daily he had gone about the business of waiting and preparing for his inspiration. He had been attendant every day for hours without the slightest lift to his spirit and the draining away of every fluid ounce of certitude that had once coursed so powerfully in his veins. He had, in his eight-hour silences in the studio room, maddened himself with thinking that perhaps there had never been a voice from God and that the ruins of the life in which he found himself had all been caused by his own folly. Only the barest light flickered in that place inside him that had once gleamed bright. Yet still he sat on, going in and taking his place by the single bar heater and letting each day's light fail in a reflection of his own diminishment.

And then, that afternoon.

He was burned to the very rim of his soul, his fingers tingled, his hair stood on end, and he moved from the studio that was already alight with the beckoning of God. At last, there He was again. God had come to him. The immensity of the rapture and vision beggered everything, and momentarily my father flew through the air. He cruised on the immaterial lightness of the spirit world like a moth and arced easily across the hallway, the thinness of himself now see-through and clear but for the doves winging about his white hair. He flew in the stairway and rose like laughter above the waves of the hosannas. My mother met him at the landing, wings beating and the edges of her hair fringed with light as he flew by and took her in his arms like a suit of white clothes, both of them hosts of the air, with God Himself pursuing with the choiring angels, in and out of each room, their pale fiery visions chasing my parents like children as they swept through the air and touched each inch of the house with their presence. The heavenly chariot was stalled outside in midair above the garden, the steeds breathing the August air, their flanks rising and falling in recovery from the speed of the long journey and their sweat falling in the form of apple blossoms into the long grass.

My father's work was over. He had pleased Him, he had lived with a purpose that had reflected the meaning of the world which was nothing but the grandeur of His creation. Glorias were being sung, the light had become more and more golden until, as God Himself approached my father and they met in midair above the window at the top of the stairs, it reached such an intensity that it became liquid and filled my father's mouth and his eyes and his ears with the sweetness of an all-consuming embrace that was sweeter and brighter and more golden than anything in this world could ever be.

11

That day only I knew what had really happened. I put aside the brutal fable I was told by the Guards and blinded out the image of the man they said had sat in front of a single-bar heater and fed into it his canvases until the house burnt down around him. It was an impossible nightmare, the kind that Guards tell in white rooms on the edge of the city, bright lights over mugs of milky tea. I heard it and forgot it. That night I had a rented bed in a widow's bungalow down the road. But even as I lay staring at the split in the curtains where the streetlight bled in, I knew my father was laughing at last amidst the angels above me.

I slipped out of the house at two o'clock in the morning and walked home. I couldn't feel any sadness. I could smell the house before I saw it, and wondered at the enormity and omnipotence of the force that had passed like a charge down the street that afternoon. The night air was choked with fumes; they entered your clothes and then your eyes and you felt the tears running. The house was a black shell against the dark blue sky. There were yellow and white strands of tape flickering in the little breeze as a warning to keep away, and as I crouched beneath them, coming in that gateway through which I remembered my father leaving us for the first time, I was already in the company of ghosts. The hall door was on the front grass; it was one side battered, one side burnt, thrown aside in a way that looked almost casual and made the opening into the house itself seem vulnerable and bare. When I entered I felt I should draw something across behind me. But there was nothing, and above my head the huge gap that was once the ceiling and then the floor of the upstairs my mother swept clean was naked heaven now. There were stars for dust. The windows had, like a family, fallen apart under the pressure and heat within the house, and my feet crunched smithereens as I made my way into the studio.

It was hardly even a room anymore, its window all air and the ceiling burnt clean away through the bedroom upstairs and on into the night. It was out through here his soul swept, I thought, and looked up into that August night that was star-flecked and clear and innocent of all the outrage of death and injustice. It was a perfect evening, so stilled and blue that it was impossible not to think of the hand that made it and to look upwards for the first of so many times to seek my father amidst the stars. I sat on a black metal something in the black space where all his colours had once been and I said a line in Latin. I said it softly, but loud enough for the ear I imagined still listening. And as the night passed over me and the cold came inside my clothes I said in turn every phrase and line I knew in Latin, sounding the air with the slow deliberate formulae of a scarcely communicative language that seemed to match perfectly the complex and unfathomable idea of God Himself.

I sat on there in the burnt-out house until the morning. The ghosts of that nighttime passed in and out of the windows and greeted me as a curiosity in that halfway place between death and living where I found myself unable to stand up and walk on into the rest of my life. My soul, if I had one, was so deeply fractured that nothing I could think of made the slightest sense. The darkness became soupy with uncertainties. What had happened? What had it meant that my father had given his life and a good portion of my mother's to the work, the paintings that he had been so fevered to create and that now were a brown dust amidst his dust at my feet? I lifted my legs off the ground and clutched them about me. If God had truly come down the street and into the house, might He not arrive now again and take me? For I could not imagine getting up from my place ever again. What was I supposed to do? *What am I supposed to do now?*

With the dawn there was the surprise of birds. They shot in the windows and flickered across the studio with giddying rapture. They perched and sang, hopelessly ungrieven, and with such relentless cheeriness that I pitched a piece of the fallen ceiling. But they would not be chased away. I fired a lump of blackish plaster, got up from my seat and rushed at them, waving my arms and roaring. But they merely flew past me to the far end of the room and would not leave through the window. There were thrushes and robins and the larger magpies, brown birds and yellow-speckled birds, birds arriving all the time in a gathering chorus, birds I did not recognize but ich flew through the air so quickly that they seemed flashes of demented energy, not creatures at all but for their singing and the thrilling urgency with which they poured forth the untranslatable and ceaseless music of life. An hour after dawn the studio room was filled with birds and I gave up trying to frighten them away. Their singing made the air so sweet

I began to gulp breaths and thought for a moment I had blossoms in my mouth. My ears were dripping honey. The birds landed on my shoulders, perched upon my knees, flew and returned on the endless song, and still did not leave me. Now the black burnt shell of the studio room was coloured palely pink and yellow and green. The colours were a dizzying mix; I might have been painting with my eyes so true and clear did the colours become as the birds trilled on. The dark dust of the floor lightened and a gust of breeze mingled it into the air. Everything was colours and music with birds flitting through it. I stood up and felt my tears fall down, only then realising that I had been crying. I walked to the front doorway in a trance and stepped outside, half-expecting to ascend on a flock of doves above all the red-brick homes of our dismayed road. I expected signals, interpretation, meaning, enlightenment, and all but fainted when a hand reached out and grasped my shoulder.

12

Angels, my father once said, must pass us in the street every day. They must be ordinary as birds, he said, and recognisable only in the brief moment of their connection to our lives. There was, according to this reasoning, a moment when you knew you were met by an angel and that whatever aid it gave you, however subtle and difficult to trace, your life was changed. When I stood outside the front doorway of our ruined house and felt the hand on my shoulder I expected at the very least an archangel, if not God Himself, and was surprised to see a small fat grey-haired man with a pained and apologetic expression. It was John Flannery. He put his hand on my shoulder, and when I almost fainted, it swept around my back and braced me against the small roundness of his body. He gave a few squeezes as a measure of condolence. His eyes were grey and fixed on me with a look that seemed to

166

urge that we should not talk about things, that it was all understood in some subliminal way between us and the best thing was to go off in his car and have a cup of tea.

The unlikeliest angel, he led the way out of the garden with his hand still firmly on my back. We sat in his car and he lit a cigarette before we moved off. A moment later he shocked himself with the realisation of how inconsiderate was the smoke that wafted through the air between us, and as the car sped along he made a sorry fuss of waving it away, as if releasing out the window the terrible facts of the fire. I said nothing. I sat in the car and let it take me away. What was I to do? I watched the road beneath the car wheels and the façades of all the dull ordinary houses where mostly women were coming and going with children, doing the shopping and walking prams through the interminable cycles of everyday. How plain and dreary it all seemed, the casualness of such comings and goings only down the road from our house where God was a visitor. For God's sake.

My angel was a bachelor. Alone in his house in Drumcondra he had cultivated a brand of good manners that was not readily available elsewhere, and he knew that the appropriate line with victims of tragedies where the father has been burnt to a crisp in the living room is to punctuate the silence with sage nods towards the surviving son. Say nothing, just look over when you come to a red light and nod twice; as if to say, Oh yes, my friend, I know just how bad it is, and do you know how you know I know? You know because I know it's so bad I can't even begin to say, you know? Then drive on.

We covered miles like this. I was not sure where we were going, except that tea had been mentioned and that my clothes smelled of birds. We travelled back through the city, got caught in traffic, sat mute together with a few brave half-nods, and then purred slowly out into the suburbs on the other side. I gradually realised that what I was supposed to do was forget. I was supposed to be making a beginning at the proven equation of distance travelled times company equals grief erasing. But it was hopeless, there were ashes on my shoes and so much of me was already dead: all my father of me dead and all my mother. What was left? I sat hunched in the sour burnt smell of tragedy and arrived at Mr. Flannery's house in mid-morning like a propped-up corpse. He turned off the ignition and staring straight at his garage door gave a slow nod. He came around to open the car door for me and reached in the hand to take my shoulder again. We went together through the doorway of a house that was almost the model of our own, except for the neatness of everything and the smell of air freshener that betrayed a life of disappointed love.

"Now tea," said Mr. Flannery, speaking for the first time in an hour and leaving me in the sitting room between the twin cushions. "Unless"—his head popped back in again, and he held a whiskey bottle—"No, no, tea." He nodded to his own advice and went out.

I think I knew then that he was not aware that he was my angel. He had no idea of the wheels and minute mechanisms of life I was only then gleaning for the first time. He didn't know—as I slowly began to see—that the meaning was in the plot, the shape, that the way and whom we met in the course of our simplest doings was so intricately and finely fit into a grander pattern that all we had to do was follow the signs—as I was following him. For otherwise everything was random and chance, and the inconsolable truth about the Coughlans was that there never had been a call from God and that my father had ruined our lives and killed my mother for no reason at all. It couldn't be true. There was a reason, a meaning, and with the smudges of the cinders still on my clothes I sat there on the sofa waiting for tea and knowing that Mr. Flannery was the next spoke on the turning wheel. All I have to do, I told myself, is follow the signs. There is something I am supposed to do next.

"Some people like honey in it. I don't. But well, that's it there. Now." He laid a tray before me and sat on the armchair opposite, his hands pressed together between his knees.

An hour passed. Perhaps it was two, I cannot be sure. The tea was cold by the time I drank it. I picked up the cup and put it down an age later. Or so it seemed. For the moment in which I held the cup became two moments, shortly ten, then twenty. And in just this way the days after my father's death became weeks became months in the familiar ceaseless cruelty of time, carrying us ever forward even when we sit still. Time does not pass, pain grows. Without exactly knowing it, I had moved in with Mr. Flannery; it didn't seem intentional, it was as if I was the forward pawn of a long abandoned chess game, a piece left in position and stalled between promise and defeat as the dust gathered. I was living in the guest room upstairs across from the bathroom. I had a set of clean and pressed towels and could sit freely in either of the downstairs sitting rooms all morning and afternoon while my host went to the office. Before he left he programmed hours of Mozart and Bach on the player and I awoke to harpsichord or piano, lying there in the bedcovers wondering how I could possibly go on.

The official government allotment for grief is five working days; it was to take five days for me to deal with my father's arrangements, settle his papers. After that I was expected back at my desk, where the vacant space I should be occupying in the room galled McCarthy like an empty chamber in his revolver. As it was, there were no papers to be settled and Flannery took care of the arrangements. I stayed in bed with Bach; I lay in the music and in the pause between the movements heard the leaves begin to fall outside. After two weeks, or perhaps longer, McCarthy himself arrived at the front door. His blue car gleamed in the driveway, and he locked it and then looked at it momentarily before turning up to the house. He used his civil service walk and brought his suit square-shouldered to ring the doorbell. I looked down at him from above, the perfect C of his combed hair, and heard the firmly pressed bell disturb an allegro. He stood back. He looked down at his car, still there, still gleaming. They exchanged smiles. Then he turned and rang the bell again, pressing it through the music like a knife and holding it there until he was sure I had heard. He was on government time; he knew his moments away from the department left it loose and idle and he wished to return. But first he would speak to me. He rang a third time and added a knock.

He stepped back and turned a look up at the house. When he saw me gazing down at him from the middle upstairs window, he was unsure for a moment and made a little wave with his right hand as if flagging from a distant shore. I waved back. It threw him briefly. Then a woman passed the gate with a child and he spun automatically to check his car, and looked up at me with sudden urgency. He waved his arm for me to come down, first mouthing the words as if I were deaf, then soon shouting at me: "Come down, open the door!"

I didn't. I watched him growing more exasperated below me, stepping away and coming back, pressing the doorbell, knocking, and giving me his sharpest eye. I could read his looks like old paperbacks: I am sorely disappointed in you, sorely. You who had been spoken of above, Mr. Coughlan, and let me down so badly. So very badly. Open this door!

I did not even shake my head. My father had once told me that when anyone is watched carefully for a little time human behaviour quickly resembles nothing as much as the random traffic of insects on a plate of grapes. Now it struck me: here he was, the portly beetle crisscrossing the Welcome doormat, unable for a moment to understand my looking down on him from another world. McCarthy's patience had a four-minute fuse; he repeated everything he had done once more: ringing, stepping back, circling the grapes, glaring, and finally giving up. When he moved away at last I gave him the same little wave we had begun with, and watched him drive away with the end of my civil service career.

I felt a flush of elation and the giddiness of being in free-fall. I got up and walked around the house; how suddenly marvellous it was to do nothing, to sit or stand at a whim, to hold breath or release it. There was nothing ahead; I had no money, no job, and only temporary lodging. When Uncle John returned in the evening to sit with me for tea I told him I was not returning to work. I was waiting for a sign.

He was a patient man, and passed me nods like biscuits. When the tea was done we sat in the long sitting room on far chairs, and the music played over us. We sat like that for a while, as if expecting the arrival at any moment of our conversation. When it didn't come we sat on, strange figures in the suburban night listening to the music and waiting for the plot to turn. Uncle John gave it an hour, then opened his briefcase and drew out files, working over figures until they blended into the scores of sonatas and concertos, returning him to the safe places of his bachelorhood. The evenings drew around us, gradually I became invisible.

I lived in the house through the autumn and winter, waiting all the time for God to speak. The little business of life clicked on without me. When the weather grew harsh and the night air thick with coal smoke, I decided that perhaps God would not visit me in the house; I needed to get out and walk and await chance encounters. So, each evening after tea, when my angel moved into his sitting room and put a match to the fire, I pulled on a coat and headed out in the hail winds where He might be waiting. What was I to do? What was next?

Tell me.

The roads were deserted and the curtained windows of the homey houses sealed in the world. Cars nosed endlessly through the dark, creatures in a purgatory of no arrival, moving restlessly onward along the curving and entangled roads of the edge of the city. So many going somewhere; if I walked more slowly maybe a car would stop. Maybe I would come across a breakdown. Maybe, what? What was I hoping for? I can't really say; something to show me the shape of the way ahead, to erase the randomness and make clear a sense of purpose.

I walked on through the night, snaking back and forth through avenues, lanes, and closes until I found myself back at Flannery's. I let myself in and went to bed. The following evening I went out again; making a routine of the empty ring around the suburb, my striding round nothingness when no God spoke. I walked into February; in March when it snowed and froze over, making hard white glass of the roads, I slip-skated out in case it was a test and destiny was at hand. In the dark that night nothing was moving; for once the roads were emptied and I could ginger-step and slide down their centre like the first man in the new world.

The streetlights lit the snow-road like a runway. At first my steps were tiny, flat slippy movements and the sudden jolt backwards of my head as I toppled. It was all edgy and expectant of falls. The city roads in the empty whiteness were beautiful with stillness. Sleep flanked them, and the grey world had vanished under the ice. Stars glittered under my feet. It took an hour to travel half a mile. I didn't care. I walked on down the centre of the runway road knowing a flight would arrive at any moment. My foot slipped but I didn't fall, and within a moment it seemed I was no longer walking but skating between the streetlights. I gathered speed, took slippy little run-ups, and threw out my hands, sliding giddily forward. And again. Down the road, a little falling-apart gallop and then the smooth rush of the skating. It was dazzling; the ice carried me like a lightweight, the houses flew by, and I gathered speed with each go, skating down the roads of Dublin, my arms flung out like wings and my coat flapping behind. I skated into roundabouts and out, through stoplights and yield signs with my eyes closed. Let something crash into me now, let the world collide with me anyway it wants. Now, now!

But it did not. I skated on through the empty suburbs, the ice coming through the thin soles of my shoes, so that only when I looked down could I be sure my feet were there. I skated one-footed, tried mini-arcs and twists to tempt falling, but stayed upright, a tall wobbling figure passing through the whiteness of the night. It seemed the city had been made vacant for me; had been prepared like a setting for the minor drama that was my sudden realisation that I was alone. Even as I skated there, it struck with a force for the first time: I had no friends, my father was dead. A pale jellied nausea turned in my stomach. My father was dead. I was alone. I made no movement and let the ice carry me downhill, feeling nothing now below my knees. My father was dead; it was as if there had been an amputation and the part that was missing hurt now. I wobbled on the ice once and then crashed headlong.

13

How long I lay there I can't be sure. Blood from a wound in my forehead mingled with the ice and made a little map resembling Norway. My feet had no feeling; there was a throbbing and a needling as if small creatures with sharp teeth were working at my forehead. My right eye was against the road, the packed ice cooling tears. I lay there and could not move, gazing down the long ribbon of frozen white until at last I saw the figure of a man approaching. Perhaps he was a dream. He was a mile away but moved with a kind of high and angular purpose that made little of the snow. He was a mile, then a half-mile, then in no time almost upon me, as if the film jumped forward.

It was my father. He was unburnt and fresh-faced, beaming at the snow. It was such a miraculous night that he had gone for a walk out of heaven while my mother was tidying up.

His fingers were warm in the wound on my forehead. His blue-blue eyes were upon me like lights, and I felt a charge of electricity rush to my toes. Dad, I wanted to say; Dad, hold on to me, please, don't let me go. I want to go with you.

And then he lay down on the road beside me. I had everything to say to him but could say nothing. All the words dissolved like snow on my tongue and we lay on in a hush, gazing starward. Time may have passed, but the pain did not grow, and in that lying-down stillness of the frozen night I suddenly began to see with my father's eyes; the star-shine, white-stippled sky, its razzle-dazzle, snow-slowed majesty, its million-berried amaze, softest and silent falls of snow off high branches of a spruce tree, powder-light, falling now as if an invisible hand had brushed by, light itself splayed across the heavens, the quality of the cool air, made, composed like music, glittering like silver.

I lay beside him and saw, saw the world infinite in detail and design, the map of its every star and snowflake exact with beauty and majesty. Then I turned to my father.

But he was gone.

1 4

Dreams, my father was certain, are the other you talking back. He never made it clear where this other you was, how exactly he lived or what he had for breakfast, but he was alive and talking in pictures when we slept. He told me this as a child while he was painting a picture called *Fragment of Dream*. It was nothing I could make out, blues and greens and perhaps a monster, if monsters exist. But for weeks afterwards when I lay upstairs awaiting sleep I had the sense to make space on the pillow beside me for a dream. My other me was fairly hopeless at talking in pictures. He was pre-primary school. Everything he said was completely muddled and made no sense. He wet his bed. He was chased by figures who moved like smears of oil paint and daubed the stairway as they came up it. His mother was a vacuum cleaner. After a while I decided to ignore him altogether and woke in the mornings with a tight criminal feeling of having erased the night completely.

The morning after the snow-walk I woke when Uncle John slipped out the door to work. I lay on the edge of sleep awhile, trying to reassemble the night it was my habit to forget. How had I gotten home? I sat up in the bed and looked out the window: the world was melted. The snow had been withdrawn in one swift movement like a magician's cloth and the grey world beneath was shown once again. The semi-detached houses across the road smoked with morning fires and left open the gates where cars had already gone into the city. The air was puffy with fumes. I opened the window and the traffic came in, its smell and sound driving through the room. There was nothing unusual or portentous. How much easier it would have been if there was a clear sign, something written in a patch of uneven snow, a pattern in the clouds. But instead there was only the humdrum nothingness, the ordinary and dull continuance of time itself, the world as we knew it.

Yet suddenly I knew what to do.

When John Flannery came home that evening I asked him for a thousand pounds.

"I beg your pardon."

"I need it. I want to make a trip."

"Well, Nicholas . . ."

"Not all for the journey. I want to buy the painting back. I want to buy the painting that you gave away as a prize."

He sat across the little kitchen table from me and put down his teacup. He was still wearing his suit. His eyes lowered to his bread and butter and left the baldness of his old head facing me. Within it ran the memories of the day he got the painting from my father, and back through the corridors to the moments he had first met William Coughlan, all the fret days of his courting my mother and the emptiness of the office on the day he had left. His own was a still life compared to it, and in the instants when he sat there across from me, his head lowered, I watched the sadness enshroud him.

"Yes. Yes," he said at last, and nodded. "You might get it back. It would be right. I'll tell you where it is."

The following morning I took the train to Galway. Uncle John left me at the station with a handshake and more nods.

"You're so like your father," he said. He stood back and looked at me and nodded, as if agreeing with some inner voice that prompted angels. And then he was gone, disappearing into the traffic and leaving me with his faith in a good world and his thousand pounds.

That morning I took the train west across the country for the second time in my life. It was no different; my father was still somewhere ahead of me in the carriages and I was travelling to bring him back. But now I had the name of a schoolmaster in an island village scribbled down on a piece of paper. I rolled and unrolled it as the train whirred with a smooth iron resolve across the soft green fields. Who was he, this Muiris Gore, the poet with William Coughlan's painting? What had he done with it? Did he value it, did he still have it? I had never heard of him. The whole idea of a single schoolmaster on an island was so swept with the romantic that it seemed unreal. What kind of life was it there? I remembered the sea off Clare, the extravagant moodiness of it, its largeness, its blue-and-white turbulence that so nearly swept me away. An island there. It was as foreign as fairy tales, and the more I dwelt on it, cut forehead throbbing on the cool window, the more the silver iron of the train that bore me west might have been the charge of knights heading for a fabled kingdom.

The plastic sandwiches brought me back. A boy younger than I bumped a trolley down the aisle and led a trail of toiletgoers. He was raw with shaven pimples. He sold me ham with cheese and I gave him one of Mr. Flannery's twenties. The plastic sandwiches came with plastic fruitcake and lukewarm water-tea. The first woman behind the trolley tried to edge past it, but the boy was having none of it. No one would pass until he reached the end of the carriage. It was his everyday power; his moment in a thin cheap white shirt and scarlet tie as he footed off the brake and moved the toileters another few feet down the train, stopping again and gruffly taking another order. When he finished the carriage we crossed the Shannon; I wondered if it was his given schedule, the measure of his days, for the journey meant nothing to him. He never arrived but shuttled back and forth across the landscape like a hare, flashing over the fields between darkness and darkness. I was exactly like him, I thought. Until today. Today I am hurtling to arrive, I thought, to get off and step into chance. For there was nothing left for me to do now; I felt I had to recover the painting before I could begin my life. I had to find it and sit down opposite it and stare and stare until I could see the vision my father had and hear the voice he heard and know the world held order and meaning, that that last fragment of his painting had some part to play, and until I found it I would not know what came next. The more I thought of it, the more certain I became: the painting had not survived for nothing. It was a clue, it alone surviving out of all the ruins of our life. And so, as damp fields flashed past and cattle stood in their mud under hedges and briefly glanced, I sat in the beating rhythm of the tracks, crossing the country with the ghost of my father and imagining that the name Muiris Gore was the next turning of the plot.

 V

1

On the morning of Isabel's wedding Margaret Gore warned her husband to behave. The night before, Muiris had met Peader for the first time. There had been a party on the island at Coman's; it began as a formal dinner with big Padraig furnishing red paper napkins and two sets of cutlery, but quickly dissolved away from the table with the men standing by the bar watching soccer on the television and Isabel looking across empty places at her mother and Sean. There was a lull between the dinner and the dancing. Peader felt awkward amidst the islanders until the drink inside him made them friendlier. Then he laughed more loudly than their jokes deserved and stood in the sweaty company in a thin disguise of whiskey.

Muiris was appalled by him. He seemed such a fool, a big weak fellow with a flabby jaw. Even when the music played he didn't seem to want to dance; he stood elbowing the counter and looking back as every shy fellow came forward to ask one last turn with the island beauty. When the music was playing, the fellow seemed even more morose to Muiris, and he had at last stepped forward to determine his character. Through the strains of the fiddling he asked Peader would he not dance. The flabby jaw opened, there was a grin and a shaking of his head. "No thanks," he said. He lifted a beer glass and looked into the drink until it came to his mouth. What was Muiris to say to him? He felt like beating him on the back with his fists; there was something about him, about his slowness, his grudging presence at his own pre-wedding that made the schoolmaster want to provoke him. Since he had arrived on the island he had shown little sign of love for Isabel. She held his arm, not his hand, and he grinned at passersby. What could she see in him? How could she have chosen him even over Seamus Beg, the small blue-eyed fellow who had sat next to her in the island school and who was dancing and spinning with her now?

"You love my daughter?" Muiris shot the question before he meant to. The two Joyces were playing a reel next to them and Peader didn't hear.

"What's that?"

"You . . . Come here. Come outside a minute."

And in a moment while Margaret Gore was wiping a fleck of dust that was grief from her eye, Muiris drew Peader outside into the night. The sudden air made the stars swim. Horan's blue boat down at the pier seemed to be sitting above the water. It was an instant before it was right again. Muiris blinked and felt the night's coolness about the back of his ears. This was his moment, he wanted it out now. He wanted an impossible proof from the loutish man before him. He held up his right forefinger.

"I want you to tell me. I want you to tell me why I should let you marry Isabel." He had blurted it out and instantly felt his wife in the night air scolding him. Peader's face screwed up, he raised his eyebrows for effect and let them land low on his eyes, then stepped back, let a little blow out the side of his mouth, threw the eyebrows again to show he meant it, and stood there grinning out at the sea. He was so surprised by the tone of the question that it took him like an attack. He felt the Master's hand on his arm turning him for an answer, and when he looked in Muiris Gore's face Peader saw his father there. He flung off the hand.

"It's not for you to let me," he said, and walked past towards the bar, growing inches of swagger in at last facing down his father.

"Wait a minute, will you? Christ, wait a minute."

Muiris had pulled him back by his jacket and saw the stars twirl and flash into the sea as a hand shoved him back and he fell sideways to the ground. The pebble gravel pressed against his cheek and the sky was huge.

It was not a blow and Peader had not intended to knock him down. He had moved to help the Master up as soon as he saw him fall, but three other men had come out and were there before him. The pub followed them out and commotion spilled around Muiris as he was put standing again. Margaret hurried out to him wearing her mortification tightly buttoned.

"I'm all right, I'm all right, I just fell. The stones are wet."

There were a few cracks, the Master and his drink, the advice he must have been giving the Galwayman, and the crowd went back inside.

Margaret Gore knew there was more to it, though she did not dare ask what. That night she and Muiris lay sleepless in bed feeling like the Mother and Father of Doom. Muiris did not mention the incident but turned on his side and stared at the truth that he no longer mattered in the life of his daughter. She was going to marry this man and her father was going to spend the rest of his days nursing the grief of her loss. It was the new blow in a life that had grown used to them. Why should disappointment and failure end now, he thought, no, I am to stand up in the morning and give away the last hope of happiness in this family. She will hate him in a year, hate me for not stopping her, and be always bearing the wound of this choice. But what can I do?

Margaret stirred in the bed. They knew they were each awake but lay beyond the possibility of words. For they knew that if they aired their disappointment the wedding would be impossible and Isabel as likely to run off and marry elsewhere. There was nothing to be done but to watch it happen, as if the whole event were some slow-motion tragedy full of horror and loss played out time and again on the starlit ceiling as they lay there in bed. Margaret moved closer to Muiris and from behind held on to him. He didn't turn but moved a hand up to place over her fingers, and they stayed like that, wordless, awake, looking at the darkness ahead while the window, open and uncurtained, let the bitter fragrance of their despair escape into the salty night air.

In the morning Margaret rose first, to find Isabel in the kitchen before her. Sean was unwell; he had turned into the corner of his bed and gestured away any attempts to get him up.

"Well, I'm getting married anyway," Isabel told him, going out into the kitchen and feeling the gloominess of the house like weights in her shoes. "Morning, Mother. I suppose you didn't want to get up today either?"

"That's not true at all. Your wedding, love. It's the happiest day of my life." Margaret paused for a second; how had she said it? Then she brought her hands together in a clap that was the on button of performance and said, "Now we have a lot to do, come on."

From that moment the house awoke and thrummed with the energy of the imminent wedding. Margaret roused Muiris, she laid out his suit and shirt, selected a tie, and then brought him tea in bed. He had slept only since the light had come up and put his feet out on the cold floor as if testing the earth for the first time. Could he stand? Could he walk? Margaret watched him from the bedroom door as he stood by the window.

"It's your daughter's wedding day," she said, and gnawed at her lowered lip. "You're not to disgrace yourself."

Then she was gone to feed Sean, try unsuccessfully to coax him from his bed, move back into the kitchen to meet the arrival of Nora Liathain, her near neighbour, who had smelled the sour yellow air of despair coming from the cottage all night. She was a widow and delighted in grief. It was company for her when gloom descended on someone else, and it comforted her to know the loss of her husband, the fine Liam, was not the only outrageous sadness God visited on the island. Margaret met her at the door.

"Everything all right?"

"Everything's fine, Nora."

"It is. Yes, fine." She paused, smelled the air. "Big day today. Yes. Yes. Anything you want doing? Will I go in to have a word with Issie?"

"Do you know we're so busy, Nora, we can't even stop for talking."

"Is that the way?"

"It is."

"I'll come over later so."

"Grand, Nora. Thank you."

"Oh, you're welcome. Anything now, don't hesitate."

"I won't. Thank you, Nora."

She was gone, but there would be others. Margaret knew that the wedding hung on gossamer; and although she didn't want it to happen she knew her daughter did, and for that reason she gave herself to policing the house from anyone and anything that risked destroying the day. She worked as if in a trance; as if it was a wedding by numbers and her entire volition that blue morning was given over to simply doing the next thing, going to the next number and the next on the preordained plan. It was the only way she could get through it. By the time she was in her daughter's bedroom brushing out Isabel's hair, Father Noel had arrived and was sitting in the kitchen with Muiris.

"Well, how are we all this morning?" she had heard his thin voice call as he came in. As she stood now behind Isabel with the brush she was listening hard for whatever Muiris might say and ruin everything. She made the strokes long and slow, craning slightly towards the door, expecting at any second the blow, the priest to come in and face Isabel: Is this true, you don't love each other?

It was fifteen minutes and she heard the glass put down on the pine table, the squeak of the leather shoes on the flagstone hallway, and the priest's approach down to the bedroom. He tapped on the door so softly it made it seem an extraordinary intrusion, the bachelor man into the room of the women.

"God bless."

"Father, come in," said Margaret.

"I won't," he said.

He was already in the door.

"How are we?"

"Fine," said Isabel, but it was lost in the louder "Wonderful, Father" of her mother.

"Great. Grand," he said, and stood, his feet in the doorway and his head leaning in. He kept it there a moment; he had heard of the trouble at Coman's the night before, there was talk everywhere of the wedding not taking place, rumours of every kind flying about the island; and so he leaned there in the doorway longer than he might, his gentle eyes and soft pink face awaiting the sharp smack of what was really happening. But it never came. And he was grateful. Thank God. How good life was when it went smoothly along like this, he thought. He was able to smile and wave a blessing, then squeak back down the hall and out into the safer air of the Atlantic once again.

"What did you tell him?" Margaret asked.

"I told him I thought the wind was getting up. I'm going to shave now. Is that all right with you?"

"Did you have a drink already?"

"What?"

"I know you did."

"I'll confess it to the priest next Saturday. I'm going to shave."

The Master walked away and took off the jumper he had pulled on for the priest, letting it fall on the floor at the bathroom door.

"My life, my life is picking up the bits of yours you drop off for me," his wife called after him.

He closed the door on her and held it there until he heard her go back to Isabel. It was a safe place. He ran the hot water and watched his face disappear in the steamed mirror; the dreadful mottled puffiness his skin had become to him, its wrinkled mess, the red bloodiness of his eyes, unlovely, unmarriable now, he thought, and doused the razor. Make something happen, make something happen was the prayer running around his mind as his hand traced the slackened line of his jaw and the seagulls began screaming outside. They were ahead of rain. He hated rain on Saturdays more than schooldays, and felt it for the children, as if it were a confiscated ball. Still, they'd all be at the wedding. They'd all be there to see this. He moved his finger along the clean shave line and pressed against his cheekbone to feel the hurt of his fall.

"Ow!"

He splashed up the cold water. He let his face drip back into the sink and then stood there, unable to move away. He was a coward. He was afraid to hurt his daughter. He was afraid to speak out and tell her the man was no good and risk her hating her father forever. He was afraid of what he thought he should do, and stood there staring at himself in the mirror praying for something to happen that might take the responsibility away from him.

"Are you coming out?" It was Margaret calling, sensing the possible weakness and ceaseless in her determination to keep the machinery of the wedding moving forward. "Are you coming out today?"

"In a minute."

"You've been in there a year."

"I have," he whispered, hearing her footsteps retreating and turning back to himself at the mirror. You bloody fool, he thought, you bloody fool. Caught like this on this day you thought you'd be so happy. Fecken eejit, who do you think you are. He's fine. She'll be all right. She's made a choice, trust her. You don't like him, but that was only a first impression. What do you know of him? Fellow'd be nervous, out here amongst us. Need to assert himself. Feel we were ganging up on him, judging every move. Put on your shirt. He could be fine, you'll see.

The mirror answered his shaven face through steam mist and droplets, but as Muiris turned from the sink and opened the bathroom window, he could not let out the feeling that something precious was being stolen from the very depths of him.

Down in Isabel's bedroom his wife was listening for the click of the lock and the opening of the door. When he came out she released a sigh and turned it into a cough in case her daughter might suspect how finely the wedding hung in the tense air. She brushed Isabel's hair as if she were strumming a Lethean lyre of forgetfulness; over and over the brush ran down, until at last Isabel asked her to stop. She stood in the room and her mother saw at once how remarkably beautiful she was. Tears started to Margaret's eyes, her chin trembled, and to stop it she called out:

"Are you out of there? Are you out?" She stammered and then

rushed from the room as if some inaudible command had been issued.

Morning in the cottage was overwound like a clock; the wedding was at two o'clock. It seemed impossibly far into the future, yet sprang forward in sudden jolts, time itself not a smooth curve but full of suddenness, leaps and stillness. It was ten o'clock; Muiris was coming out of the bathroom. It was midday and the bells were ringing the Angelus on the radio as Margaret found a stain on the dress. How could there be a stain? Yet there it was; the dress that had come from Galway lying now on Isabel's bed unzipped from a plastic suit bag and revealing a clear brownish mark on the right hand side below the hip. It looked like the island.

"Shit!" It was Isabel, turning to the window and the slappy sea. "Shit." If this was a sign she had expected more.

"We can save it," said Margaret, trying to disguise the certainty of the bad omen.

"Look at it."

"Don't worry, Issie. We'll get it out."

Half-past one o'clock and mother and daughter were still bent over the stain, still working with water and vinegar and bread soda and salt. At last, twenty minutes before the ceremony, they thinned the discoloration but spread through the fabric an unforgettable air of bitter vinegar that everyone who was in the church that day took for the scent of a doomed marriage. While the women were in the room the father of the bride sat with his mute son in the back bedroom. There was nothing between them but the crying of the gulls and the growing pounding of the restless sea. The bridesmaids, Sheila and Mary O'Halloran, had arrived at the house and stood in the deserted kitchen picking at the baked ham and confirmed in the belief nothing was going to happen. Then time sprang forward; it was two o'clock and Isabel came from her room trailing her mother, the dress immaculate and her brushed hair carrying slivers of light. She was ready. Nora Liathain came across to sit with Sean, feeling comfort amidst the uncleared lumps of his sadness. She pressed Isabel's hand with bent brown fingers that felt like thorns, and then stepped back to watch the procession begin.

They were to walk from the house to the church. When Muiris opened the door he felt he was letting out the world, and his step on the front flagstone was wavering and unsure. His daughter clutched his arm. Margaret walked behind them with the bridesmaids, the little party of brightness going out the door and heading down the stoney way between the walls, their clothes fluttering on the sea wind. It was a short walk and not one of them spoke. They moved in a trance, each of them gazing ahead at the stone church and wondering in their own way if something was about to happen. If there was to be a sign; if there was to be something, then surely it would be now.

The wind threw the scent of vinegar and perfume. Muiris felt the bruise in his cheek smart and his daughter's hand tight on his arm. Did she want him to do something? Did she want him to steer her past the door or through it? He could not look at her and walked with her beauty on his arm like a glorious bouquet that was shortly to vanish. When they got to the church door they heard the music and like a slap felt the hot breath of the swollen crowd. There was a whoosh and a flurry of glances, and the all but inaudible sound of the island hearts breaking as the most beautiful woman amongst them came forward to marry the stranger.

There was nothing to be done. Yet even as he led his daughter up the aisle the Master was awaiting something, some spectacular interference, the church to burst into flame or the roof to blow off. He kept his eyes straight forward on the tabernacle and beyond Father Noel's completed smile. He heard the noise of the wedding dress rustling on the floor like a low fire and the small squeaking of the new shoes on the shone floor.

Now.

Now. Anything? Something?

But there was nothing. In a moment the bouquet slipped off his arm and the wedding began.

2

On the morning after the newlyweds sailed to Galway to begin their honeymoon in Connemara, the island slept in the bittersweet dream of their most beautiful woman gone. The dreams were thick as twisted blankets and tripped even the donkeys moving on the beach. No one was awake but Nora Liathain. She had not gone to the wedding and had passed the evening visiting in and out of the Master's cottage seeing to Sean. At any minute she had expected the wedding ceremony to collapse and violence to erupt; when it hadn't she bore the disappointment like a secret blister she consoled herself would burst later.

Of course it would.

She was cleaning the inside of her kitchen window when she saw a stranger coming up from the ferry. She rubbed a circle on the glass, saw him, and felt the blister tingle. She was at the door in a flash. He was a tall young man with a high forehead and his shoulders stooped forward. As he came up to the houses the widow called out a greeting to him in Irish, then swiftly added: "Hello."

She watched him coming towards her. "Rain coming." She called the cheerless news cheerfully across the little scrub of her garden, her hands going into her housecoat pockets.

He stopped on the rough road.

"Are you looking for somebody?"

"I am. Yes, the Master . . ."

"Is it his daughter?" She shot the question before he had finished; here it was, the tingle on the blister beginning to rage already. She knew.

"What? No, em . . ."

"Is it Isabel?" she said, a narrow smile darting to her eyes. "Only she's married. Yesterday. You're too late." She paused to allow the shock to register; she waited to see his heart break there in front of her and his doleful recruitment into the ranks of the grieven alongside her. But there was no sign.

"Isabel?" he said.

"Not that she loves him. I knew that. We all knew that. Probably did it to spite you. That's the way with her, of course. Wild as that." She nodded towards the sea and the man turned to look at it. The ferry was making its way back to the mainland and was already small in the grey mid-distance.

"Which house is Gore's?"

"They're asleep. They're all asleep. I'm the only one awake. My husband's dead, why would I be sleeping?"

"I'm sorry."

"You're in love with her and she's gone. But she's not dead. That's something," said the widow, throwing him the consolation like a breadcrumb and watching his puzzled lost expression with a little comfort.

"Which house did you . . ."

"There. That's them. But she's gone, I tell you."

"Thank you." He stepped away from her to cross the narrow way to the Master's house.

"You're too late," she called after him, but he did not turn back. "Everything's always too late!" she shouted in case there was still any hope left in him as he went in the little gate and up the garden path to knock firmly three times on the front door.

3

Isabel was locked in and trying to get out. The walls of the long corridor were timber and were leaking water and Muiris was hurrying along them trying to find the door. But there was no door, only the hammering of her fists on the wood as she tried to call to him to save her. He scrambled on, his hands running along the rough timber and feeling the splinters needle into his fingertips. Still, she was calling to him. He was frantic to find her and cried out her name to let her know he was near. But where was she? Where was the door? It was dim and tilting, a grey murk was on everything. When he turned to look behind him, it was the same as the way ahead.

"Isabel? Issie? Issie?"

Still, the hammering of her hands on the wood: one, two, three.

And then everything shaking, the wood dissolving, the corridor crashing into bright light that hurt like sharp pins in the irises of his eyes as Margaret shook him awake with:

"The door. The door. There's somebody, Muiris."

He took in the world in a daze. Was it really there? For an instant he imagined it was still the morning of the wedding and not the one after. Then he moved his head and felt the kicking of hoofs against his temples.

"Muiris! Go on."

Another three knocks; he held his hand across his eyes as if shielding a blow and sat up out of the heat of his dream. Who could rise with any hope into the world this morning? Why was there such light? As Muiris moved his toes to the cold floor, he felt he needed to steady the earth or he would get up and fall down. The light was relentless and unreal, the gap in the curtains a straight rip of sheer white he turned away from. No, better not to look out. He moved out of the bedroom in his pajamas, expecting calamity. For who on the island would be awake that morning? Who would not know to avoid disturbing him?

Or perhaps. The thought that his daughter's married life had lasted only a single night flashed through his mind; it was not beyond her. He reached and opened the door expecting Isabel but found Nicholas Coughlan.

"Mr. Gore?"

"Who are you?"

"I'm here about a painting."

The Master was lost; the morning air was slapping his face from sleep but the world was still senseless and badly made. That blue sky with the grey clouds, the island herd of donkeys that had followed the stranger up from the beach and were standing now like a chorus at the garden gate, Nora's eye at the window of the cottage across the way. And the painting—what painting? He stood and said nothing and looked at the young man in front of him.

"I'm Nicholas Coughlan," he said. "My father did a painting . . ."

The widow was trying to listen with her grey eyes, so Muiris reached abruptly to the visitor's shoulder and drew him forward. "Come in. Come in." The cold was rising up his legs. "Here, sit down in here, I'll get something, I'll be back."

Nicholas sat in the kitchen that was still scattered with the remnants of the wedding preparations, ribbons, needle and thread, scissors, the cut-off stems of carnations and water-speckled cellophane, the leftover quarter of the wedding cake that had been carried home by Margaret in the tipsy moonlight and then crashed to the kitchen floor when she put it down too close to the table's edge. What had been rescued had a battered look.

"Now." Muiris was back in trousers and socks, his pajama shirt loose and lending him an air of vague dissolution. He reached for the kettle. "We're in a terrible mess here, but we can make tea anyway." He waited until the water ran, then said it for the first time in his life. "My daughter got married yesterday."

"I see. Congratulations."

The Master held the kettle in the air, paused between the continuance of his life and the surging memories of his vanished daughter. Congratulations; it flooded his ears like mockeries. He blinked his eyes briefly to escape falling down and said, "It was nothing to congratulate me for."

"Muiris!" Margaret Gore stepped into her kitchen as if she were coming to rescue her life from ruin. She walked forward in her dressing gown and took the paused kettle from her husband's fingers without a glance at the stranger. First things first; first she had to keep the world turning, to prop up her husband and usher away the winged shadows of despair she saw beating about his shoulders. He had to carry on; they had not come this far, through the unending struggle of light in the island dark, only to surrender to gloom now. She was resolved on it; his heart was broken, so what? Carry on.

"Morning to you." She nodded to Nicholas. "Muiris, will you wake up Sean for his breakfast?"

The Master went out and his wife knifed the bread. "It's yesterday's loaf, I've none made this morning yet."

"I'm fine. I don't need . . ."

"You'll have tea and something anyway."

She didn't look at him while she spoke. She swept her arms along the countertop and gathered up the debris of flowers and cellophane and threw them all in the bin. Mustn't pause, keep going. She rubbed the place down and held her lower lip in her teeth when her hand stopped at the photograph of mother and daughter on the windowsill. "You don't know Isabel?" she said.

"I'm sorry?"

"This is her." She picked up the picture and gave it to him. "My daughter."

It was nothing; it was a natural gesture, but one that she would remember later when everything had changed and she would wonder what might have happened, how the world would have spun on differently, if she had never shown him the picture.

He looked at it and gave it back, not yet aware of whatever spore or dream had blown from it and that his life was changed already. She was a beautiful woman in the picture, that was all.

"This is a visitor. This is Sean, my son." Muiris wheeled Sean in in his chair and Nicholas held out his hand. Sean didn't move and Nicholas touched his limp fingers only briefly. The wheelchair was pushed in by the table alongside him.

"I'll make the tea."

"Sit down, you," Margaret commanded him, and buttered the wedges of brown bread while the kettle started singing. The three men sat mute a moment under the force of her personality, then Nicholas told them why he had come.

"My father is dead," he began, bringing to their own grief his personal portion and telling them the horror of the Dublin afternoon as if it were a grim fable or folklore, something of the ancient days, and not part of the dull and tawdry dramas of everyday. The Gores said nothing. They sat amazed about him, ignoring the tea and the bread before them, spellbound within the story. There was something in the telling of it that struck each of them at once with the same dread familiarity: that moment William Coughlan began painting, the day the boy's mother died, or the manner of the father's death all echoed in their stilled minds the calamitous moment when Sean's illness first struck; how lives shattered with the fall of one day's light.

Nicholas told the story and the tea cooled. (Outside in her garden, gardening nothings, Nora Liathain leaned to the west, listening for an explosion. Here surely was the girl's lover; at any moment would tragedy not engulf the house? Perhaps there would be lamentations, shrieks, and tears; she knew these. These were familiar company. Perhaps she'd understand the nature of loss even more if all she came in touch with fell weeping beneath it. She waited in the salt breeze and on the low shore saw Father Noel walking his sins in a whiskeyed S to the church.)

When Nicholas reached the part of the story that was most recent, he did not hesitate but told the assembled family that he had met his father on a snowy road in Wicklow shortly after his death. He said it without exaggeration or comment, as if it were the most natural thing in the world, and perhaps for this reason it struck Muiris and Margaret as just that. His father had not told him to get the painting, Nicholas said. But when he awoke the next day it was clear to him that that was what he was to do. "There is a plan," he said, "in everything. According to my father. We only have to figure out what it is. Read the signs."

Read the signs. Margaret held up the bread plate and passed it to the visitor. Muiris kept his eyes fixed upon him. Read the signs. Even Sean seemed to be listening; to each of them it was as if Nicholas Coughlan's arrival at their door on the morning after the family had shattered was already a sign of something. He was like no one else they had ever met, and might briefly have been part of some strange shared family dreaming. Sean nodded in the wheelchair, and when Nicholas caught his eye, he grinned at him.

"My husband won the painting for a poem," said Margaret. "Didn't you?"

"Yes," and then to Nicholas, "I didn't know what the prize would be."

"He didn't even enter. I had to enter him."

Nicholas said nothing. John Flannery had told him about the competition and how the painting had been given to the schoolmaster. What he wanted to know now was whether he could buy the painting back. He sat there in the island kitchen, having filled the air with tragedy and gloom, and took another hot cup from the second pot of tea.

"We'll go see it," said Muiris, and rose. "I'll just dress myself." In an instant Margaret was after him to bring something back from the shop if he was going up to the school. She left Sean in the kitchen with Nicholas and carried an unfolded bundle of premonitions down to her bedroom.

"Do you want more tea?" Nicholas asked.

The invalid shook his head slightly, and the two of them sat there in a silence that was not heavy but hopeful, on the cusp of something that was greater than both of them. Nicholas picked up the dishes and put them in the sink, and as if it were the easiest thing in creation, Sean began to hum a reel very quietly to himself. It was as if a small bird had appeared in the room, though the doors and windows were closed. Without turning from the sink, Nicholas knew at once it was one of the birds from the burnt ruins of his father's house, and as he rubbed the dishes he heard the melody with the fondness of refinding an old friend. Read the signs.

"You shouldn't have done those." It was Muiris, buttoning his shirt and reaching for his jacket on the back of the door. "She'll kill me for letting you," he said, and paused suddenly, imagining he heard the thrumming of wings, only to turn and witness the tune Sean was humming. It was too soft for real music, too thin and fine to embroider the air, but touched the father so deeply that he had to turn away his eyes lest the tears run from them.

Although it was barely above a hush Margaret had heard it as she threw Isabel's bedsheet in the air, then crossed her arms to fold it: that joyful music. She came down the hallway of the cottage with her lips pressed together. As she stood in the kitchen door and looked at her son humming the tune, with the two men stilled on either side of him, she too saw a lone white bird flying in the kitchen air, and as sudden laughter at last broke out from a trapped place inside her, she knew that healing was beginning

4

Nicholas and the Master went out to meet the donkeys. The little herd had not moved from the front gate and Muiris waved his hands in the air and yahooed to little avail. The animals stood over to one side to let the men through and then followed along to the school in single file behind them. (Nora Liathain knew it was a bad sign. A very bad sign.) The late-morning air was blustery and quick gusts flapped their trouser legs, drying Nicholas's and making the Master uncertain in his step. He didn't speak about Sean; he dared not, but already felt the providence of the young man and leaned on him when a loose cobble in the road almost toppled him.

"Must put that right."

Still, Muiris walked shakily onward with his son's half-tune in his ear. Something was happening, a key was turning in the world and he felt it with every step, opening his eyes extra wide and yawning his mouth to be sure he was fully awake and it was not the brandy and whiskey playing God. The sea was in the air and his face was damp and freshened. His breath was taken away in quick gusts and blown like blossom over the cottages on the western road where no one was yet awake.

"There's the school, over there," he said, pointing. "It needed a bigger wall, the picture, to show it right, and the houses are small enough you know." He paused. "I thought it would be better here where the boys and girls could . . . Well, you'll see."

With the donkeys still behind them they reached the school. Muiris unlocked the door and stood back for Nicholas to go in before him. It was a small building and needed repairs; the gutter hung loose along the eastern gable, the orange paint peeled annually, as if the Atlantic were each year trying to skin the fruit and devour it altogether, and yet Muiris was swollen with pride as the stranger entered. He closed the door behind them and the room grew quiet.

"There it is."

He needn't have said it. Nicholas was already before the picture, standing amidst the small desks, the taped-up watercolours of the Junior Infants class, the laminated maps of Europe and the United States, the picture of the Sacred Heart, and the two blackboards. He was standing there, unable to move, drawing quick shallow breaths and looking up at the only evidence that his father had once been right. There it was, the picture painted that early summer down the coast of Clare when Nicholas had almost drowned and his father had pulled him from the waves. It was a picture of raging colour, a fable of greens and yellows and blues that to the schoolchildren was the raw material of the making of the world; it was Aesop and Grimm, it was Adam, it was the sea and Cuchulainn. Nicholas leaned back against one of the desks. Behind him the Master said nothing; he was remembering the poem Margaret had submitted and felt one of the sudden waves of emotion he was given to, the quality that made him seem soft to the islanders. His eyes were watery and he held his lips tightly together to stop his chin jumping with the feeling he had for her.

An age passed. The light in the schoolroom dimmed and then brightened quickly, then dimmed again, as if time were fast-forwarded, leaving only the men still, waiting there in silence before the picture. Clouds flew by.

In travelling across the country Nicholas had had a simple intention: to see the painting and then to pay the teacher for it and bring it back with him to Dublin. But now, leaning back on the desk in front of it, he lost that certainty. He didn't want to move it. It looked so right against the schoolroom wall with the long windows showing the sea either side of it. He didn't know what to do and was relieved when at last Muiris spoke.

"You can have it, of course. But I'll miss it."

"No."

"I will."

"No, I mean I don't think I should take it."

"You don't like it?"

"It's not that, it's . . ." He turned and looked at the older man. "How do you know what to do? How do you ever know?"

"You don't. I don't," said Muiris, coming forward. "You ask for prompts, I suppose, don't get any, and then just pick one thing or the other. Anything can happen. It's all chance."

There was a loud thump; the front door flew open, and with an expression of dumb curiosity a donkey's head appeared.

5

When the two men walked back to the cottage, they noticed the mainland had disappeared. The island, it seemed, had floated free in the wind and was screened about now with a moving rain-mist. It veiled them as they came up the stone path. The donkeys were no longer trailing them but had huddled on the southern side of the schoolhouse, their great heads lowered as if listening to ghost stories in the grass. Nora was in the kitchen when they got there. She was saying a prayer over Sean even as he was humming a lighthearted tune called "Donnellan's Favorite." Margaret was standing back by the kettle. She met her husband's eye as he walked in and stood there.

"It's a miracle," said Nora as she finished the prayer. "He's coming back to you." She stepped away to watch the effect of the prayer, but Sean simply hummed on, going directly into "The Widow and the Sparrow."

"He hasn't stopped since you left," said Margaret, not quite knowing how to speak in front of Nicholas and feeling a strange tingling in the small of her back standing beside him. "I think it's something you did," she said to him.

"I didn't do anything."

"He just sits usually. He never lilts. He never does anything like this."

Muiris put his hand on his son's shoulder and sat beside him. He tried to catch his eyes, but it was impossible, for they flew high along the ceiling with the notes. He gestured to Nicholas to sit down, and Margaret turned to the kettle singing.

"Father Noel should be here," said the widow, "to say a few . . ."

"Stop." It was the Master. "We don't want anything like that. We don't want everyone coming in peering over us."

"But it could be God's own . . ."

"Nothing. God's own nothing, same as He done for years. Now go home, Nora."

"But it . . ."

"Go home. Thank you. Goodbye."

His voice turned around and out the door. It was bad luck, the way he was treating her, she knew that; very bad luck. Not proper at all, and she crossed the little way to her house in the rain comforted only by the knowledge that the Lord would see her rewarded in another's punishment.

"Will you talk to him? He seems to respond to you."

"Me?" said Nicholas.

"I don't know," said Muiris. "I know nothing about anything. I'm the most ignorant man in the world to understand what anything means, but I have never seen my son like this in years and you came in here this morning and . . ." He waved a hand at the music that had already filled up the kitchen air. "So, will you talk to him?"

"What will I say?"

"I don't know that either. I don't know."

Nicholas looked from the Master to his wife and took the mug of strong tea that was put before him. He felt the weight of their expectations like leaden hands pressing on his chest and had no idea what to do. What did it mean? He had done nothing to their son. He had no gift. He was only there because of his father, because of the brief chance that had brought the painting that was his father's last handmark in the world to this house. It was for that he had come, and yet moments after seeing it he had lost all certainty that he was to bring it away with him. And now this. The tall thinness of himself shook under the burden of the moment; he was shaking beneath the table; trickles of sweat ran from his armpits with the sensation of a cold blade passing down his skin. What was he to do? He put the mug down on the pine table and turned into the music.

"Sean," he said.

And at once the notes stopped.

That night Nicholas slept next door to Sean in Isabel's emptied room at the end of the cottage. Muiris and Margaret lay awake beneath their opened window and turned to the starless sky their utter amazement at what the day had brought them. Their son was coming back; he had spoken to Nicholas and seemed to have discovered in the visitor an invisible connection back to the real world. The Master and his wife were cracked with hope; it split them open to their very heart and lay vulnerable and bare all the private dreams and aspirations of father and mother for the only son. Their night bedroom was peopled with images and an unheard music made them dance. They moved closer together in their pajamas and gazed out the window for the signs of tomorrow, wishing it would hurry, lest whatever spell or miracle had visited the cottage be gone by morning.

Nicholas too could not sleep. In the air that was still sweet and heavy with Isabel's beauty, he floated questions on the night like moths. What had happened? He had done nothing; it was true. All he had done was ask the man questions, was to look at him, and yet there it was, the transformation in Sean so clear and evident that it may as well have been another man sitting in the chair before. Still, it kept coming back to him: he had done nothing. It was a chance, a coincidence. His reason for being there at all was chance; it could have been another house, another poet winning the prize. It could mean nothing. How could he make sense of something so random? He turned in the covers and stirred up the perfume of the young girl's dreams. He thumped the pillow and let out without realising the tortured half-sleep of all the nights she had lain there blaming herself for what had happened to her brother. Her guilt swirled in the air like a fine dust; it caught in his throat and he began a coughing fit that lasted minutes. Tears streamed from his eyes and were soon flowing so steadily that he realised with shock they were whole rivers of grief. He turned his face into the pillow and wept it wet, weeping out of some deep and uncharted abyss within himself, some place that had needed no prompting but like a finger touch on a magic rock opened flowingly on the night. He hushed himself and tried to swallow the gasps in case the others heard him, not yet knowing that they had already awakened Nora Liathain in her back bedroom and that all the island air was glassy and sharp with sorrow. Men coming home from Coman's bowed and were struck by flying shards of it.

Nicholas felt the loneliness of the island immensely in the night. Perhaps because the mainland was screened off and the island seemed to sail miles into the black nothingness of the Atlantic, he felt more keenly a sense of cut-off and abandoned desolation. It was a mirror of his life: this nowhere in the sea. What had he done? Why had he come here? What lives these were out here on the rock and what part had he among them? The more he thought on it, the more it seemed a reckless and stupid will that had driven him to come there, when all he was feeling was the loss of his father. Loss, loss, loss. The word passed across his chest like a knife opening his flesh and spilling his organs. How much easier it would have been to have been wounded, to have lost a limb, to stumble through the day one-legged, flap one-armed, and show: this much of me is loss, this much hacked away by grief and despair.

But he lay in the bed, weeping and whole, and missed his father. His entire life, it seemed, was that tall man and his high forehead. His growing up and adolescence had been in terror and admiration of him. He had thought nothing for himself until he thought of his father; had no real friends because of him, had loved no one because of him; was here now because of him. It had all been so wrong, so forced and unfree; where was his own life? Where was the meaning if it was not in what the old man had done? His eyes tightened, across the boards of the ceiling he let a flash of anger: Jesus, what am I doing? Why did you burn everything up? Why didn't you think of me? Why? Why?

Nicholas called the question out loud as if it might summon his father, and Margaret Gore appeared in his doorway.

"Are you all right?" His tears had dampened the room.

"I'm sorry."

"It's no crime."

She stood there in her nightgown a moment, saying nothing, looking at him, the young man from Dublin weeping in Isabel's bed. She waited. He lay there and looked at the ceiling and said nothing. She opened her hands slightly as if trapping or releasing a small bird and said simply:

"It'll pass."

And then she had left him. The tears dried up as quickly as they had come and Nicholas fell into dreams of birds and flying islands that smelled like girls. He moved through rapturous cloudy skies where dolphins leapt and the colours kept changing through all the hues of his father's painting; he was lucent and lambent, and touched with flowers that looked like fire. He smelled the smoke, and then awoke to feel the cottage take shape around him in the girl's bedroom. There was toast burning on the top of the range.

6

Nothing in the natural world is random was the principal tenant in William Coughlan's philosophy. Witness the salmon swimming out into the vastness of the seas, the unmappable and unmarked immensity of water that was almost beyond dimension to the solitary fish; and then his return, the staggering leap up river and the glittering homewardness that brought the salmon back again. Why? because just so it was meant to be. It was the scheme of things. Once you understood the scheme of things, he said, you had no worries. What was right was right. It was undeniable, there was a place for everything; everything God made fit somewhere.

Just so, that morning, despite his own doubts and the moisture of his tears still drying off the air, Nicholas Coughlan found himself fitting into the life of the Gore family in their cottage on the island off the western coast of Ireland. Although it had no apparent logic, no clear reasoning in the scheme, when he turned in his bed and looked about him Nicholas felt less a stranger than he had done the night before. His feet, when he swung them onto the flagstone floor, found their place as if it were already familiar. He stood by the bedroom window and looked out to see the mainland had returned. The sea was brimming and full, slapping at the coastline and stirring up the gulls to a raucous hovering dancing only inches above the water. The air was full of home fires, and the three chimneys he could see from Isabel's bedroom all painted an alarmingly slanted eastward plume of smoke across the breeze.

He went into the kitchen and was welcomed to his breakfast. Sausages rolled in a sizzling pan, eggs slid and landed with a soft slap on his plate, and the Master threw him down three slices of bread as he buttered them.

"Muiris!"

"Well, he needs it. Look at him. Thin as a greyhound. Give him another sausage."

Sean sat next to him in his wheelchair. That morning he had awoken with music in him and greeted his mother for the first time in years with "Ryan's Favorite" as she came in to dress him. Now he took the egg that was fed to him and looked across at Nicholas with a grin that kept appearing, as if the same joke was going back and forth across the networks of his mind.

In a little while Muiris had risen from the table, given his wife the first look of happiness he had found within himself in years, and gone out the front door to open the school. He told Nicholas he would see him at three o'clock and stepped out onto the garden path as if it were the first page in a wonderful and surprising novel. He carried the tune his son had been humming as he went across to the school, and even when he opened the door and the children rushed in, the tune somehow slipped in with them and he heard it faintly flying about the schoolroom as he sat at his desk.

"Well," said Margaret when he was gone and the happiness he had given her was still warm as dough in her fingers. "What do you plan for today?"

It was the middle of a bright and polished morning by the time Nicholas wheeled Sean down the bumpy path and out the garden gate for a little tour of the eastern shore. It was not exactly what he had planned; it was like everything else now, falling into place. He had gotten up from the kitchen table with no real idea of what to do, looked out the window at the swollen sea, and realised he had seen nothing of the island. Then as he turned he found Sean's eyes and a slanted smile upon him.

"Yes, yes, of course, yes." It was the woman's warmth flowing over him when he asked to take Sean that was so surprising. It was as if he were a paddleboat being whooshed forward on a great wave of her good feeling and hope. He felt it buoy him up and was flushed and amazed, seeing himself briefly through her eyes as a figure of fate and pulling on his coat like a storied character cloaking to face the enemy.

"Well," he said, moving out of the mother's gaze at the door and then closing the angle through which Nora Liathain peered so intently. "You'll have to tell me where to go." Sean swung his weight a little to the left and the chair followed it. Once they found the right path, bumping along the windy way, Sean began to hum again, and a lively music accompanied them, along with a cluster of donkeys.

"You're not really sick, sure you're not? I know you're not. You hear everything I say and you could answer me if you wanted. But you just don't want to. That's what it is."

They were at the cliff edge and the sea roiled like an illness below. Nicholas talked while the wind blew off bits of his hair. He had no indication whatsoever that Sean was listening to him, but he talked on as if to an attentive audience who must hear what he had to say.

"I thought about that. After my father died. Saying nothing. Doing nothing. Just sitting there, or lying in a bed. I had a man take care of me too. Same as you. Could listen to Mozart all morning if I wanted, lying in bed. Put on enough music on the player to go all day. Imagine. Didn't have to hum it either. It was just there. Like angels, my father would have said. That was the kind of thing he said. Music there, like angels. Or Latin. Do you know Latin?"

He waited a moment, but Sean said nothing, was still and gazing out into the moody blundering of the water on the dark rock.

"I do. I learned a good bit of it. No reason really. Just like picking up stones on the strand or something. Latin. He loved the sound of it. At least I think that was it, I don't think he understood it. One time we sat in a barn out of the rain and all his paintings ruined by cattle and he told me to say the Latin. I couldn't get over it. Like it was a blessing or something. Can you picture it?"

Nicholas paused but was not expecting an answer. He was speaking to the invisible world, to the Atlantic air and the broken water below. "Latin in the rain in a barn somewhere in Clare. *Cetera per terras omnes animalia somno laxabant curas et corda oblita laborum.* Virgil. All creatures throughout the lands easing their cares with sleep, their hearts forgetful. Something like that. He liked it. I thought it was the music maybe, just sounds. I did it other times too. When I came in from work one time and he was sitting by the table with nothing on it: as if he had sat down to his tea and there was nothing there, as if he'd only just discovered how alone he was—that's the thing in my family, we're like three alone people, and we forget it for a while and then it jumps up. It's there. Well anyway, there he was when I came in, sitting there, stooped a little over the table where he took his tea. And I came in and he said—there were tears in him somewhere, he was all edgy and broken up—Say some of it for me, will you? I don't even know for sure what he meant, but that's what it was anyway, the Latin, the music of it, like angels coming out of the ceiling, he said. And I started and came to a word and he stopped me suddenly. He looked up and tears were running down his eyes, and do you know what he said? He said *Amor*. Just that. He sounded it out. *Amor*. And then said my mother's name. Bette. *Amor* Bette."

Nicholas stopped, and again the sea and the wind and the seabirds blew over them.

There was a long, windy nothingness, a rawness coming up the cliff that made the gulls hover and dare long slow arcs over the rocky promontory. The sky was moving white clouds before a shower and bringing them in like half-dried sheets about the island. High above the two men's heads on the eastern cliff, in the unseen and white airiness that was all unmappable kingdom perhaps a door blew open or a curtain drew back, for in a moment, unbidden and clear, Sean spoke for the first time.

"Help me stand up," he said.

7

In the Master's classroom the tune was still playing. The more he kept looking down over the children's heads, the more Muiris seemed to hear it. It wasn't long before he was seeing it too, thin ribboning veils of the music in blues and faded yellows moving through the air and back again like the falling cloths of passing spirits. The children seemed not to notice particularly, but were in very good form, he noted. Not even O'Shea was causing bother or flopping himself about in the desk like a landed dolphin. No, it was to do with the music in the air. At first he thought to ask them, did they hear it, but the moment passed and he let their ordinary faces look up at him in the room waiting for their work. If they heard it, it was in some inner ear, he reasoned; it was playing someplace just beyond everyday hearing, but there nonetheless. And as clearly as it was playing, it was also clear to him that it was his son.

While the scholars did their Irish Who What Where and Hows, Muiris sat at the top of the room and listened and watched. The coloured veils of the music kept passing up and down the room, pale and fine and near-transparent. At twelve o'clock he got up from his high chair to walk down the classroom and see if it made a difference. He reached the door and turned and saw with amazement that the colours he was seeing were exact and soft emanations from William Coughlan's painting on the back wall. His head spun, he put his hand down on Nuala Ni Ceailligh's desk and thought he would fall over. He blinked and looked again and saw the same thing. There was a trembling, something was moving that should not have been. Like a clock, the children had stopped in a single moment; their faces were turned to him, as if to reset the world and get it going, for what they had just seen had astonished them out of the domain of words and writing. There it was, look! They turned as one and looked back up the room even as Master Gore was wandering forward between the desks, moving to the eastern window in a dumb and wavering amazement. The children's voices were humming suddenly about him, there was noise where there should not have been, and a rising beat of excitement and confusion coming through the music that was growing louder and wilder in his brain, until he at last reached the top window and pressed his fingers and his forehead against the cold pane to feel something solid and real as he looked out and saw there, there, the stranger and his son walking across the island towards him.

8

By the time Nicholas and Sean reached the school, the children were already outside to meet them. The Master made it only as far as the door and stood feeling the wind on his wet face and watching as the children ran forward and yahooed the little herd of arriving donkeys that had come trotting up behind. The children kept looking at Sean's legs, but he kept his eyes on his father and walked steadily in the gateway of the school. When he was within fifteen feet of him he stopped, and then hurried forward as Master Gore collapsed in hard and uncontrollable spasms of released grief. He slid down to the ground and his body convulsed and the cries that escaped him rent the air and stilled the children. (The Widow Liathain stirred from her fire when she heard them and went immediately for her boots.)

It was too much; it was simply too much for him. The Master was racked with it and reached up his hand blindly and took his son's warm fingers for the first time in years.

"I'm sorry," Muiris said, and crumpled like an old newspaper, showing dark water stains on the front of his shirt.

Nicholas and Sean helped him up. The commotion outside the school had already caught the attention of several of the islanders, and as the three men headed back to Margaret in the house, there was a gathering cluster of old fishermen and widows and children about them. They looked at Nicholas as much as Sean for the evidence of the miracle and followed across the stones in a whispering throng that was flecked with the giddy cries and yelps of the freed schoolchildren. The Widow Liathain came out to meet them and sucked in her cheeks as if receiving blows. It was a minor holy carnival, this moving crowd with the three men at the front. Muiris was walking a few inches above the surface of the island, carefully placing his feet and taking each step across the air with the concentration of a tightrope walker. He mustn't fall down, he mustn't fall down and wake up now. He must make it to the house. He reached out and held on to Nicholas's arm to keep himself from floating any higher and let his swimming eyes go without blinking as the world turned watery before him.

What was this? What was happening? In the windy walk from the cliffs to the schoolhouse and then back to the cottage, the impossible questions flapped like sheets in the two men's brains. Nicholas was sure he had done nothing; he had not touched Sean nor prayed nor even been thinking particularly of him when he had stood up. It was nothing to do with him; it was idle chance. It was random and wild, and yet as he was walking in the garden gateway and feeling the crush and trample of the people behind him, he could already feel interpretation and judgment alighting like blackbirds on his shoulders.

With a joint sigh the three men arrived at the cottage door and were on the instant of knocking when Margaret Gore swung it open and threw up her arms to air her son's wheelchair blanket. It blew sharply westward out of her view and left her dumbstruck and staring at the crowd in her garden.

"Mother," said Sean as she came inside the hoop of his arms with such fierce strength his face reddened. She pulled back after a moment, took a sniffle from the air, and drew the three men inside the doorway quickly before turning and closing it sharply with her backside, even as the islanders were stepping forward to come in.

9

The crowd stayed in the garden; as if the aftermoments of miracle might still be descending on their heads like dust or fire. They bundled in hope and faith, but with little charity, each of them privately wishing their own separate redemption, their victory in the Lottery, the glut of fish or the house falling down on their enemy. The widow gave out her predictions like black missalettes. Nothing could come of this. It was something very strange, very wrong. What had the stranger done to him? She was happily dispensing gloom when Father Noel arrived looking for his housekeeper and the explanation for no morning tea.

"What is it?" he asked.

"Sean Gore walked, Father."

"The Dublin man made him walk."

"He did. He did, Father."

The priest shushed them, and waved them hopelessly back towards the gate. He was a quiet man who sought quietness, and was suddenly alarmed at what had landed in his parish. Panic prickled in his lower stomach like a bag of needles. It was the kind of thing you wished on your worst enemy this: miracles. Let the bishop have them, give them to Galway, but not here. Why were they always happening in out-of-the-way rural places? God! His shaven jaw stung in the salt wind and he rued the new blades he had bought at O'Gorman's.

"Outside," he said to the faithful. "You should get outside. You should all go home. Go home now and . . ." He wasn't sure of his words; they were caught on needles. "Go on, I'll . . . I'll find out what . . ."

The crowd moved back outside the gate, but did not go home. They were like a wave returning when Father Noel turned his back and stepped up to knock on the door. Miracles! This family, they were odd people, you could put nothing past them. He palmed the door firmly and kept his back turned from seeing his power over the congregation fade as they came forward in a surge to see. He let himself imagine he was the figure of order in all this, going in to set things right, and kept himself upright and proper at the cottage door. When it did not open he knocked again a little louder. Of course there was commotion in the house; they were excited and noisy most probably. He stood and moved his stomach to the left to relieve the sharpness of anxiety, but kept his back to the fisherman and children. He waited, the wind played with his trousers. The smoke from the fire within made the air grey as the sea, and looking upwards Father Noel thought to himself that this was one of God's little tricks. One of His little trials. Oh yes. Just wait, and knock again. Be patient.

He knocked again, trying hard to make the action seem even gentler and more mild-mannered than before. He shifted his weight, looked down at his knuckles, checked his watch, felt the eyes of the islanders on his back, and quite suddenly realised he could hardly breathe. They were crushing him from ten feet away with expectation and judgment. He raised his fist and banged on the door again. And again. Damnit. Come on, come on. Again he raised his hand and beat there on the wood, growing hot and dizzy and wild with anger and impatience as the wind off the sea blew at his back and his cheeks reddened and bled high colour around to the thickness of his neck. He felt the door locked against him and kicked out at it with his polished right shoe, getting no reply, and feeling the bag of needles explode in all directions within him as he turned away and walked falteringly through the parting crowd and out of the garden.

10

It was Margaret who had locked the door and had the three men sit mute in the kitchen while the priest banged outside. She was too dumbfounded to react, but knew instinctively this was one of the moments of her life. She could feel the enormity of a presence in the house and blinked the water that kept welling in her eyes when she looked across at Muiris holding on to Sean's hand. She put on the kettle for tea and drew the curtain. She tried not to look at Nicholas, but kept catching the strange pale face of him like a light beam as she took out the mugs. Who was he? What had brought him here? And what had he done to make Sean come alive so?

"I'm fine. I feel grand," said Sean, replying to no question but feeling swift flights of them like arrows coming over the air.

"I didn't touch him," said Nicholas, turning towards the mother his own dumb amazement, the blankness of himself. "It was nothing. I was talking and then . . . He was just fine, like you took a blanket off him or something. I didn't do anything."

"Of course you did," the Master told him. "Who else did it? There was nobody there. And he hasn't . . ."

"Stop!" Margaret turned sharply from the part of the wall she had been studying. "Stop. I don't want any talk about it. It's not right. It's bad luck. Just . . . We'll just. You're feeling all right now, Sean?"

"Yes, Mam."

"And you've no pain?"

"No."

What she was going to say, how she was going to marshal the events into a code of practice, a line of interpretation, the men never knew. For she came across the kitchen like a flowing tide and fell about the neck of her son, clasping him with gratitude and grief and letting the salt of years run free from her.

That evening, while the crowd lingered outside the locked house and novenas ascended like fireflies into the moony Atlantic nighttime, Sean played the fiddle for Nicholas and his parents. Muiris brought out whiskey for the visitors from the parlor and mother and father danced in a red-checked gaiety they hadn't known for decades. The kitchen swayed, its floor thumped in rhythm, and shortly the little house itself sailed off on the music. It was hypnotic and free; the slides and reels turning the air into spun thread and the feet stepping away on a journey that went round and round the floor and off into the place beyond thinking.

Nicholas sat across from Sean and watched him like a puzzle. It made no sense. It had been nothing, and yet inside the house it felt like a miracle. He took a sip of the whiskey and let it burn down his throat. Muiris stepped free of the dance and topped up the glass, turning back to Margaret within the beat. And so on it went, the parents dancing, Sean playing, and Nicholas drinking a hasty road into oblivion. By the time he collapsed on the table, everything in the house was dancing, chairs twirling tables and pictures jiggling on the walls. He closed his eyes and his mouth gaped at the wilder visions in his brain, then looking again he saw the table crashing upwards to meet him.

By midnight the crowd outside had moved to Coman's and only the widow next door was watching the house for wings descending. She felt a blow of disappointment when the lights were shut off and the music stopped. The island settled in a whispering and excited nighttime, and within each cottage the story of Sean Gore left husbands and wives sleepless in their beds, feeling the sudden chill knowledge that while they were thoughtlessly churning through the day perhaps God Himself had passed along the island roads.

11

For two days and nights Sean did not leave the house. The Master stayed at home and the school was closed. Then, on the Friday morning before six o'clock, the fisherman Seamus Beg took Sean and Nicholas in a small boat to Galway. It was Sean's idea; he wanted to be there to meet Isabel returning from her honeymoon. He wanted the mischief of the surprise and told Nicholas he'd have to catch her when she fainted. The Master and Margaret agreed on the plan, only because they found it impossible to say no. Events were swimming along at their own pace; there was a quickened sense of plot, an air of verb, and the mother and father felt themselves pulled along within it. What could they do? To tell their son that they didn't believe he could manage himself off the mainland when he looked like a grown man? To tell him they couldn't be sure to trust the humble and quiet visitor who seemed to have brought about the miracle? It was impossible; the parents found all arguments blocking up within them. Besides, they agreed, with Sean and Nicholas gone for a couple of days they could go about and dilute the thick reverence and superstition that was smelling like incense all over the island.

So, on the Friday morning, Margaret woke the boys in the darkness. Muiris rose in his suit, bed-wrinkled and tuft-haired, and prepared the ten-pound notes for Seamus Beg. They sat together for the last sausages in the house and took tea in gulps. Sean was giddy and drummed his knife and fork lightly. When the three men were about to leave for the boat, Margaret turned off the lights before opening the door. She dipped her fingers for the holy water that had dried up on the little sponge in the font and so blessed their heads drily in the doorway. The wind came in the house, the sea was broken and bits of it flew on the air. In the half-light beyond the garden wall something moved, and for an instant it might have been the waking camp of the vigil; it was the donkeys. Margaret pressed Sean to her and slipped into his coat pocket a letter for Isabel. She turned to Nicholas and felt her words blow away; she wanted to say, Thank you, she wanted to say, Look after him, she wanted to say, For whatever reason and however you have come into our life you are welcome and that nothing they could do or say could repay whatever it was that had been done to bring about this miracle, she wanted to say that she felt his goodness like a shawl about her and that she had not slept a single moment since it happened but had beseeched God and the stars and the sky that whatever it was, whatever fall of light or opening door, that it would not close or darken again. She blinked her eyes and the men stepped from her.

They hurried down to the pier like spies and met Seamus Beg in his woollen hat spitting for the wind. He blessed himself when they came.

"He won't sink my boat?"

"He won't." The Master offered the money. "He hasn't been saved to drown. You're safer with him than anyone else."

The fisherman scowled into the weather. "Get in so."

"You'll come back to us," Muiris told Nicholas, holding his hand before the water separated them. "I'll give you the painting."

The passengers sat in on wet benches and felt the frailty of the boat as the engine gave an oily cough and shuddered. The sky was still dark and bruised heavily with clouds, the mainland lurked in a gloom, and as the boat pulled away the Master held his arm up in a slow wave, his fingers reaching for the unknown heavens and his mind wondering what could happen next.

VI

1

Some things do not bear much telling. I think my father knew this. I think he knew how words can sometimes flatten the deepest emotions or pin them like wild butterflies stunned out of magnificent flight, flimsiest souvenirs of what moved and coloured air like silk. Better to imagine it. Imagine music playing, imagine light falling through clouds into the morning street and the scent of the island following us as we walked to find the shop. Imagine there was nothing unlovely in the world, and that we walked as proof of miracles, our feet barely touching the path and smiles playing on our faces as the thousand birds sang in the sky. Imagine goodness floated from us into the city air and cars slowed to unwind windows and breathe the thick perfume that smelled like white candles and fresh linen. Imagine one of the aches of the world had secretly mended, and music heralded the news, rising along allegro with notes like joy and laughter pealing as we opened the door.

This is how I came to see Isabel Gore for the first time.

VII

1

When Nicholas returned to the island with Sean five days later, Margaret Gore saw in a moment that the worst had happened. She did not need to make enquiries; she brought the two of them their tea in the kitchen, and as she slid the plate of buttered toast down before Nicholas she detected in the air about him the smell of crushed roses. She knew, and without further ado began planning how she would hide the news from Muiris. He was a man, she reasoned, and less likely to detect anything; but it was the poet in him she worried about, the part that was neither man nor woman but more a solidity of scented air. If he sat alone with Nicholas for any length of time, surely he would see it too: the man was in love.

At the tea table Sean was quiet and ate ferociously, wolfing the toast and nodding to the bits of news his mother told him. Father Noel wanted to see him. There had been a Mass for him. Nobody in the place had been talking about anything else since he left; and of course they blamed her for letting him away.

"Your father's useless, of course, can't speak up for himself. Unless it's to roar at somebody, and then it's the drink talking and not him."

She brought fried eggs before them. "Eat them now."

She stood back a step and watched how Nicholas pulled away a fraction from the eggs, confirming her suspicion that love was making butterflies in his stomach.

"Perhaps you'd prefer something else?"

"I'll have that." Sean tilted the other plate and slid the eggs together. "He's a bit queasy after the boat."

"Just tea, then," said Margaret, pouring him another mug and looking down at the hopeless figure of him, slouched there at the table. She knew without asking. She felt she had known all along, as if the moment he first stepped through the door she had half-read the signs, the something about him that was not ordinary, that was equally touched in some sense with tragedy and miracle. But she had only half-read them then. Now it was all clear to her: he had been smitten by Isabel. Even as he was sitting there staring at the table she knew he was thinking of her, sickening for her and breathing down all the channels of his being the bruised and rosey scent of her daughter. She longed to ask, but could not, and so stayed about the kitchen while the two men ate, running her cloth over the taps and along the sink while the sea in the distance frothed with laughter.

"So you both had a good time?"

"Brilliant."

"That's good."

"Galway's great when you can walk in it," said Sean. "Anytime I was there before was only for doctors. This time, though, it was great. Just great. Is there another egg, Mam?"

When she saw Muiris coming towards the garden, Margaret felt a lump of dread rise in her throat; he would come straight in and ask about Isabel and the truth would come out. He had finished school an hour earlier and his arrival now meant only one thing: he had stopped for the two or three drinks that burned away the tiredness of the teaching and left him in a quickened, excited state, liable for anything. She saw him coming from the window and turned to the boys.

"Don't say too much now to your father. He'll be tired."

Muiris opened the door with a swing and was inside before his wife could meet him in the hallway. "Well, are the men home?" His face in the kitchen doorway was a red moon tilting, and joviality flushed his expression to the point just before laughter. He touched his son's shoulder and squeezed it.

"Well, what did she say? Was she astonished?"

"They're tired from the boat, let them eat."

"She nearly fainted. Didn't she, Nick? Nearly passed out in the shop."

The laughter escaped through every pore of the Master; it bubbled freely out of him and he sat down to hear more.

"Nearly passed out?"

"She did. Nearly. Nearly dropped on the floor when she saw me. Ran up and kissed me. Told her about your man here and she kissed him too. Good job there was nobody in the shop."

"Good job." The father nodded, feeling with a little surprise the tears tilt out of his eyes.

"Not that there's ever anyone in there, I'd say. We didn't see one the whole time. Did we, Nick? Not a single customer."

"They ran when they saw you in there maybe," Margaret cut in, and lifted the dirty dishes above them to the sink, where she could hold her lip with her teeth and wait to see if her husband caught the scent of hopeless love. Look at him, she thought, glancing back at Nicholas while her son passed fragments of the story to his father. Look at him, look at the pale washed-out look of him as he sits there, as if all the blood and feeling of him were elsewhere. Look at the half-bowed head, the forward stoop in his neck, the way his lips seem to quiver on no words and only the roses in his nostrils hold firm the picture of her.

"Every day?"

"Every day. She said he could either take care of the shop himself or close it, she didn't give a damn which, she was coming out with us."

"Good girl."

"She can drive his van. We went out to Oughterard."

"My God."

"Didn't get back until. Some times we had, didn't we, Nick?"

"Any talk of her . . . Might she be thinking of making a visit anytime soon? Did she say?'' Muiris had let the image of his daughter swoon up before him, and with it the sweet fantasy of the family all being back together, complete, unified and isolate, beyond the press of time. The sentiment of it was like a spring river on which he whooshed along, an involuntary passenger of the feeling.

"You boys go on and let the Master have his tea. Ye can talk later. Go on. Let ye get tidied up. Had they no water for washing in Galway?"

Margaret ushered the men from the room and set the table before her husband.

"What did you ask them that for? Isn't she only gone? Isn't she only married and you're asking is she coming back? Making a right fool of yourself, that's what you're doing.'' Her voice was sharp and in pieces, as if the silence she had kept in her mouth were a plate of glass and was now spat out in shards. She brought the teapot and put it before him. "You went into Coman's, of course.''

"I did.''

"You didn't even think to come home to see them.''

"I knew you'd want your interrogation first.''

"I didn't ask them anything. What was I doing, only praying that he wouldn't be coming back in a wheelchair. What have I been doing the past five days, only that. You're the one who wanted him to go and see her. You're the one who couldn't wait.''

"Will you stop?''

"And do you know why? I know why. Because you thought it would bring her back. I know the kind of fairy-tale thing you think . . . I know . . .''

"What's the matter with you? For God's sake, Margaret, what . . .''

"Nothing.'' She caught her lower lip between her teeth again and held it this time, harder. You see, she thought, you open your mouth for a second and everything flies out. She turned away from her husband and rubbed at the greasy pan while he drank his tea and felt the effects of the whiskey slip from him. He was like a balloon losing gas behind her, and as she looked out at the blue beaten sky she regretted having been sharp. She took from the

Stanley oven the apple tart and cut him a deep triangle she dribbled with cream; not too much to stop his heart.

"Here. The apples are still a bit sour."

"Lovely. I'm sure it's delicious."

His eating softened the room between them, and after a little while he said, "Margaret, you don't mind if I bring the two of them to Coman's with me for a bit of the evening? People'd like to see Sean and we can't keep him hidden away. You could come yourself."

"No." She let the lip go an instant. "You go and enjoy yourselves. Don't be too late with them, will you?"

"Of course I won't." The Master stood up and backhanded pastry crumbs from his lips. "That was a delicious tart, Margaret Gore," he said, bringing her the empty plate, "as usual."

She did not know what time it was when she heard the men's footsteps returning on the garden gravel, but the stars were brilliant and the sea was sleeping. She read the crunch of their footsteps like Morse and knew that gaiety not gloom was bringing them home. She lay awake but turned from the door so that when her husband at last came into the bedroom carrying his shoes he judged her asleep and said nothing. When he sat on the side of the bed a waft of whiskey and smoke rose and crossed her to the window. Margaret lay absolutely still and tried to read in the final moments before Muiris fell soundly asleep if he had guessed what was wrong with Nicholas. But she could not tell. When she whispered to Muiris some minutes later, she got no response, and so slipped from the bed, standing a moment to look down at him in the starlight, a curled figure still in his trousers and vest, a hand dangling over the edge of the bed as if to pick up dreams.

Margaret moved out of the bedroom and stood in the dark hallway. The cold of the floor rose swiftly and she pressed her toes down against it, walking slowly quietly forward until she was just outside the door of the visitor's room. He could not be asleep; of this much she was certain. No matter what he had taken at the bar, alone in the room now the scent of the roses would be back in his mind. He would not be sleeping. Holding her breath to keep it from giving her away, she leaned her face forward to the door and heard nothing. Nothing. And then the small noise of writing.

She moved away and breathed. He was writing. Of course he was. She should have known; he was the kind provoked into hopeless words by strong feeling. But this time words would not dilute the feelings, Margaret knew. No, he was fuelling the fire, he was writing a love letter.

She stole back along the hallway, more certain than ever that Nicholas had fallen hopelessly in love. When she came into the bedroom her mind was already flicking through the myriad possibilities of what she could do. She laid herself delicately like fine china back into her nestled place in the blankets. But she could not sleep. She knew Nicholas was not sleeping, and now all she had to figure out was if Isabel was. As she watched the stars turning, she imagined she saw the hopelessness and grief of all romantic love, the sorry and tarnished fable of moonlight and rapture spinning down into the unremitting and grey disappointment of everyday; how the glamour flashed so briefly and the cheats of beauty and promise and courage and youth rang like mockery beaten off the shallow stars. She felt the impossible yearning and sorrow from the room down the hall. She felt it as if it were her own and was not surprised when there were tears on her cheeks and the air was thick with the bitter perfume of broken rose stems. She knew the pages Nicholas was writing as if it were her hand across the paper, and the longer the night drew on, the more clearly she knew that he was still writing, still looking out the window at the blind sea and imagining the face of Isabel. She swallowed lumps of regret like purple blossoms, but not for a moment did she let herself imagine this might lead to happiness. It could bring nothing but grief, and Margaret Gore must do everything she could to lessen it by stopping it as quickly as possible. She resolved to lie awake in the bed as long as Nicholas was continuing to write. But some moments before Cian Blake opened the first door on the island to look out on the pre-dawn sea, she slipped without help into a soft and pink dream and was lying there smiling when Nicholas finished the first letter to Isabel and went outside and down to the shore to wait for Mrs. Hurley to open up the post office.

2

Margaret had awakened with a jump. Quite literally. There had been a castle and a narrow high window and someone below. But the jump woke her and she had turned to Muiris to find that his bloated and unshaven face seemed to have swallowed whole the dazzling face of his youth; it was nowhere, but she had met it in the dream and stepped out of bed with a peculiar unease. The day was already blowing and the boats in the harbour knocked and squeaked with discontent.

It was only when she stepped out into the hallway and saw Isabel's room door open that her heart quickened. Where was he? The bathroom was empty, Sean was still sleeping. And the kitchen? No, he was gone. She hurried back to Isabel's room and went inside. Without a moment's hesitation she threw herself into a frantic search for the letter, but couldn't find it. Everything else was as it should be; he was not gone, even the pen and paper were there by the bedstand, and the faint but persistent odour of fallen apples, but the letter. What time was it? Where had he gone to?

"Muiris!"

She turned the moment the answer came like a cannon shot to her brain, and she was back in her bedroom throwing off her nightgown as the Master stirred himself. He lifted his head a fraction to see her naked by the window and lay back imagining himself in a painting by Rubens.

"Muiris, get up, we're late. Wake up, do you hear me?" She lifted a cold hot-water bottle from the floor and let it flood on him.

"Jesus!" He cried out as if struck, but kept his face in the pillow.

"Make your breakfast. I've to go out. Do you hear me?" He made no noise and Margaret scanned the room for something else to throw on him, finding his shoes and tossing them in the general direction of his back as she went out the door.

It was two minutes to half past nine. The day was blowing in her face as she slipped out the little gate and headed directly across the cobbled way for the post office. A flock of gulls were wheeling on the wind like escaped newspaper. The smoke from O'Leary's plumed sharply eastward and made it seem the sky was sitting low on the island, as if the gods had come down and were assembled in the invisible, pressing the pillow-clouds with their great thighs and gazing down at the Master's wife hurrying out to try to stop Fate itself. She wasn't sure yet what she would do; it was a letter, she knew that, and she must somehow intercept it without Nicholas knowing. It was what a mother had to do. It was right and vital; it was the only way she could hope to halt the progress of a doomed and hopeless love that could bring nothing but grief.

The wind carried Margaret to the post office, barely allowing her to breathe as it gusted in her face and brought with it the smells of salt waves and frying eggs from Coman's. The bell above the door jingled when she entered and she stepped inside to nobody. Then, from inside her kitchen the slow weighty voice of Aine Hurley called blindly out to her.

"There in a minute."

It was a minute the gods had not counted on, and it gave her time to peer in over the small counter and see there on the small table scored with scribbled additions and the myriad inkings of thumped stampings a first letter of the morning, addressed to Isabel ni Luing in Galway.

"Ye're all out early this morning." Aine Hurley appeared with flecks of toast in the corners of her mouth. She was chewing softly as she reached the counter and waited until she had finished before allowing herself any business. She was sixty-two years old and had buried two husbands, a fact she carried with her as if in testament to her own hardiness and longevity. Haste, she reckoned, had killed both of 'em, and she was obliged to make up for it by a slow and careful manner, handling each moment of her life several times before letting it go.

"Now, Margaret." She looked across at the Master's wife. "What's the news with you? We had your visitor in with us already."

"Well, that's it actually, Aine."

"I was hardly even in the kitchen, he was knocking the door."

"He had a letter . . ."

"Rushing about, do you see."

"He gave you a letter."

"No good, I told him. You can't be rushing around here."

"No."

Margaret waited while the sea sighed.

"He posted a letter all right."

"That's why I came over, Aine. It's to Isabel, and he was supposed to leave it open for me to put something in and he forgot. So if you could give it back to me. I'll just take it home and bring it back again to post this afternoon."

"Forgot something?"

"Yes."

There was a long beat, a flickering moment as if a hand were pedalling an upside bicycle of Time and the minutes spun in free-wheel. Then Aine Hurley turned and looked behind her at the letter on the table.

"That's because he's rushing, d'you see? Dublin man, of course," she said. "Two countries, Tom always said, Dublin and here. Only pretending to be the one." She flapped the envelope once and nodded, handing over the letter and not noticing the sudden lift of the sky, the all but imperceptible changing of the wind as the gods flew back to wherever and Margaret Gore strode out the door with Nicholas Coughlan's first love letter in her hand.

3

Dear Isabel,

I write these words not knowing if you will read them. I am in your room and cannot sleep. I can do nothing. I have never written a letter like this before. I don't even know if it is a letter, but it's after midnight and I can't stop thinking of you.

We returned to the island in the middle of the afternoon. I could hardly speak to your mother when she sat us down in the kitchen. Everything seems unreal now; did it really happen? Have you ever felt something so powerful and intense that in the moments afterwards it seems to be part of your skin itself, part of your smelling and tasting and breathing, and nothing else exists but those moments, those memories. Here you are with me in your room, here tonight. I write that down and close my eyes and sit and wait and you are here. Past and present at the same time. Here and not here. Here you are standing inside the shop door in the long grey cardigan when we bundled inside, a kind of brightness flooding from you, and the way your eyes filled instantly with tears as if a sharp arrow had struck you. I can hardly believe I am writing these things to you; the touch, that first touch that was nothing to you, your hand on my arm as Sean was explaining and you steadied yourself against me and turned and looked at me. That moment has changed everything for me. How absurd and foolish I feel even writing that; I feel like an elephant before a rose. Forgive me. I only have the courage to write these things not fully knowing if I will send them.

When you closed the shop that first morning and we walked down the street, the three of us, you kept laughing and looking over at me. We bumped against each other; the swaying way you have of walking, of owning the road, and that scent tangling about me. Was it then? I don't know. I know nothing about why things are or how they come to be. Everything can seem so random and muddied and outrageously planned at the same time. Do a million lives run parallel or are each two singled out to meet? Here you are in these hundred memories in my head and I am lying in your room with the sea all around me. How did this happen? I came here for my father, to find the last part of him from the wreckage of our life, the semblance of some reason as to why and how everything was. And I find myself coming in a door to meet you.

You. You.

I wonder how, in five days, the world could change so much. You are more beautiful than anyone I have ever seen. Is that wrong to tell you? I close my eyes to see you even now. And of course it's wrong. Of course it's hopeless and stupid and leads into a roundabout road of nowhere. She's just married, I tell myself. She's newly married and in love with him. So where's the sense of it? Where's the plan, the order, the rightness of coming together you're supposed to feel, the touch of inevitability my father like to call God? I came two weeks late and look what happened. Someone is laughing at me. I know I didn't cure Sean; it was nothing to do with me, and yet if I hadn't arrived for the painting, if I hadn't met him, if, if if . . .

See how the pieces fall together even when they belong to different puzzles. Isabel, Isabel. You kissed me on the third night and the pieces flew in the air. On the street with cars passing. Not even hiding. Your hand around my neck and my falling so much farther than the distance between your face and mine. I think I swooned, something flew out of me. You said nothing and drew back and then kissed me again, your hair falling across our mouths and your fingers coming to touch my face as if to make sure there was more of me there. I tasted almond on your fingertips and felt for the first time the overwhelming rush and desire to devour someone, to eat and bite and have every part of you, to lose myself and you utterly in that moment on the street and stop the clocks and hold the stars and let nothing be beyond that moment. If only life could be that, could reach a moment and stop there on the instant of ecstasy. But no. The cool air swept across my face and the kiss was over. You said nothing. You stepped back and you took my arm and we walked. Did I dream it? Did we say nothing at all but walk together around by the docks, my mind lost in the falling apart of reason and the huge high tide of desire washing red over everything? It was scent and taste and touch the world was made of, not words. Even when you left me that night to go back to him you said nothing.

What can I write to you? I write these words to feel your eyes reading them. To feel in that way at least I am touching you and we are linked in the flickering of each letter as I write it down and you gather it up. But I want more. I want to see you. I want to hold you. On Thursday when you met the two of us I thought Sean knew already. I thought it must be painted across my face, or that the thump of my heart was amplified deafeningly as you came to the guesthouse in the morning and beamed to tell us Peader was looking after the shop for the day and we were heading for Connermara. Do you know I could not breathe when you sat at the breakfast table alongside me and touched my hand? Did you know then? There is such life, such wild gaiety in you that even sitting beside you was like sitting within some fabulous carnival of feelings, a spinning carousel that carried me flying forward in sheer terror and delight as I felt your fingers under the tablecloth travel up my arm.

That day. The day on the road to Oughterard. Was that the moment I knew?

The truth is, I don't know. I don't know what you feel. I feel I can hardly breathe. Have I written that already? I don't even know what I am to say; I love you. I have fallen in love with you. I cannot wait not knowing if and when I will see you. Will you write to me, please?

Please?

Nicholas

4

Even as the words were printing themselves forever across the yellowed pages of her mind, Margaret Gore fed the letter into the fire. She scolded herself silently for the tears that kept coming to her eyes and chewed on her lower lip until it was raw as meat. It was the innocence and purity of the passion that had struck her like a spear, and even when she got up and heated the iron and thumped the Master's shirts, it was still hanging at an alarming angle out of her chest. Nicholas had not returned, and she knew without enquiring that he was off alone, brooding amongst the rocks and sighing away the time until the return post tomorrow. Now it was not enough to simply ask Muiris to send him away. The passion was already too far gone; he would simply go to Galway, wait for her, and then; Peader was a violent man, it didn't bear thinking of, and as Margaret pressed the iron on the buttons she knew now that they must keep him there until the love had subsided or been broken.

This was not the way the world should be. This was not the world she had begun with, not the one she had carried in her basket going past the fishing boats in Donegal on the first days after meeting the poet Muiris Gore. This was not the place of happiness hereafter; and even as she knew the grief she was causing in burning the letter, Margaret imagined she knew more intimately the grief she was saving. And this was the world she had found out she lived in: the world served better by the burning of the love than the living of it. She knew this was true, and yet still the spear swung madly out of her, and all day and afternoon she was on the point of wild and hysterical weeping. When Muiris came home from the school she stood in the kitchen, frozen, and waited to see if he noticed anything unusual about her. When he said nothing, she pointed at the line of empty bottles near the sink.

"What are these?" she asked him.

"What do you mean?"

"What are they?"

"They're bottles."

"And where do they go? Where do we put them? We put them outside in the bag, we don't put them here by the sink, do we? But why am I always the one to be carrying out your bottles that you leave here by the sink expecting God only knows why that I've nothing better to do but to come along after you and carry out to the bin that's only ten feet away and still too far for you to bother. Answer me that. Why?"

It was a question too difficult for the Master and he looked away out the window at nothing.

"Maybe you could take your shirts into the room yourself," said Margaret, and walked past him out of the kitchen, the spear in her chest smashing against the doorjamb as she passed and Muiris's face lost in the hopelessness of understanding her and the half-dozen shirts with their wrinkles pressed into them and arms ironed across the chest as if shielding outrageous blows.

That evening when Nicholas returned for his supper they could each feel the melancholy of the sea seeping off him. His hair was matted and his shoulders huddled with a heavy dampness. The stillness within which he had spent the day was as obvious as the weather, and as he sat at the table even the movement of a hand reaching for the salt seemed an intrusion on his gloom. His mood was like a thick cloak of rain, and from the paleness of his face Margaret could tell at once that illness was imminent. Since the night before he seemed to have lost some of his hair. His forehead gleamed under the bulb, he was whiter than paper, and while Margaret was turned away from him cleaning the knife after the butter she realised he had sent all his colour to Isabel. She could hardly look at him and was glad when he got up from the table, thanked her for the food, and said he needed to lie down.

Sean and Muiris disappeared to the pub, but not before the Master had made a grand opera of washing the dishes and drying them too, of folding the dishcloth and wiping the table and demonstrating for Sean the importance of sweeping out under the table and not only around it. He finished and parked the brush and looked around the kitchen, but not at Margaret sitting in the chair with her magazine by the range. He left the cleaned room as his token of love and took his jacket with a flourish, as if something had been proven.

Margaret looked up only when he had gone out. She saw the sparkle in the room around her and sighed loudly, knowing that another battle was over. She moved herself in the chair but got no relief from the spear in her chest, and then went and opened the door to hear and interpret the noises from Nicholas's room. He was collapsed on the bed was her first conclusion. He was lying in that terrible silence of memories, hearing only the constant inner voices repeating over and over the scraps he could remember of what Isabel had said. He was listening to his memory talking, and trying to use the exact inflection of her voice. He was lying in the stale air of the room and trying to breathe through nostrils of recollection the scent of roses that came out of her hair. He was lying there with his mouth open and his lips touching each other and then opening on the air, trying with hopeless and bitter desperation to find that taste of her his lips could not remember. He stroked his chest with his hand and felt the heat of himself, trying to make the fingers of his hand her hand, trying to be her there with him. In the silence at the other end of the house Margaret knew what was happening, knew that he was searching in the room for the tenth time for the scent of her, that he was lying down on the floor and pressing his face against the mat where he imagined her stepping out of bed morning after morning, that he was looking out her window and lying on her bed and smelling the tight mothballed air of her wardrobe for traces of her, not yet knowing that the effort of bringing Isabel to his mind, that the urgency of his dreaming, was making him ill.

There was a knock at the door. A snake of fear leapt up Margaret Gore's throat, and it was a moment before she could swallow it again and go out into the hallway. She opened the door on the night and felt the sudden damp forescent of autumn brush past her. Father Noel allowed it to pass and then asked her if he could come in. Margaret closed the door behind him with Judgement and the sin of destroying the love letter made her face burn scarlet all down the left side. When the priest had sat down in the kitchen, Margaret angled herself so that he spoke only to her right profile.

He had come, said Father Noel, to see how they were managing.

"Grand, Father," said Margaret, hoping that the lie did not burn out on her other cheek.

"And the visitor?"

"Yes."

"Is he staying on?"

"For the time being, Father."

"I see," said the priest, seeing nothing and detecting less. Certainly not the sudden murmuring that had begun in the far bedroom that Margaret heard and knew at once was her daughter's name, sounding over and over into the feather pillow.

"He's happy so?"

"He is, Father."

"We never spoke rightly about that . . ."

"You'll have a glass . . ."

"What? No no, I won't, thanks, Margaret."

She was standing behind her profile, leaning one hand on the back of the chair and wondering if she was going to start coughing to smother the calling and groans from the bedroom. The kitchen door was open a crack.

"I thought maybe . . ."

"It's best to forget about it, Father."

"Exactly. I mean as long as we both . . ." He lost his words even as he approached the very thing he had come to say. "He's not making any claims, and it's not like he's going to be going around laying hands and em . . . well." He let a pause finish for him and looked up at the ceiling.

"No, Father."

"No," he said with some finality, and tapped his fingers twice on the table. He stood up at a moment when it seemed to Margaret the calling of Isabel had grown to its loudest.

"How is, how are the newlyweds getting on?"

"Oh," said Margaret, exploding in a series of sharp staccato coughs as she ushered the priest to the front door. Only when he was outside under the windy stars did she finish, "Fine, Father. Thank you."

"Right so," he said, and stepped off into the blind darkness.

For hours that evening Nicholas filled the house with the restlessness of his lovelorn spirit. He paced, turned about, lay on the bed, and stood absolutely still, hoping in some way to relieve the pressure on his heart. For minutes at a time he succeeded in chiding himself out of the rapture, touching briefly on the reality that he had seen the girl for only five days, that she was married, that nothing could come of it: he sucked on the air of this easier pain and then fell back into the longing, memories, and acute desire that were the familiars of his condition. By twelve o'clock Margaret could still hear him moving about, and as she went past his room to lie sleepless on her bed, she thought for one rash moment that she glimpsed through the crack of his door white birds flying about in the feathery air.

5

The following morning Nicholas was sick. He did not come in for breakfast and the Master went to his room to see what was wrong with him. While he went Margaret spooned two boiled eggs from the pan onto Sean's plate and held her breath to see if Muiris would find out the truth.

"He's staying in bed," he said when he came back. "Must have caught a bit of a cold yesterday out about the island."

"That's it," said his wife, relieved.

"Stomach must be at him. He turned over and let out a groan when I mentioned an egg."

It was a telltale sign, and Margaret was surprised and even a little disappointed the Master did not know it. While she drank her own tea and looked across at him, she wondered at how far he had fallen from knowing the nature of love and recognising the fluttering heartbeats that could be heard now in all corners of the house. Was he deaf as well as blind to it? Could he not smell the perfume of his daughter, the sweet air of bruised roses that had drifted through every room during the night, brought there by the intensity of the lover's dreaming? How could he not know? She sipped at her tea and watched him more carefully than she had in weeks. But nothing, no sign of his having the faintest idea of the calamity that was happening not twenty feet away. This piece of wood I'm married to, she thought, this hopeless man in a bottle.

Her son, she imagined, was nearer to it. Sean must know, he must have seen it happening in Galway. He would be Isabel's accomplice, she reasoned, and handed him another two slices of toast.

Nicholas did not get up that day. Nor the next. He waited for the post and told Margaret he was expecting a letter. Would the postman know to bring it to him here? Perhaps there was a letter waiting down at the post office? Had anything come today?

It had not, and Margaret watched the news register in tiny lines around his eyes as Nicholas fell back on the bed and waited once more. His illness worsened. Dr. Doherty, a new doctor for the island, arrived by boat on the Tuesday and included Nicholas on his rounds.

"It's a fever," he told Margaret outside the room.

"It's lovesickness," she said, amazed at another man not noticing the heavy suffocating fumes of roses in the room, the scent of which thickened when the window was open.

"His hair is falling out," Margaret said to confirm her statement. The doctor looked at her and let his baldness reply. "I'll be back next Tuesday," he said, "unless it worsens."

And it did. Three days later Nicholas was still in bed. No letter had come and he had fallen through the floor of longing into the place where love seemed impossible and the image of the beloved more real than the physical world. She was there with him. He alone saw her, and in his fevered and delirious imagining she lay beside him and he tasted and touched her, swept himself about her, and clung there against her whenever no one was in the room. He fell in and out of this reverie, its happiest and most willing victim, whispering to Isabel to come back even as Margaret carried his untouched soup bowl back out to the kitchen.

After five days, in a moment of clarity, when the wind blew in a great gulping breaths from the east and showered the island with the germs of a dry cough that had overtaken most of Galway, Nicholas wrote Isabel a second letter. He was not well enough to take it to the post office himself and so instead trusted it to Sean.

But Sean, in the week since returning from the mainland, had grown lazy in the use of his legs and was happy when his mother offered to make the journey to the post office for him. He gave her the letter, and that evening when she had ushered the father and son out of the door to Coman's, Margaret sat in the kitchen by the opened door of the range to see how the love was progressing.

6

Dear Isabel,

No letter has come from you. I cannot wait any longer and must write again tonight. It's a kind of madness, I know, this continual haunting in my blood. It runs along my arteries, I feel it in every part of me, a longing to be in touch with you, to be writing down words that you will read. Even when I stop my hand briefly on the page it is to feel your breath paused there above the paper, resting with me there. There. In the place where for an instant there is a shared peace. I think your mother imagines I am losing my mind. I notice the way she looks at me, as if expecting at any moment I am going to stand on the table and start screaming. She is still thinking of Sean, I think, and what happened, and looking for proof or something hidden that might reveal another truth.

Nothing in my life has prepared me for this. To love you. It is hardly even what I think of as loving. I have to see you. I feel a compulsion like fire inside my skin. Do you understand? Do you know what this is like? Even as I write I hear voices telling me: She has forgotten you already. Already you are nothing but a fleck of dust blown into her past. You were that day on the road to Oughterard, but now, nothing, you've vanished.

I don't believe it. This is no such thing as chance. Everything fits somewhere. It has to. If you knew the story of my father; if you knew, you'd know everything has a reason. There was a reason why. There had to be, and a reason why you came that day in the car on the road to Oughterard. You drove like a snake down the middle of the road, thirty miles before you told us you couldn't really drive. And then letting Sean try and looking back at me, and smiling.

I am going mad. I am. I am still there. I am still in the stopped car on the side of that road, and Sean has gone out across the boggy fields and you are laughing and then you are kissing me. And your kiss is like this sweet fire. Like this unreachable sweet sweet ache deep inside me. How trite and stupid it all sounds. God, I cannot write it. I cannot even get near it. O Isabel, Isabel, is a bel. Please. I want. I want . . .

Please please please write to me write to me please

N.

7

The letter was fed to the fire and Nicholas's illness raged on. He was lost in the abyss between worlds and could neither go about in this one nor fully return to the one he had left behind. He waited in a burning agony for the letter that would not come. He supposed a dozen excuses every hour as to why it did not and lay in the bed and tossed the covers through the afternoon, torturing himself with the sweet thorns of memories. His mind was vivid with Isabels and when he was alone in the room he could all but summon any number of them into the room; here was Isabel with her fabulous hair falling to one side as she bent to kiss him; here was Isabel telling him he was different from anyone she had ever met; here she was holding his hand up and kissing his fingers and laughing at the disbelief marching across his face; here was the woman holding his head to her breasts in the questhouse room on the night before they returned to the island, her hand moving on his hair, and when he lifted his face pressing her finger to his lips not to speak when she told him she did not deserve real love. All these moments floated through Nicholas's mind sweeter than fantasies; but they were shipwrecked now amidst the sickening seas of rejection. She had not written, and now his stomach churned and his face blanched. He tried hard to swallow the grey lumps of hopelessness but vomited every meal. His trips through the house to the bathroom began to punctuate every day; the degree of each day's passion measured by the time between eating and expulsion. If the vision of the girl was strong enough he could hold the food for two hours; but if the voices of reason, the words of sense were ringing in his ear telling him no love could be so, that the woman didn't care for him, and that besides, nothing could come of it, then the meal lasted barely five minutes. With each bout of vomiting came a strange aftercalm and Nicholas would return to his bed with a beatific smile, as if the rioting of his innards were a valid testament, a bouquet he offered into the silence.

Although the entire village on the island had begun to suspect something awry and the unmistakeable scent of broken rose stems was easily detected in the vomit, Margaret Gore tried desperately to disguise it and burned holy candles made of beeswax in the bathroom all day. She told her husband it was the kind of fever she had seen once before, and that it would surely clear up in another week. When Muiris suggested maybe Nicholas should be moved to the Regional Hospital in Galway, she looked at him as if he had seven eyes and she could not figure out on which to focus. No, no, not at all. He would be fine, she told him, and opened her mouth wide in the hope of freeing the balloon of guilt caught in her midriff.

In the aftermath of his cure, Sean was a village curiosity, but soon grew weary of answering how he had felt, and spent the days lying about the house or taking long walks to the far side of the island. Although he did not yet know it, he was on the point of deciding to leave the island and go to England, following a destiny that was as unclear and haphazard as the patterns of flies and that would soon have to face the extra difficulty of a half-heard half-dreamt vocation to the priesthood. For now, vaguely aware of the precipice ahead, he wore a thick coat of brooding even in the blue air glistening with high gulls. He had, for the time being, abandoned music, and when he sat in with Nicholas in the sickroom he was neither company nor solace.

So the days ran on like a ragged wool, neither loosening nor gathering. They became nothing; they were waiting days between the hitch and stitch of the plot. Nicholas remained abstracted and ill, and Margaret covered for him as best she could. When the high sound of soprano singing emanated from the bedroom and flowed throughout the house, she turned up the radio full volume and drowned out the love madness with the one o'clock news. When Nicholas called Isabel in the night and risked waking the house, it was she who slipped from her room and opened the door to quiet him as he stood naked and holding a huge erection in the half-moon, his eyes closed and his mouth kissing and biting the nipples of the soft Isabels of the air.

There was nothing could be done but to wait it out. Margaret Gore knew what love was. She knew the enemy of love was time, that the world wrinkles dreams quicker than skin, and that when nothing happens, when no letter comes and no touch happens, the passion collapses. There was a time, she knew, when the absence of kisses was stronger potion than kisses themselves. But just so, after that was a time too when absence of kisses was a grim and hollow feeling that drew out until it filled every inch of the soul's million miles. An emptiness you were full of. She waited each day and watched for it to begin filling in Nicholas Coughlan. When she sat him in the armchair in the kitchen and changed the bed-sheets, she thought she could detect in their scent the first faint aroma of juniper berries that was always the smell of loss after the death of a loved one. (In her cottage across the way the Widow Liathain almost fell from her chair when she smelled it too. She moved to the window and put the old prune of her face into the air. When she knew the scent came from the Master's house, she began at once spreading the news of his imminent demise and preparing for his funeral.)

Four days after the second letter Nicholas wrote a third. He wrote it without hiding in the middle of the afternoon. He had run out of paper and asked Margaret for a page and an envelope.

"I want to write to Isabel," he said.

She was taken aback momentarily and did not dare to meet his eyes.

"That would be nice," she said to the curtain, finding that the hem of it suddenly needed studying and waiting there until she was sure her face showed nothing once again. "I'll bring you a piece of paper." She paused and chanced to look at him: this hopeless long pale figure with his high forehead and his intense eyes, his lips bruised from biting and the rubbing of the back of his hand backwards and forwards across them. "I'm sending a letter myself. I'll post the two of them," she told him, stepping out of the room stunned at how easily the plot had conspired with her. It was a kind of blessing really. It was an encouragement, a proof that she had not been wrong in what she had done and was going to do. How many more letters after all could he write and not get a reply? Surely he was nearly burned out?

She brought him the paper and sat in the kitchen listening for the telltale signs of the writing of a love letter, the sighs and groans, the frustrations, the accompaniment of violins you could just make out beyond the screaming of the gulls outside. But this time there was nothing. He was quiet. The room was stilled and only the clock was loud, punishing the arrival of four o'clock with a particularly fierce striking.

Perhaps he had fallen asleep? Perhaps the moment had come when the passion had at last slipped from him like a too warm blanket and he was free? Margaret rose in the kitchen and walked down the flagstone floor until she was outside the room. She had become accustomed to the whole range of excesses that Nicholas was now prone to and expected anything: he might have been crawling on the floor and sniffing for the ancient clippings of Isabel's toenails and it would not have surprised Margaret. He might have been naked on the bed with the sheet of the letter pressed against his sex and the fumes of the roses maddening in ecstasy his delirious brain. It might have been anything and not shocked her. But still, when her brown eye reached the crack of the door and she leaned forward and peered into the room, the vision she saw there stopped her heart.

Nicholas was sitting on the edge of the bed and wearing a kind of whiteness that shone so that Margaret could not be sure if it was his clothing or his skin. He looked like a light and not a person, so intensely was he burning with the electricity of desire. The air of the room was the quality of white satin; it seemed to have fabricated itself and hung in huge loose drapes from the ceiling, billowing slightly all the time as the hundred doves passed by it, their wings thrumming softly and moving the air as if with the finest of lace fans. Nicholas shone, but next to him was the figure of a taller version of himself. At first Margaret thought it was done with mirrors; it was a trick of reflection, or a doubling of vision due to the dessert spoon measure of cough medicine Muiris had had her take that morning. She tried her other eye to the door, but the picture remained the same: there they were, two men bathed in a fabulous whiteness, one sitting in the chair, the other on the bed, and neither of them saying anything to each other. They were simply gazing. When she pressed her face closer and tried to focus against all the shining and light, Margaret could see the second man was older and he was smiling.

But saying nothing. When at last he rose and moved towards Nicholas the whiteness of the room grew even brighter. Margaret felt heat rushing up at her from the floor; it was as if the light were fluid and filling upwards within her. When it reached her head she felt her feet rising off the floor, then she saw the white birds flying out of her mouth, and then she fainted.

8

She had a touch of what Nicholas had. That's what the Master decided, and consigned his wife to bed, where she lay like a woman who had seen a vision. She didn't dare enquire if her husband had noticed anything about Nicholas and so lay in bed for the rest of the day in mortal terror of what might be in Isabel's bedroom. She gave free rein to her imagination, and over the course of the hours she lay there it took her through a full compendium of spirits and ghosts, angels and devils. But when Nicholas finally appeared at eight o'clock, knocking on her door and coming in to see if she was well, Margaret noticed no change in him, except for the alarming disappearance of his hair. He was greatly improved, he told her. He felt lighter, and his eyes were steady and clear for the first time since returning from Galway. He was weak, of course, but in a couple of days, he said, he was sure he'd be all right.

"I did write the letter," he said.

"The letter?"

"To Isabel."

"Oh yes."

"Will I ask Sean to post it for me now, as you're sick? You could give me yours and I'll put them together for him."

Oh no. No no no. Margaret raised herself against the pillow and made a show of strength. She'd be fine tomorrow, she assured him. It had been an overdose of cough medicine, that was all. She was sorry she had alarmed him just outside his room. No no, she'd take the letter all right. She'd post the two of them to Isabel tomorrow.

And so Nicholas Coughlan handed over the third letter of love for Isabel; and for the third time Margaret Gore fed it to the fire when her son and her husband were out in the night.

But this time was different. It took a greater effort. When she lay in her bed and held the letter in its envelope, there swept over her a sudden chill. She felt the goosebumps about her calves and chafed her ankles together as another round of debate opened in her mind: Her daughter was capable of anything; she had married a fool who was entirely unsuitable for her and now had this man burning like a Roman candle and losing all his hair for her. She had married the wrong man, but she had married him, and that was that. There was no going back, the world was not reversible, and although Margaret imagined the certain dullness and disappointment of the life ahead for Isabel with Peader, she was right to believe there was no other option. Of course she was. These letters were nothing but disaster. What could come of them?

She flapped the envelope softly against her lower lip, waiting for the argument to come out strongly in her favour. When it did and she was happy she was doing the right thing, she took it in her dressing gown and went down the hallway into the kitchen, pausing only for a moment when she thought she heard the sound of writing coming from Isabel's room.

She opened the door of the range so the turf glowed orange against the bars of the grate and then, as a clatter of heavy rain spilled loudly onto the corrugated roof of the back kitchen, she opened the envelope. At first she thought she was mistaken; it was a blank page. But no, there in the lower half of the white sheet was the full message of the third letter, one word:

Love

And nothing else. Not I love you, not her name, and not his. Neither the slightest blemish nor spot of ink anywhere on the page. At first Margaret thought there must be something traced, some secret message held up to the light or the mirror, something beyond this. But if there was, she could not find it. Just the one word. Just *Love*, and nothing else. She sat and held the page in her lap, laid her head back against the rest, and felt the surprise of tears running into her ears. It was too pathetic, sending this to her, a page with one word. The hopeless yearning was flowing off the page and filling her mouth with the taste of lemon juice; it made everything smart, as if the world was suddenly stung in every wound and no balm came. This single word on the page, this despairing and inaudible cry that was both a question and a statement, an expression of fact and of aspiration, of present and future melted together in the one note, the four letters of Love. It was too much for her: What was he thinking? Had he fallen beyond language now, abandoned himself to the grim silence, the vast wordlessness that eats all love and leaves only the empty hungering sound echoing off the stars? Margaret held the page away from her and looked at the fire. God, she thought, what am I supposed to do?

And not expecting an answer, she blinked away the tears, lifted the page with the word Love, and fed it into the fire.

9

Everything, said Muiris, would soon be right as rain. It was two days afterwards and Margaret Gore was back on her feet. Nicholas had emerged from his fever and walked out on the island for the first time. Sean went with him, and Margaret watched them from inside the net curtain on the front window as they ambled toward the foreshore and met the herd of donkeys coming to greet them.

"He seems well," said Muiris. It was Saturday and he was sitting in the armchair he preferred over most other pleasures in the world. "He's over the lovesickness anyway," he said.

"What?"

"Tell me you didn't know."

"Didn't know what?"

"What I'm talking about. Of course you know."

"I don't."

"Then you're not my wife. My wife knows."

"And how do you know?"

"You have to ask that? Isn't it plain enough? Couldn't you tell the moment he got off the boat coming back from her?" He paused and let register the comfort of the chair: how does one chair become so comfortable? "Of course you could."

"Why didn't you say anything?"

"Say what? There was nothing for us to do. It was in the hands of the gods. Things like that you can't, you have to let them be what they are."

"You're a fool, do you know that?" Her voice broke in small

glassy pieces, and when she turned her eyes on him Muiris could see the pain he had put there. "Gods! Is that what you think? Is that what you really think?" She fired the question and left the room before he had even begun picking the shards of it from his face. Well, he thought, she is even more hurt than I imagined she would be. And then, settling himself farther into the chair, he let his eyes dream and wondered how many years ago it had been and just who it was his wife had secretly loved and not left him for.

10

Love does not pass; it simply changes shape. It takes a different form when it meets an obstacle that will not move. The obstacle Nicholas met was the silence from Isabel, the absence of any reply and not the slightest sign that she was for one moment thinking of him, never mind returning his feelings. It was not a rock, it was a mountain in the middle of the road; it was the overwhelming and audible prompting that he should at once forget all possibility of seeing her and leave the island to return across the country in the hope that distance would dupe memory and desire die with time. The nothing he woke to each morning, the no-news, the constant and firm rejection that was awaiting him when he opened his eyes in her bedroom and knew instinctively there was no letter from her would have been the vanquishing of another emotion. But not this love.

It was too foolish to give up.

Three weeks after he had returned to the island and one week after the third letter, Nicholas Coughlan began writing about his father. He began it as an explanation, and under his father's prompting. He sat at a small table he had carried into the bedroom, and when he raised his hand and ran it across his head, he felt the gleaming pate of old William. At first Margaret supposed he was at another letter, but when a week went by and her vigilance in watching any movement towards the post office was not repaid, she began to realise this was something else. She dared not go to the door and peep in for fear of seeing an outlandish vision, and instead steadied herself with the thought that the love was dying. She had not spoken to Muiris about the lovesickness again because she feared he might be gifted with omniscience in her company and that he would know at once about the burning of the letters. Instead, she waited out a new course of action, and put aside her fears that the spots appearing on the back of her hands were the rising to the surface of her sins.

A clutch of warm days came together and the island was suddenly infested with swarms of flies. They rose out of the rocks and moved like a dirty gauze in the tepid air. The fishing boats in the harbor were alive with them, and the islanders took to walking about with caps or headscarves in hand, batting at the insects and praying for the wind to clear them. But the sea stilled and the sun beat down, so the flies embroidered themselves against the blue backdrop and flew in endless random patterns in and out of the doors and windows of every cottage. Except the Master's.

It was Margaret of course who noticed it. She heard the talk of the flies in the shop and the post office, she saw them everywhere and flicked a child's school copybook she brought with her as a fan. But when she entered the garden gate and stepped in home the flies did not follow. She alone did not have to keep her windows closed, but did so in the hope that no one else would notice the purity of love causing the absence of the flies. Perhaps, she tried to tell herself, it was the scent of dying love that kept them off. Perhaps it was the clicking noise of the keys in the old typewriter that Muiris had got for Nicholas, and that now clicked all day in the back bedroom though the sun shone brightly outside. It might have been many things, but secretly she knew.

The evening she first noticed the absence of the plague of flies Margaret at last counselled Muiris that it was time for Nicholas to leave. She was no longer afraid that by releasing him from the island he would go directly to Isabel. It was fading away, she had decided. His lovesickness was passing off, as all men's passion does, and she comforted herself with that grim reality as if confirming stones in her shoes. It was unlucky to keep him any longer. Give him the painting and let him go back to Dublin, she told her husband in urgent whispers as he sat on their bed peeling off his sweated socks.

"Why this, so suddenly?" he asked her. "Can't he stay as long as he wants?"

"He should be going. What can he do here? There's nothing for him here. Tell him in the morning." There was a quality of lead pellets in her voice. The Master felt them in the back of his neck and closed his eyes.

"Do you hear me, Muiris?"

He lay himself down on top of the bedclothes without replying and brought his hands together on his chest as if praying. When the whisper came again he was deciding if this was ground for taking a stand on, or more of the treacherous and giving bogland of marriage.

"Muiris?"

He faked sleep, even when her hand rocked his shoulder, retreating instead into the separate and private peace of the bed. And there they lay in the humid flyless darkness, each pretending to sleep while the constant and faintly muffled noise of the typewriter keys clicked away into the island night.

In the morning Muiris was off to the schoolhouse before his wife could confront him. He raced away in his rolling gait and breathlessly batted the million flies that met him on the path way. Behind him he left the strangeness of his life and blew sighs of relief that he could escape into the school and a world where everything made sense.

Margaret decided to leave it to her husband to tell Nicholas. It could be done that evening; and with the sweet scent of this resolve filling her like a roomful of tulips, she dedicated the day to being as pleasant as possible to the visitor. She brought him in a tray of tea and buttered scones midway through the morning. And even when he paused only for a moment to acknowledge her she did not let the slight poison her mood; neither did she let the sight of the scattered pages everywhere around the table worry her unduly. After all, he would soon be gone, and she had done her job well. It was only later in the afternoon, after she had brought him roast chicken and potatoes and the last of their own carrots and parsnips, when she paused in her magazine and felt like a palm pressed on her shoulder the sudden stillness in the house as the typing stopped, only then, that she felt the alarm ring. She listened the length she had grown accustomed to for the change of paper, but the time stretched on without any typing. He had stopped; everything had paused; it was as if the island itself had slipped through the crack of Time and no fly buzzed and no wave fell on the shore as Margaret sat at one end of the cottage holding her breath with a sudden premonition while Nicholas Coughlan gathered up the many pages for the final letter to Isabel.

When he appeared in the kitchen doorway Margaret's heart nearly stopped. He had the sheaf of the pages in his hand and she could tell from the clear rose prints on his cheeks that he was still thinking of Isabel. This was worse than before; this was not madness and infatuation, this was not dreams and fantasies, the tossed bed of desire and the sleepless yearning for touch. This was more confirmed and resolute, and Margaret had to swallow hard to overcome the knowledge that Nicholas now had the look of a saint. He was going to the post office, he told her. Had she anything she wanted to include?

"I'll do it for you," she heard herself say.

"No, I want the air."

"But there's flies . . ."

"Really?"

She went to get up but found a tall white man sitting on her lap. He smelled so sweetly of eucalyptus that at first she forgot the world and took the heavenly scent of him like a rapture. He sat across her with his long legs out in front, and although he held her there from moving, he weighed nothing at all. Margaret tried to release her hands from the armrests but was unable to, she just squirmed a little in place. She opened her mouth to tell Nicholas not to send anything to Isabel, to tell him she knew of his passion and that it could bring nothing but ruin and grief, but when her lips were open a dozen white birds flew inside her and no words came out. She could neither rise nor speak, and simply sat there in her kitchen looking up at the tall and balding figure with the light beaming from him.

Only when Nicholas had closed the door after him and headed down the path was the older man gone too and Margaret suddenly free to get up and look out after them. She moved the curtain at the front window and saw with further conviction that the natural and supernatural conspired, for the island air was free of flies.

11

Nicholas carried his bundle of pages down to the post office. He bought an envelope from the lower counter and then moved along to wait for Aine Hurley to take her time and come up and join him at the post office one.

"That'll cost a lot," she said, taking the package and reading the address without further comment. She weighed the largest of the love letters and told Nicholas Coughlan four pounds would bring it to Galway.

"When will it get there?" he asked her.

She took this as some judgment on herself, some slight on her performance, and pursed her lips before answering: "Tuesday," and then adding with only the lightest of her entire armoury of ironies, "God willing."

"But it's Friday," Nicholas told her.

"Is it? Thank you," said Mrs. Hurley, feeling the small bristles of her moustache standing.

"Couldn't it get there tomorrow?"

She looked at him as if he were the newest species of Martian to arrive on the island and shook her head.

"No."

"It's only . . ."

"No."

The bell above the door jingled and Nicholas turned to see Margaret Gore arriving. It was the briefest moment, the slightest particle of time in which no thought happens and the plot of life leaps forwards into the vacuum; or perhaps it was the invisible prompting of the tall man standing beside Nicholas, perhaps he pushed his son's arm, for in a flash Nicholas reached to the counter and drew to him the already stamped and paid for envelope for Isabel. He took it and turned, held it to his chest, and walked out the door.

He himself wasn't sure why. He had no sense of threat or danger but was guided by that steady nudge that walked him quickly from the post office and past the amazement and dismay of the two women. He was walking towards the shoreline before he knew it, before he had had time to marshal reason and select his next action amidst the galaxies of the improbable that were now his life. He felt his shoes sliding on the white sand; it was as if the world were giving away beneath him and he was not sure why, but he walked on towards the water. From the post office door Margaret Gore was watching him and held her breath in a gasp as she realised he was so far lost in the dementia of loving that he was about to walk across the sea to Galway.

His shoes drank the edge of the cold sea with a million mouths, and Nicholas looked down to feel with surprise that the froth did not pillow him. His ankles stung even though he had stepped only three feet into the water and now walked along just off the island shore with the envelope of the love letter clutched against his chest. He looked out to the mainland and felt his heart release a half-dozen butterflies at the sight of sunlight piercing down through mottled cloud. Was the world conspiring with him or against him? Who was walking him now? And where? The sickness was rolling in his stomach. The salt in the air burnt his eyelids and it was a moment before he realised the gulls were gathering behind him, rising and landing again and again as the waves came in and sucked back, signifying something so deeply misunderstood. He walked on along the edge of the island, neither quite on the land nor in the water.

Leaving the post office and coming down to the shore Margaret Gore shepherded him at a small distance, fearing at any moment she was to witness his drowning.

Where was he going? What was he doing with the fourth letter? Did he know she had burnt the others? She felt certain he did and had a sudden longing to cry out to him. But from up the Long Road she saw out of the corner of her eye Nora Liathain leaving her cottage and coming down to see what was happening, and the moment passed.

Nicholas walked four hundred yards along the edge of the island, his trouser legs drenched with the sea slapping across them and the letter held high against the spray. He seemed to Margaret to be walking aimlessly now, but she knew enough of the deviousness of love to keep following; she wouldn't put it past this loving to have gifted him with sudden omniscience and insight just to keep itself alive. It would hardly surprise her if it had even allowed him bi-location and the Nicholas she followed was not the Nicholas who wrote the letter at all. She was burdened with possibilities, and as the wet sand took her footprints she let rush ahead of her the bare-toothed dogs of her maternal drive to save Isabel. But when she saw Nicholas walking in the water up to the mustard-coloured boat of Seamus Beg de Blaca, she felt defeated at last. The sand held her and she could walk but not move, the way tragic lovers travel in dreams. She saw Nicholas hail the boat as it was pulling out to sea and then standing to his middle in the water and speaking with Seamus Beg for a moment before handing over the envelope. The boat sailed away, Margaret walked in the empty space, and Nicholas let himself fall at last like a long sigh into the waist-high sea.

12

And there was the ending.

If only there were endings. If only the moment arrived when there was no more longing, and the story froze and was stilled beyond grief and disappointment and age and death. But it was the plotting not the ending that mattered. For the world, after all, is quite simple. Even the most convoluted plotting, the wildest chance and outrageous coincidence fit like measured cogs into the vast wheel of everything.

There is a meaning; there is sense to everything, Nicholas thought, as he drew himself up on the shore and lay down soaking on the white sand. It all fits together perfectly, he said out loud, and burst out laughing, not at all surprised when he saw it fly like ribbons of white satin from his mouth.

He looked out and saw the boat now small in the distance taking the letter to Isabel. It was the fourth letter of love. *Amor*, he said, sounding the air with it, thinking of the journey of that love letter and not knowing that the other three had burned, and laughing out loud as he watched it go, but not quite hearing the boom laugh of his father lying next to him. If she does not come with this letter I am wrong, Nicholas thought. But she will.

"She will because she will," his father said, beyond Nicholas's hearing but clear enough for Margaret Gore to hear it with a hopeless dread as she stood in the sand a hundred yards away.

"She will come," Nicholas said aloud, "she will," and was suddenly aware that the reason was quite simple, that it was because that was how the world fit together, not how we plan it, nor with a shape we conceive, but with a crazy pattern of its own that runs through all the twists and griefs of everyday unto the point of me lying here knowing I am to love her and the plots of love and God are one and the same thing. She will come.

He lay on the beach beside his father and watched the western sky moving slowly above him, the planes of blue air ceaselessly and easily fitting together and so softly coming apart. Until the moment his mother arrived and sat with them. The three of them sat there then in a place not exactly chosen, but for whatever reason a place where Muiris Gore could see them as he stood on a child's seat and turned with a screwdriver the left of the two screws that held William Coughlan's painting to the wall. The screw turned but did not loosen, and for fifteen minutes Muiris kept turning and turning it in vain, unable to understand until his legs grew tired that there was a reason and a way beyond the laws of science. It was only when he had abandoned the effort and stood down to rest against the front desk that he noticed for the first time that the picture of the painting was in fact a huge image of a very old man. He blinked to make it vanish and had to sit down when it did not. Then he laughed. And laughed. It was laughing Margaret Gore heard as she turned home and was startled when she looked over at the school on the little rise of rock and noticed it shining. When her husband came out of the doorway he had lost twenty years and she saw him across the distance with a quality like a fall of light coming towards her. Everything was lit. Golden birds flew, and as the islanders came to their opened doors they caught the white smell of eucalyptus wafting in from some Africa of the mind. Even the fishing boats would arrive with the scent of it in the evening. There was eucalyptus in the pillows of the whole island, the unmistakeable scent of the world's loving.

It did not matter then that none knew that a storm would take Seamus Beg in its hand and toss the last letter of love into the Atlantic, that Isabel would never receive it, as she had none of the others, that the wait for a reply would last three more weeks and two days. There was in the air that moment a rare feeling of healing, of things lifting and coming together, of the story being carried suddenly forwards, the great whoosh on which everything suddenly rises and flows, and you know a great spirit somewhere is watching down.

It was in the air at that moment, and at that moment, at the beginning of the discovery of new love for Muiris Gore, Margaret Gore felt the tears streaming from her eyes with sudden foreknowledge, knowing now that at last Isabel would arrive home on the island to tell Nicholas that she had fallen in love with him, that she was pregnant with Peader's child but that she never intended to see him for the rest of her life, that she had not for a single moment since Nicholas had left the island been able to breathe without thought of him, that the way ahead was no more clear than the way behind, but that it was the way for them, for all that; that the plots of God and Love came together and were the same thing, and that loving Isabel Gore was what Nicholas Coughlan was born to do.